For Claudia and Oliver,
my wild olives

PENGUIN BOOKS

The Olive Sisters

Amanda Hampson grew up in New Zealand and moved to London in 1976. She spent her early twenties travelling, finally settling in Australia in 1979 where she has been writing professionally for more than a decade. Amanda's non-fiction titles include *Battles with the Baby Gods: Stories of Hope* and *Take Me Home: Families Living with Alzheimer's*. Amanda lives with her partner on Sydney's northern beaches and has three children and two grandchildren. *The Olive Sisters* is her first novel.

For more information please visit
www.amandahampson.com

The Olive Sisters

AMANDA HAMPSON

PENGUIN BOOKS

PENGUIN BOOKS

Published by the Penguin Group
Penguin Group (Australia)
250 Camberwell Road, Camberwell, Victoria 3124, Australia
(a division of Pearson Australia Group Pty Ltd)
Penguin Group (USA)
375 Hudson Street, New York, New York 10014, USA
Penguin Group (Canada)
90 Eglinton Avenue East, Suite 700, Toronto, ON M4P 2Y3, Canada
(a division of Pearson Canada Inc.)
Penguin Books Ltd
80 Strand, London WC2R 0RL, England
Penguin Ireland
25 St Stephen's Green, Dublin 2, Ireland
(a division of Penguin Books Ltd)
Penguin Group (India)
11 Community Centre, Panchsheel Park, New Delhi – 110 017, India
Penguin Group (NZ)
67 Apollo Drive, Rosedale, North Shore 0632, New Zealand
(a division of Pearson New Zealand Ltd)
Penguin Group (South Africa) (Pty) Ltd
24 Sturdee Avenue, Rosebank, Johannesburg 2196, South Africa

Penguin Books Ltd, Registered Offices: 80 Strand, London WC2R 0RL, England

First published by Penguin Group (Australia), 2005

7 9 11 13 12 10 8 6

Design by Miriam Rosenbloom © Penguin Group Australia
Cover photographs by Amy Neunsinger and Marc Grimberg/Getty Images
'I am Woman' – words and music by Ray Burton/Helen Reddy © Irving Music, Inc./ Buggerlugs Music
Co. All rights reserved. International copyright secured. Reprinted with permission of Universal Music
Publishing Pty. Ltd.
'In the Cool, Cool of the Evening' from the Paramount Picture *Here Comes the Groom*. Words by
Johnny Mercer, music by Hoagy Carmichael. Copyright © 1951 (Renewed 1979) by Famous Music
Corporation. International Copyright secured. All rights reserved.
Typeset in 10.5/15.5 pt Sabon by Post Pre-press Group, Brisbane, Queensland
Printed and bound in Australia by McPherson's Printing Group, Maryborough, Victoria

National Library of Australia
Cataloguing-in-Publication data:

Hampson, Amanda, 1954– .
The olive sisters.

ISBN 978 0 14 300399 1

I. Title.

A823.3

penguin.com.au

One

I STAND ON the threshold of the house. My father's boots sit beside the door, the shape of his foot preserved in leather. I have only come because he's gone and I'm only here because I'm desperate. A desperado, you might say.

It's thirty years since I saw my father and now, as I stand looking into the darkness of the house, I realise this is the day I have dreaded. Indifferent to the significance of the moment, my daughter Lauren sits in the car parked in the driveway. I can hear her twittering into her mobile. Mercifully, her voice drifts away with the shrilling cicadas as I step into the cool silence of the house.

The old farmhouse is divided by a wide hallway that connects the front and back doors. On the walls of the hallway are photographs of my father, Jack, wearing a series of hard-hat and dirty-overall ensembles with enormous earthmoving machines in the background. Some photos have a date and location scrawled on them: Broken Hill 1955; Tennant Creek 1962; a bunch of blokes outside a pub, arms flung casually over a mate's shoulder, daft grins for the camera – Mt Isa 1967. I had similar photos of him in my schoolgirl album.

My father was my hero back then. Always absent, always somewhere more interesting.

To the right of the hall are two bedrooms; both open onto a wide verandah that wraps around the house. To my left is a living room with a kitchen at the back. Every surface is cluttered with books, lumps of rock and chipped mugs sprouting mouldy growths. Spiders have spun delicate palaces of lace in every corner. It smells sad and abandoned. Signs of a solitary life.

'Oh my God, what a dump!' Lauren calls as she sprints on a tour of the house. 'It's so dark and musty – why are all the curtains closed?' She joins me in the living room, pulls back the curtains and wrestles with the French doors until they burst open. A shaft of sunlight penetrates the room, illuminating a star field of floating dust.

This house once belonged to my grandparents. Jack moved here sometime after my mother, Isabelle, died. She always knew he would come here; she thought it strange that he had such affection for the house when she, who grew up in it, had none at all. But I can imagine Jack liking this house; it's simple and solid. It lacks pretensions of any sort.

'I'm tired,' I say, sitting down on an old brown sofa that appears equally exhausted. It looks as though much of the furniture belonged to my grandparents. Jack's idea of furniture was more along the lines of a couple of crates with a plank across the top. He was suspicious of style. The two old sofas would be his; the twenty-year-old television definitely. But the polished wooden table in the kitchen with its plump curvaceous legs and the dark dresser carved with flowers and leaves – definitely not. It's as though there are layers of lives, imposed on top of one another. It's too depressing for words. I can't possibly live here. I just can't.

'You can't be serious about living here.' Lauren flops down on the sofa beside me. 'Things can't be that bad – this is *grotesque*.' She savours the word.

'They want my car next week.'

'Your beautiful car,' she sighs.

'I don't care any more. I'll just buy a cheap get-about.'

'Living in a dump, driving a wreck. It's so not you, Adrienne.'

'I have everything I need,' I lie. It's my new mantra.

'Really?' Her eyebrows collide with her dark fringe. 'Where's the bathroom?'

She's right. I didn't see a bathroom either. We tentatively get up off the sofa and head for the back door. On the verandah there is a sort of lean-to with a striped plastic curtain for a door. Lauren glances at me to see how I'm taking it. She pulls the curtain aside.

'Hmm, no spa I see,' she says sweetly.

I smile bravely.

The garden and lawn are wildly overgrown, neglected as they have been for almost a year. The house is completely enclosed by trees and hedges gone berserk. Attached to the back verandah is an old pergola smothered in grapevine. We wander down the steps and stand knee-deep in grass. I've been bracing myself to tell Lauren something she won't want to hear. Now seems as good a time as any.

'The other thing I have to tell you, Lauren, is that you're going to have to pay your own rent and uni fees next year,' I say abruptly.

'What?' she screeches. 'How am I going to do that? This is all *your* fault. You've wrecked everything. Why can't you start another business or just get a job like everyone else?'

The lawn is a soft green meadow. I have a sudden overwhelming desire to lie down on it but Lauren will tell everyone I'm going mad – and maybe I am.

'Look, I've just done three hours of driving, Lu. I need to rest,' I say firmly, trying to claw my way back into you-child-me-adult territory. 'Why don't you explore the farm – or something . . .' I falter at her pinched face and narrowed eyes. She's nineteen years old and I vacillate between treating her as an equal and, if that fails, a pre-schooler. No wonder she behaves like one sometimes.

'You know I *hate* the country.' She stalks back to the car, mute with fury.

I sleep on the sofa for an hour, dreaming of my beautiful apartment; of my white bedroom, where every morning I would wake to see the edge of the world where sea meets sky. Gone . . . all gone. The sadness is a dead weight pressing on my chest. I'm too sad to cry. That apartment was my dream. My fortress. It took me twenty years to get there. I probably waited too long to sell it, convinced there was some other way out of the financial tangle I was in, convinced there would be a reprieve. I didn't deserve this punishment. It wasn't my fault. There came a terrible, terrible moment when I looked around and realised that my home was truly gone; that some other dreamer would soon inhabit its light-filled rooms.

It hurt like a lover's betrayal. I thought we were forever.

It's late afternoon when I wake with a sense of urgency. We need to make a space for ourselves, tidy up the kitchen and find some clean sheets for the beds so we can sleep tonight. Tomorrow the removal truck will arrive from Sydney with the few things I still own. I need to be ready.

I stand at the front door. Lauren is in the car still, on the mobile. I'll need to choose my moment carefully to tell her that her phone belongs to the company. I walk over and open the car boot, pull some of the bags out and carry them back to the verandah. 'Come on, I need your help.' She ignores me. 'Lauren!' Scowling, she slowly gets out of the car.

'I'll call you back,' she mutters into the phone.

'Look,' I say with a big smile, pulling out two pairs of crisp white disposable overalls and pink rubber gloves. 'Aren't they just divine? We'll look like the avenging angels of cleanliness. There they go – Saint Brillo and her sidekick Ajax, ascending to heaven in a white tornado.'

'They're grotesque, Adrienne; you're not a saint and —'

'I gather grotesque is the word of the week,' I snap. 'I'm bloody tired of it. Just last week you were going on about becoming more spiritual – grotesque doesn't sound very bloody Zen to me.'

'I will never tell you anything again!' She snatches a pair of overalls from me and marches into the house. I don't need to have the last word. Really I don't.

'Good!' I shout after her.

We do the basics in silence, the bathroom and the kitchen benches, and clear off some of the rubbish into bags. It's years since I did my own cleaning. A stranger to domestics (apart from complaining endlessly about the cleaner), Lauren hasn't got a clue. She flops the cloth around ineffectually with a sulky look on her face. But I'm actually surprised at how satisfying it is to do work that requires little thought but is so involving at the same time. I've had too much to think about these last few months.

'Yoo-hoo! Hello. Oh, you look like those people who clean up after nuclear accidents.' The solid shape of a woman is silhouetted in the doorway, the bright afternoon sun glowing at her back. She comes towards me with her hand outstretched. I just have time to slip off my rubber glove before she grasps my hand, shaking it vigorously for a woman easily in her seventies.

'Mrs Oldfield – Joy. I'm just down the road. I heard you were coming up, thought I'd drop in to see if you needed a hand with anything.' Despite the warm afternoon she is wearing a light raincoat, trackpants and jogging shoes.

'Heard from who?'

'Oh, you know, round and about. You must be Adrienne,' she says, her curiosity a little too obvious.

'I am, and this is my daughter, Lauren.'

'I've brought you some tomatoes from my garden, and a lettuce. Jack's lettuces will have all gone to the wallabies,' she says, lifting a carrier bag out of her basket and handing it to me. She looks around the room. 'Grief, you've got your work cut out here. I've got a couple of hours – let me give you a hand.'

'That's very generous, Mrs Oldfield, but I couldn't expect —'

'Thanks a lot,' says Lauren, shooting me a warning look.

'Perhaps we need a proper plan . . .' I venture, slipping on my managing and directing mantle.

Mrs Oldfield smiles. 'We'll be right, dear. We'll muddle through.' She fossicks around in her basket and pulls out a carefully ironed cotton floral wraparound. She's come prepared. Removing her raincoat, she hangs it on the back of the door and slips into her wrap. She switches on the mutinous vacuum cleaner we have struggled to get working for the last half hour, gives it a swift kick and together they roar off down the hall.

In one bedroom there's a double bed and a pile of boxes, in the other are two single beds, some bags of old clothes and stacks of newspapers. We decide to tackle the smaller room with the single beds first. We strip the worn and yellowing sheets from the beds and discard them in the bin, carry the mattresses out into the sun and prop them up against two large fruit trees. Lauren's expression throughout this operation is like that of someone who has found an entire dog turd stuck to the bottom of her shoe and is trying to clean it off with a wholly inadequate twig. It's all a little too sordid for her, poor love.

Next, we start to clear the boxes, mostly full of newspapers and old mining books. There is something so utilitarian about the way Jack lived here. No adornments, no comforts; just the dusty accumulation of life.

'When I was a child everything my mother had was beautiful,' I say wistfully.

'Didn't you say she made wedding dresses?' Lauren asks.

'She was just a dressmaker, I suppose, but she made christening gowns and wedding dresses – debutante gowns were

7

the thing in those days. She embroidered and made lace. She used to make our sheets and pillowcases. My father was more of a pragmatist; I don't think he ever really cared for that sort of thing. I see nothing of hers here. None of the lovely things we had. He probably sent the lot to St Vinnie's, knowing him.'

Lauren narrows her eyes, thinking. 'Did you see that big chest in the hall with a cloth over it?'

Moments later we stand in the hall, scanning the bits and pieces sitting on top of the chest. Without a word between us, I open the mouth of a garbage bag and Lauren sweeps the lot into it.

'Extreme feng shui!' she giggles. Things are looking up.

The box is full of at least some of the things I have just described to Lauren. There are soft cotton sheets and damask bed covers, all folded carefully with withered sprigs of lavender tucked inside. There are many things I haven't seen before – perhaps from my mother's early life. Pillowcases embroidered with plump cherubs and enshrined with tiny knotted rosebuds. Double sheets adorned with hearts and flowers. Folded pieces of satin, silk and organza, neatly coiled lace and satin ribbon – my mother's unfinished symphonies. When she died, Jack took everything from her flat, so he must have packed this chest. Perhaps even he couldn't find it in himself to throw it all away. As I touch the richness of the fabric, I can almost hear my mother's voice. A brittle fragment of grief from somewhere in my chest journeys through my body until even my fingers ache with it.

Lauren shakes out a single cotton sheet with 'Isabella' embroidered across the top, elegant in pale pink. There's another just like it, but the stitching – blue and rather wobbly – reads 'Rosanna'.

'Who's Rosanna?' asks Lauren.

'I've no idea.'

'Rosanna?' repeats Mrs O, who has suddenly materialised, bent over and pulling dusters from her magic basket. She straightens up and looks at me. 'You don't know who Rosanna is?'

A heartbeat. It is as though the three of us are suspended in the open space between question and answer, drifting like birds as we wait for a current to move us to the next moment.

'Should I?'

I see Mrs O watching me carefully. 'Rosanna and Isabelle were sisters.'

I'm stunned. 'No. Can't have been. My mother never, ever mentioned having a sister.'

'That's weird . . .' says Lauren. 'Is she in prison or an asylum or something? Locked in the attic, perhaps!'

Mrs Oldfield raises an eyebrow and gives her a look I imagine she refined on her own children over the years. It proves to be effective with Lauren. 'Rosanna hasn't lived here for a long time. I didn't keep in touch with her.'

'Well, I . . . I have to say that I am shocked,' I stammer, sitting down with a jolt.

'It would take more than that to shock *me*,' says Lauren, ever the opportunist. 'I thought *Jack*, who was, after all, my grandfather, was dead – until I happened to see a letter saying he *had* actually died.'

They both look at me oddly. The odd one out – that's me. I've lived all my life as the only child of an only child, and the same fate has befallen Lauren. But now I find that's not quite true. Suddenly I feel I've been short-changed. I have an aunty! Perhaps there are cousins as well. Aunt Rosanna. Aunty Rosa – sounds quite cosy.

'Well – I'd better be on my way,' Mrs Oldfield says, breaking my reverie. 'Got my grandkids coming for dinner. Which reminds me, you'll most likely get a visit from Darryl Leeton. He's been wanting to get in touch with you. You'll know the Leeton boys when you meet 'em – second-generation earthmovers – they all shout. Don't ask him inside, whatever you do.' She gives us a wink, slips her coat on and is out the door.

I watch her drive away as I sit down on the front steps. Lauren comes and settles beside me, quiet for once. Both tired, we watch the evening descend, infusing the garden with shadows that fade from plum to grape. It's a relief to be still, but I have a niggling discomfort at the Rosanna revelation. That crevice of distrust that opens when you realise you have been deliberately deceived . . . Why? What else don't I know?

We eventually rouse ourselves and move into the kitchen to find the food we brought from the city this morning. I open our bottle of wine and arrange the camembert, olives, tomatoes and baguette on a plate and take it outside to the pergola. There's an old, quite ornate, metal table and four matching chairs decorated in a vine-leaf design and a rectangle of light from the kitchen falls conveniently on the table.

The trees become stark silhouettes as the moon rises quickly behind them, glowing like an alien spacecraft. It rises so swiftly that the trees seem to tear its light to tatters, then suddenly it's full and plump again, sitting smugly above the distant hills. Within minutes a distant dog howls a lonely song.

Lauren cups her ear. 'Hark! A moonstruck bushie? Or the ghost of Jack Bennett, come to haunt you for misrepresenting him as a dead person?' She laughs, throws back the last of her wine and goes into the house – to update her friends on this latest drama, no doubt. Within moments I hear her shrieking with laughter, then a door being kicked shut, then silence.

This is what it will be like when she's gone. Dark and empty. I make myself experience it. I try to summon my inner warrior; the one who allowed me to speak on podiums to hundreds of people, negotiate million-dollar contracts across polished board tables and command a whole army of people. It seems my inner warrior has been replaced by my inner wraith. I'm slowly withering away.

The grass is already damp with dew as I make my way across to the gate that divides the garden from the murky world beyond. I hold fast to the gate to prevent myself being sucked into the blackness, and hear myself howl into the empty night. Even my howl sounds tentative, though God knows I've plenty to howl about.

It's barely light when I'm woken by a series of thuds and shrieks as Lauren, sitting up in bed, hurls her shoes across the room. Noticing I am now awake, she turns her attention to me.

'That was a disgusting little disgusting mouse! This place is totally *grotesque*! I'm going home tomorrow, even if I have to catch the train. I have to look for a job, anyway,' she sniffs, getting out of bed.

Not quite awake, I sit up and look out the window. Rain beats a steady rhythm on the tin roof and it has formed a pale silken curtain around the house. I feel trapped.

Lauren calms down after a shower. Water soothes her, as it does me. I can hear her humming something smooth and bluesy.

'Tooooast?' she yodels. I'm forgiven. Toast is the mainstay of our relationship. For us it's a meal rich with tradition and infinite variations. Our darkest moments are redeemed by the hot, crisp, buttery comfort of toast. Sweet puddles of raspberry jam make us sigh with familiar relief. It's one of the few things we do for each other. We say 'Toast?' instead of 'Sorry'.

I had the foresight to bring my espresso pot with me rather than pack it. I hear it getting up a head of steam and the fragrant promise of fresh coffee lures me from my bed.

'What's the plan, ma'am?' says Lauren, as I totter into the room. Chirpy now, she sits down at the table.

'We need to clear some space for the stuff the truck will bring. We'll just zoom through Jack's boxes, make sure there's nothing important and then chuck the lot.'

'How is all your furniture possibly going to fit?'

'There really isn't much. Most of it was leased.'

She opens her mouth, closes it again and finally says weakly, 'That's lucky.'

The air inside the house is damp and stuffy, almost claustrophobic. 'What season is it?' I sound like a bad actress feigning amnesia but I really have lost track somehow.

'Hmm . . . I saw the other day that there are only thirty-five shopping days till Christmas. So it's late spring? Early summer? Sprummer?' says Lauren, spraying toast crumbs everywhere.

The living room is dark, even with the lights on. If I know anything about Jack, we won't find a bulb over 40 watts in the whole place. We decide to drag one of the two sofas outside onto the front verandah and carry the boxes out there so we can work in some light and comfort.

After much getting up and down and rearranging things, we are finally settled side-by-side on the sofa with a stack of boxes at each end. The rain has eased and the air is cool and fresh, like a tonic. We sit in silence, lifting handfuls of papers, old newspapers, clippings about mining and dredging operations, mineral sands analysis reports and the like from the boxes, flipping through them and sorting them into Keep and Throw categories.

'Look at this. It's your mother's birth certificate,' says Lauren. 'Listen. Child: Isabella Margherita Martino; Mother: Adriana Carmela Martino; Father: Francesco Giovanni Martino. Oh my God! We're Italian!'

'*We're* not Italian, my mother's family were. You only have to look around the house to work that one out. That dining table, the china cabinet – all straight out of some Neapolitan nonna's front parlour.'

'Why didn't you ever tell me? Is it a secret?'

'I don't know if it was a secret, exactly. My mother didn't *look* Italian; she was quite fair. You and I look more Italian than she did. I'm not sure she was ashamed of it, but she certainly wasn't overt about it. I don't think I ever heard her speak the language.'

'How cool is this?' cries Lauren. 'I've always wanted to be Italian!'

'You've always wanted to be Italian? Since when?'

'Italian or French, or something exotic. Just not nothing.'

'We're not nothing – we're Australian.'

'You know what I mean. It's like we're camped here on someone else's land. Anglo-Saxons don't have ethnic pride. We don't have any songs.'

'What about *Waltzing Matilda*?'

'Billies and billabongs – hardly an anthem to inspire all humanity,' she says loftily. 'The problem is, we haven't suffered enough repression.'

'I'm sure that could be arranged,' I say irritably. 'Why don't we take a break and go for a walk or something?'

I get the withering look. 'Mother – it's raining, the grass is wet *and* the whole place is probably teeming with snakes. Let's just get this done. You go through this document box and I'll handle the other big ones.'

When did my daughter take charge, I wonder? Perhaps she's always been in charge; she was a bossy little girl. She often seems to feel that life has gypped her; she has the idea that other people have what she wants, or what should be hers. When she was about four years old she insisted her then-nanny was stealing her dreams, and began to follow the poor woman around, spying on her, until she got spooked and left, as they all did eventually. Her boyfriends are the same. They never stay long; she runs them ragged. Perhaps the same could be said of me. I've been told, by more than one man, that I am 'high maintenance' – whatever that means.

The document box is smaller than the others, an old hat-box with a lid. There are a few dog-eared photos like the ones in the hallway, some of myself as a baby and others when I was older with my mother; she looks unhappy in every one. I'm ashamed to admit I never noticed. Beneath the photos I find some technical drawings of a piece of machinery that appears to be for crushing grapes. My birth certificate and my mother's death certificate are also here, and a small box made of polished wood, hinged on one side. I open it. Inside is a letter and a black-and-white photograph of a woman. She's laughing and her mouth is wide open, showing off her beautiful teeth. Dark eyes sparkle with mischief. A thick braid of black hair rests across one shoulder. There's something about her I've seen before, some quality that reminds me of Lauren at her happiest.

The envelope is addressed to Miss Rosanna Martino, 74 Riley Street, Adelaide. The postmark is 5 August 1956. I was two years old. The address has a line through it and 'Return to Sender' scrawled across the envelope. I turn it over. The sender is Jack Bennett, 3 Cromer Road, Broken Hill. I take out the letter and unfold it.

Darling, darling Rosa,
I can't live my life without you. I've tried and failed.
You are a part of me I never knew existed. You are my
life and I will never stop loving you. I miss you every
minute of every day. Please write, please come. I am
waiting for you.
All my love, Jack.

It's so strange to see my father's familiar hand express such foreign emotions. I'm shocked. Bewildered. I simply don't know what to make of it. The bastard. The shit. He has reached out from the grave to disappoint me one last time. Did my mother know? She must have. No wonder she never mentioned having a sister. She was a secretive woman anyhow, never gave much away. She always described herself as 'private', as if she imagined herself to be somewhat enigmatic. It was the same thing in my eyes. The door to her inner world only ever opened a sliver, and you only saw what she wanted you to see.

I haven't been lucky in love myself. Judging by this letter I would have to say that I have never really experienced love. I've never known the sort of passion that renders people powerless. I've never understood how people can abandon husbands and children or cross the world to be with their lover. I can't imagine what it is like to be prepared to die – or kill – for love. The letter is so raw and honest it hurts to read it.

I sit there looking with new eyes at the photograph and there comes a slow, dawning realisation that Rosanna is part of my life. Who is she? Where is she now? Without my ever knowing it, she has undoubtedly played her own part in my relationship with my father and, perhaps, even in our eventual estrangement. As a child I thought I was the source of his unhappiness; that I was somehow the catalyst for his discontent, his angry restlessness. I thought he never stayed long at home with us because of me. Later I thought perhaps my mother just didn't hold onto him tight enough. It seemed to me then that my mother was unfathomable and my father unattainable. Not just to me, but to one another.

'Are you crying?' Lauren sounds alarmed. Crying is not something I do.

'Of course not,' I say, quickly slipping the letter back into the envelope. 'It's just a sad business cleaning up other people's lives.' I used to be more honest with her but lately there's been a lot I've hidden, lied about even. Things I don't want to talk to anyone about, let alone to someone who judges me as harshly as Lauren does.

She reaches out and takes the photograph off my lap. 'This is Rosanna, isn't it? She's got my eyes.' She gives me a brilliant smile and flutters her eyelashes.

'But you've got her teeth,' I smile. I'm going to miss Lauren when she goes tomorrow, which I have no doubt she will. 'You can take my car back to Sydney when you go,' I say on impulse.

'Really?' she throws an arm awkwardly around my shoulders in a burst of affection. 'But what will you do?'

'Mrs O said there's a bus down to the village. Surely Jack must have had a car. I wonder where it is. Will you stay just one more day?' I implore. I hate the wheedling tone in my voice. My generous offer is instantly denigrated to the status of premeditated bribe. But she agrees.

It's almost dark when we hear the removal truck come bumping and splashing up the long driveway. It pulls up covered in purple jacaranda blossoms, with a large branch perched on the roof.

'Yer wanna get yer trees trimmed, missus. Truck's just

17

had a bloody paint job,' says the driver, springing from the cab. He's a nuggety little fellow of indeterminate age. Blue eyes burn from a face baked as shiny as a glazed bun. He nips around to the back of the truck, unlatches the double doors and slides the ramp down before his offsider – a good-looking twenty-something boy in a white cowboy hat – has even made his way to the back of the truck.

Cowboy brightens up and looks a bit keen when he sees Lauren. I watch him taking in her hipster pants and bare midriff. His eye snags for a moment on the ring in her belly-button. He tilts his chin a little; the eyelids droop slightly. It looks like something he's practised in front of the mirror for hours, along with his Elvis impersonations. In that infinitely delicate way that young women hone their mastery of men, Lauren snubs him. There's a glance, a dainty sniff and an almost imperceptible flick of her glossy bob of dark hair, culminating in a bored gaze into middle distance. The poor chap is visibly crushed. She's got it down to a fine art.

The two men work tirelessly, lugging box after box of the remains of my life. 'Where does this go?' and 'What about this one?' is the extent of the conversation. The driveway is wet and muddy and soon the verandah and floor are tracked with dirt.

Lauren moved out of the apartment a month before I did, so I have no one else to blame for the abysmal labelling of boxes. I actually have no recollection of doing it, lost as I was in a dark miasma of my own making. Finally, it seems a better idea to direct all the boxes into the shed, which appears dry and safe enough. I can leave stuff in there that I don't want to unpack. I won't be staying long. God knows where I'll go, but I simply cannot stay here.

From the depths of the shed I hear Lauren give a scream dramatic enough to land her an instant role in a B-grade horror flick. I run outside to see her standing on the front steps screaming and flapping her arms madly. As I get closer I realise she is pointing to her bare belly, on which there is a big black slug. Repulsed though I am, I do try to flick it off for her. It's stuck.

'It's a leeeccchhh!' she shrieks. '*Get it off*!'

I can't touch it. I cannot put my fingers on this thing. Where are my rubber gloves when I need them? Unfazed by Lauren's yelps, Cowboy opens the cab door, grabs a small salt container from the dash and sprinkles a bit on the leech. It releases instantly and rolls fatly down Lauren's leg and onto the ground, where it disgorges dark-red blood into the mud. As I lead her inside – she's still shuddering and hyper-ventilating – Cowboy gives me a broad grin and a slight lift of the eyebrows. Says it all, really.

It's midnight before we get to bed. I'm desperate, desper-ate for sleep. On the other side of the room Lauren is asleep already – worn out by all the excitement, no doubt. The room smells musty and dusty despite our cleaning efforts. I suddenly feel ill with despair. I used to be so tough, so fearless – nothing touched me. Where is my courage now? Perhaps it wasn't courage, just bravado. Perhaps I've always been a coward.

I think back to Lauren screaming about the leech and I can't help smiling. A hiccupy sort of giggle bubbles up. It's probably nervous exhaustion but suddenly I'm helpless with laughter. I put my pillow over my face to smother the noise. My whole body shakes with laughter, tears stream from the corners of my eyes. As I gasp for air I realise that, for the first time in months, I'm breathing. It feels good. It feels really good.

Two

ROSANNA AND ISABELLA were like two shells of the same nut – two parts that when joined fitted perfectly. Isabella – three years older – was serene and as elusive as a promise. Rosanna – curious, intense and volatile – ran towards life as though it were running away; Isabella watched with interest, dusted her sister off when she stumbled and fell, but seldom cautioned her.

'*Matta*!' their father would call Rosa when she defied him. Crazy. He and Rosa would argue until they forgot what they argued about or which side they were on. Isabella rarely defied her father but often, when Rosanna was in full flight, a smile would play around the lips of the good daughter.

The two children lined up their dolls on a blanket under the shade of the mandarin tree. Isabella sat cross-legged on the rug as she carefully stitched pieces of satin cloth together to make her doll a gown. Bored by delays in the game, Rosanna climbed the tree. Clinging to a precariously fragile limb, she plucked the hard green fruit and hurled it down at the recumbent dolls.

'*State attente*! *Presto*! Falling rocks. *Chiama un medico*!'

'Rosa, we did not agree to play emergency. The princesses are going to the ball and if you don't help yours prepare, there will not be any princes left for them to marry. It will be a great disgrace for the kingdom,' cautioned Isabella, without lifting her gaze from the needle and thread.

'Perhaps they can marry the doctors instead?'

'No. Only nurses can marry doctors. That is a different game.'

Rosa climbed down and lay spread-eagled on the rug, consumed by boredom. 'Why are princesses always English?' she demanded.

'Well . . . I'm not sure. I think because the English are very upper-class people. And they have lots of palaces and castles for the royal people to live in.'

'So are Australians English?'

'Sort of, I think. But they don't have any palaces, so, of course, there aren't any princesses.'

'So wogs can't be princesses.'

'I don't know how you can even let that ugly word come out of your mouth, Rosa,' said Isabella, intent on her work.

'Wogs and dagos. Dogs and wagos. You pretend you don't hear, but it doesn't make any difference. We're wogs.'

'There, I've finished,' said Isabella. 'Doesn't she look beautiful?' She got up and took the doll into the sunshine. She smiled a dreamy smile and danced the doll on the breeze, admiring the play of light on her creamy gown.

22

Franco and Isabella stepped out of the searing afternoon sun and stood inside the dirt-floor barn that served as the Duffy's Creek stock and station agent. Franco made his way to the counter while Isabella wandered behind, looking at the high-piled sacks of feed, dog food and fertiliser. Around the walls hung coils of ropes, bridles, wet-weather gear and hats.

The man behind the counter was intent on his paperwork. Franco tried to attract his attention with a greeting. The man grunted but didn't look up.

'I want to buy the fer-*dil*-liser, please.'

The man looked up slowly. His smirk made Isabella's chest feel so tight she could hardly breathe. She wanted to run, to fly up into the rafters where she could perch unseen.

'Whaddaya want, mate?'

Again Franco placed emphasis where there was none. 'I want the fer-*dil*-liser,' he asked. 'Please.' Isabella heard him relinquish his last vestige of power in one pleading note.

'Can't work out what yer saying, mate. Why don't youse learn English? That's what we speak hereabouts.'

Isabella moved closer to her father. The man's eyes slid across to her, challenging the child to compound her father's humiliation by speaking for him. His eyes were dull with some sort of nameless hatred she found impossible to understand.

'Come on, Babbo. Let's go,' she murmured.

'Good idea, girlie.' The man abruptly went back to his paperwork.

Isabella pulled her father towards the door. As they stepped out into the white heat of the yard the man called,

'Fertiliser won't help youse, mate. Yer can't grow that fucking dago-food in this country.'

Isabella and Franco sat side-by-side in the front seat of the old truck. Knuckles white on the steering wheel, Franco stared straight ahead, murmuring a stream of invective, like a spell, under his breath: '*Figlio di puttana, stronzo . . .*' Gutter talk, her mother called it. Isabella picked a rag up off the floor of the truck and carefully wiped the dust off her shoes. It wasn't what the man said. It was the way he said it. The disgust.

When Rosanna was strapped by the nuns for speaking in her native tongue it confirmed Isabella's belief that her origins, her language and, daily, her school-lunch, conspired to shame her. It strengthened her resolve to quietly divest herself of everything that marked her as different.

Everywhere she looked she noticed details that didn't fit. She and Rosanna were like a couple of walnut trees trying to blend into an apple orchard. The feasts their mother prepared for lunch were a smorgasbord of smells that invited snorts of disgust, whispered remarks and explosions of laughter from the other girls. She longed for flat white sandwiches containing nothing more offensive than a beige slice of devon. She just didn't have the heart to tell her mother.

Mrs Martino took the high ground on these matters; her standard response to her daughters' humiliations was to quote an old proverb '*L'ignoranza fa rima con l'intolleranza*' – ignorance rhymes with intolerance. Isabella nodded her head in agreement but wondered privately what to do with this piece of information. She didn't want to become ignorant or intolerant, but more pressing was how to avoid the attentions of those who were.

Isabella severely angered her father only once. She was fourteen years old and he discovered she was calling herself Isabelle Martin at school.

'Do you really believe this little "o" at the end of your name is the villain?' he shouted, striking her with the full force of his anger and frustration. For days he could barely meet Isabelle's eye for shame. She lay on her bed and thought about those 'little o's and how they turned up in ugly words like wog, wop and dago and was determined not to take hers back.

The most cutting punishment for Isabelle, however, was to witness her sister's relentless efforts to be accepted. It wasn't that she tried hard to fit in – it was that she was stubbornly oblivious to the fact she didn't. Rosanna continued to invite girls home from school, who, despite their promises, very rarely came. And Isabelle hated it when they did come, because they gathered evidence that, sooner or later, would be used against them.

'Charlotte Furnell has only invited six girls to her birthday party and I'm one of them,' Rosanna announced proudly over dinner one night. 'Mr Furnell is going to collect us in his car – it's a Chevrolet.'

Charlotte was the most popular girl in school; everyone knew that she owned a horse named Bunty and had once flown in a plane to Queensland.

'I don't think you should go, Rosa,' said Isabelle anxiously.

'I *am* going and all the girls are getting new frocks, Mamma. We're going to have afternoon tea at Charlotte's house and then go to the pictures in Tindall and Mr Furnell has arranged to have a special birthday message for Charlotte up on the screen before the movie. She'll be famous!'

Franco laughed. 'Famous for turning twelve?'

'I can go, can't I, Babbo? They're very high-class people.'

'What's so special? We are very high-class people, child,' said Adriana. 'And we can't make a new dress every time you get a party invitation. You can wear the white one you had for the school formal.'

Rosanna leapt up from the table. 'I want a party dress, Mamma. *Please*. Blue with little white polka dots and a wide belt.' She spun around, her hands clasping her waist. 'And a swirling skirt. Just buy me the material – Bella will make it for me, won't you, Bella darling?'

'Sit down, girl, you'll ruin your digestion. Bella can cut down my dress with the pink roses for you.'

Rosanna scowled.

'Perhaps you shouldn't go,' repeated Isabelle quietly. Rosanna pretended not to hear.

On the day of the party, Rosanna was up at dawn to complete her chores and boil up the copper for a bath so she could wash her hair and be ready for Mr Furnell's arrival.

'Ah, roses for my Rosa. What clever and beautiful daughters I have,' said Franco when he saw Rosanna in her cut-down frock, hair smoothed into a ponytail. 'And what time is the famous Charlotte arriving?'

'She'll be here at two; I'll be the last one to be collected.' She showed him the embroidered silk purse Isabelle had made from scraps of fabric as a present for Charlotte.

Isabelle sat on the front step with her sister as she waited. 'You could still change your mind,' she whispered. 'I could meet them at the gate and tell them you're not well.'

'Silly goose – stop worrying.' Rosanna gave her sister a kiss on the cheek.

At two-thirty Rosanna announced, 'They're just running late. I'll go to the gate and wait there. You stay here.' Isabelle watched her walk down the drive. She seemed smaller, as though she had lost her adolescent bravado and slipped back into childhood.

Isabelle continued to wait on the step, listening for the rumble of an approaching car. At four o'clock Rosanna came back up the driveway, chin held high. She was silent as she passed her sister. She went to her bedroom, took off the dress, rolled it into a ball and put it in the bottom of the chest of drawers they shared.

'Mr Furnell's car probably broke down,' said Rosanna when she returned, sitting down on the step in her old work clothes. Isabelle nodded. She tried to put a comforting arm around Rosa's shoulders but was blocked by a black look and a raised elbow. Rosanna sprang up and ran – towards the river or the fields – as fast as she could.

On Monday morning, as soon as they got on the bus, Marcia Simmonds slipped into the seat in front of them. She twisted around to look at Rosanna. 'What a shame you couldn't come on Saturday, Rosanna,' she smiled. 'We were just turning into your road when Mr Furnell said, "She's not one of those Eyetalians, is she?" Of course, Charlotte said you were, and I hate to say that he was quite horrified. He turned the car around. Charlotte stuck up for you but he got really cross and said that everyone knew Italians were thieves and he wasn't having their kids spying in his house. So unfair.' The sisters said nothing, their faces impassive. Marcia flushed a little. 'I thought you should know, anyway.'

Rosanna lifted the lid of her school case and feigned absorption in its contents. Isabelle looked out the window. Perhaps now Rosanna would understand that in order to survive they needed to blend, to become as bland as devon on thin white bread.

The first time Jack Bennett saw Isabelle Martino was in the Duffy's Creek council offices. He had gone there to research some land titles for a new mining operation to be set up near Bateman's Lake, some 40 miles west of the town. He happened to be standing in the foyer when Isabelle materialised out of the shimmering heat of the day. A beauty in her late twenties, she wore white and carried a parcel wrapped in brown paper; she held it aloft, intriguingly large and soft, draped across both arms. The heels of her shoes clicked an even rhythm on the tiles as she passed him and headed down to see Nobby, the town clerk. Jack usually avoided Nobby but today, he decided, he would make an exception.

In Isabelle's presence Nobby was transformed. He radiated charm and allowed Jack to lean in the doorway without his usual caustic remarks. She laid the package across the clerk's desk. For a moment they both stood looking at the parcel as if in the presence of something sacred.

'Please, sit down.' Nobby gestured towards the visitor's chair. Isabelle sat. Nobby's secretary, Mrs Moss, and three of the typists crowded into the doorway, forcing Jack to stand inside the office.

'Well, it's a big moment.' Nobby rubbed his hands together. Isabelle smiled at him; her fingers formed a steeple in her lap. He undid the string and opened up the paper to reveal a gown in vivid red, trimmed in black velvet and – Jack leaned forward for a better look – 'Rabbit!' Jack said with surprise.

'Traditionally the robe is trimmed in sable, but I thought —' Isabelle began, sounding uncertain. Jack noticed her hair. Swept up in a rather old-fashioned French roll, it was the rich dark gold of bush honey. Little tendrils swirled at her nape; she fingered these nervously, smoothing them into submission.

Nobby lifted the mayor's robe carefully off his desk as though it was alive and might be dangerous. The typists whispered and giggled among themselves. Silly bunnies, thought Jack.

'It's perfect,' said Mrs Moss, who understood what was required in this moment. 'Just perfect. No one would ever even know it was rabbit. Our new mayor will look quite splendid!'

Taking that as approval, Isabelle stood and bobbed slightly in Nobby's direction. Jack was interested to see how the town clerk would respond to being curtsied to. Still standing, Nobby laid down the robe and gave a slight bow in return. Without a word Isabelle slipped out the door. Nobby followed her, sending the bunnies scurrying.

Jack leant over the robe and gently stroked it; the fabric was so soft it seemed to melt beneath his fingers.

'Get yer great mitts off that,' snapped Nobby, stepping back into the room. 'Are you here for any particular reason? Go and bother them down in engineering.'

Jack ran the length of the corridor and skidded into the foyer just in time to see the Italian's old truck pull away, Isabelle's face, ethereal as in a Renaissance painting, was framed in the passenger's window.

He knew of the local Italian and his daughters but would never have guessed that she was one of them. They had a small acreage and grew some crops, the surplus of which was sold in a roadside stall with an honesty box chained to it. He had bought apples or tomatoes from it occasionally. It took Jack several days to construct an excuse to call on the family and he did so before his nerve failed him.

It was well known that the mother rarely left the house and did not speak English, so it was unfortunate that she was the first person he encountered. She was sweeping the verandah and looked up with alarm when she saw Jack's Prefect round the bend in the drive. She stood quite still as he pulled up, then suddenly dropped her broom and scuttled off around the side of the house.

'*Franco*! *Franco*!' she shrilled.

Jack waited beside his car and finetuned his story as the minutes dragged by. Finally Franco appeared and greeted him warmly, as though he was always ready for an unexpected guest. A stocky man, almost a head shorter than Jack, he wore no hat, his black hair thick and luxuriant for a man in his fifties. He washed the dirt off his hands under the yard tap so that they could shake hands and Jack was struck by the energy and force behind that handshake. He was led around to the back of the house and urged to sit under the shade of the vine-covered pergola while Franco went inside calling to his wife, who had disappeared. Jack waited patiently, fingers idly tracing the vine-leaf design of the wrought-iron table before him.

'Is beautiful, yes?' Franco joined him at the table.

'Yes, very lovely.'

'My wife a city girl, from Genova. When she come Australia her father send many beautiful furniture with her. They think Australia it's a wild place and we must bring everything,' he said with a conspiratorial smile.

'It *is* a wild place,' replied Jack.

Franco nodded thoughtfully. 'Ah, *si*, *si*, she's wild and generous. Good earth. We grow everything here. *Paradiso*.' He gestured grandly towards what Jack knew to be a modest land holding of less than thirty acres. All the time he wondered about Isabelle's whereabouts. Perhaps she was inside the house, lying down during the heat of the day.

Franco talked on and on about his farming methods and the success he'd had with different crops. His accent, combined with his rapid English interspersed with Italian words, made it difficult to distinguish one from the other and impossible to follow everything he was saying. Occasionally Jack completely lost track of the topic but continued to nod sagely at what he hoped were appropriate moments until he caught up again. He began to feel like the suitor in a fairytale who comes to woo the princess but cannot get past the lonely king. He had no opportunity to put forward the pretext for his visit; Franco was clearly just delighted he had come.

Mrs Martino reappeared with a tray laden with coffee, cake and a plate of small crescent-shaped biscuits. Despite the afternoon heat she was dressed from head to foot in black. She didn't look at Jack, but had an exchange of words with her husband. Jack listened for a moment, thinking some sense might come out of it. It sounded like a spat but it was always hard to tell with foreigners. In the Broken Hill mines he had worked with blokes from Hungary, Yugoslavia, Germany and Italy, and most could barely speak any English. He found smoko more relaxing when they didn't attempt to make conversation but talked quietly among themselves. He liked to let the sounds wash over him like a song that required nothing of him.

He sipped his coffee, although he would have preferred a cup of tea or even a beer – it was almost unbearably strong. The sweet offerings, soft, crumbly and flavoured with almond, were delicious and he was embarrassed when he realised that in his distracted state he had eaten the lot.

Mrs Martino did not sit with them but melted back into the shadowy interior of the house. Franco rubbed his hands together with what appeared to be glee.

'So, Mr Jack. You are a man of the out door like me? A farmer?'

'Engineer.'

'Building?'

'Mining.'

'Ah, you work under ground, I work the top!' said Franco, as though they had truly established a commonality. 'Come,

come and see what wonderful gifts this generous woman grows on the top.'

They made their way through a small gate to an area where the vegetable gardens were as abundant as the ones Jack had seen the Chinese grow but on a smaller scale. Staked tomatoes, lettuces, beans, asparagus, cucumbers, carrots – Franco's face glowed with pride as he invited Jack to admire the compost he had created to enrich the garden beds. He dug out handfuls, crumbling it through his fingers to demonstrate the friability, colour and texture. Catching a fat worm around his finger, he lifted it to his face and murmured 'Hello, beautiful,' before replacing it almost reverently on the heap.

'Do you know these herbs?' asked Franco. '*Salvia, rosmarino, basilico, origano,*' he recited as he tore off a leaf of this or that and crumpled it under Jack's nose. 'I will give you some for your wife for cooking.'

'Thanks all the same. But I don't have a wife and my landlady wouldn't have a bar of herbs, I shouldn't think,' said Jack.

Chickens of every colour and pattern roamed the garden. Franco picked up a speckled marmalade hen, tucked it under his arm and stroked its head absentmindedly. He led Jack down a track that crossed the creek to show him his orchard, introducing him to each and every tree as if they were members of his family. There was still no sign of Isabelle. Franco seemed to sense he was losing his audience and suddenly remembered he hadn't yet played his trump card. 'Ah! I know why you come. Come, please, this way.' He discarded the chicken and set off at a trot back towards the house.

Veering off past the garden beds, they headed towards a large weatherboard implement shed that stood on the perimeter of the garden. As they stepped inside Jack was surprised to find the interior light and airy. The long wall that faced the hills was made completely of old windows cobbled together like a quilt of glass. It was hot inside but many of the windows had been opened to catch the first hint of the promised southerly.

Dazzled by the light, it took a moment for Jack to take it all in. The entire surface of the floor was covered in shallow boxes and other containers. Hundreds of cuttings were sprouting in tins and crates of every shape and size. This, he realised, was a propagation shed. And there, at one end of the shed, her hair tied back in a scarf and wearing a faded cotton frock and gumboots, knelt Isabelle. She was intent on her work and hadn't seen the men enter.

'Isabella, Rosanna! Come to meet Mr Jack.'

Isabelle sprang to her feet, startled. She glanced around as if looking for an escape route. Now she was standing, Jack could see that there was another figure working behind her. Rosanna also stood; slipping her arm casually through her sister's, she drew her towards the two men.

Franco introduced his daughters in a formal manner and, not knowing quite what was expected of him, Jack offered his hand. Rosanna laughed and shook it firmly with a muddy paw. Isabelle blushed and slipped her hands behind her back. Before Jack could say a word, Franco spoke to Rosanna in rapid Italian.

'*Scusi*, Mr Jack. I ask Rosanna to tell you, tell about the olives,' said Franco. 'Her English, it is perfect.'

'You've come to see the olives, have you?' asked Rosanna, looking Jack straight in the eye. He was within a few feet of Isabelle and playing for time. It was all getting rather complicated and difficult. Both women watched him and one at least seemed to see right through him. He was intrigued by how different they were: Isabelle so gentle and fair, so fragile; Rosanna more solid like her father, her long dark hair carelessly tied in a knot. She had pushed her sleeves up as though readying herself for a fight and her feet were bare and dirty. Jack wasn't sure he had ever met a woman quite like Rosanna and he wasn't sure he wanted to now. Feeling like a fraud, he assured her that he did, indeed, want to know about the olives.

Rosanna shot him a look of pure scepticism softened only by a hint of amusement. He had a feeling she was going to provide a dragon for him to slay before the day was over.

Three

I DREAM THAT I am standing on a hilltop looking across a wide green valley. In my arms I hold a crumpled sheet, as pale and fine as mist. I try frantically to fold it and make it orderly, clutching it to my chest, but the wind curls around me, teasing and tearing at the fabric. Finally I give up and throw it to the wind. But the wind doesn't tear it apart as I feared; it lifts it gently and it rises in a plume to the heavens.

It's not quite dawn when I wake. Lauren snores softly in the other bed. I used to love to watch her sleep when I came home late at night. She still sleeps like a ten-year-old – limbs flung about, mouth softly open.

I make myself tea, take it out onto the verandah and curl up on the sofa. I'm not in the habit of getting up this early. Anything to escape the sense of dark foreboding that has become my soul mate. The garden is quiet and still, apart from the occasional bird trilling in anticipation of dawn. The teacup warms my hands and there is a moment when I feel comforted, a moment when I feel calm and certain. But it's only another moment before I feel it all weighing down on me again.

I see my father's boots, still there by the door, awaiting his return. I called him Dad until my mother died. After that I thought of him as Jack, if I thought of him at all. I get up off the sofa and slip my feet into the boots. I stand for a moment, waiting for what I don't know. Direction? They're too big and ten times heavier than my usual heels but there is a safety in that. They are like small life rafts that will take me through the sea of grass. I clump down the steps and wade across the back lawn to the scene of last night's howling episode.

Standing on the barred gate I get a better sense of the land, now a dull monochrome in the half-light of dawn. Thick grass is growing up around the trees that are dotted through the paddock. Fine fragments of mist drift like wispy veils. The land rises towards rounded hills. Beyond them, I can see the first blush of the rising sun. As it creeps a little higher it suddenly shoots fingers of gold down the valley. Each moment they stretch closer towards me, illuminating tree after tree as the kookaburras set up their cry of 'Looka-kookalookalook!'

I open the gate and walk into the field. Behind the hedge an old truck sits quietly rusting. I hoist myself into the back and then onto the roof of the cab. From this higher vantage point I can now see that the trees are planted in strict rows. As the sun tips over the hills and pours a river of light down the valley, I realise there are hundreds and hundreds of trees and I've seen those silver leaves before, shimmering in the groves that grace the terraced hillsides of Tuscany. It's like discovering an orchard of silver clouds floating in perfect symmetry in your own backyard. Caught unawares by its beauty, I feel a rush of emotion and find myself blinking back tears.

I climb down off the truck and make my way through the grass to the nearest tree. I have to look closely to see the tiny green baubles, the promise of fruit to come. Encircling the trunk beneath the grass is a lacy skirt of olive stones, the flesh a feast for birds.

In the kitchen Lauren opens cupboards and bangs them closed, barely glancing in each one.

'What are you looking for?' I ask, coming in the back door.

'Food,' she says without stopping. Bang. Bang. Bang.

'You expect it to jump out at you?'

'Yes! There's nothing to eat!' She stares hard at me. 'Jeez, you look a dag in those boots. You'll be chomping on a bit of straw and linedancing next. Moving here is such a stupid idea. Believe me.' She gives me a patronising smirk.

I feel a sudden rush of red-hot fury. I'm angry. Really fucking angry.

'How the hell do you think food gets in cupboards, you selfish spoilt brat! You just don't *get it*! Sometimes life turns bad and there *is* no food to put in the cupboards. How dare you sneer, *sneer*, at me when I'm trying to get my bloody life back together?' The only weapon in sight is a tea towel – she's lucky – I pick it up and flick it as hard as I can across her bare calves.

'Shit! You don't have to throw a hissy fit about every little thing!' she squeals. Her face is pink and twisted up with anger. She grabs another tea towel off the bench. 'Hah!' She darts forward and I give a yelp as the tip connects with my left ear. We stand two metres apart, glaring at each other.

'Having a bit of a ding-dong, girls? Tea towels at forty paces?' Mrs Oldfield suddenly appears, unbuttoning her 'all-weather'. I've got to keep that front door closed, though that would probably only slow her down. She takes a coat hanger out of her basket and hangs her jacket behind the door. My ear throbs.

'Coffee, Mrs O?' Lauren looks as if she's suddenly started to have a good time.

'Why not?' replies Mrs O as she lifts a large plastic container from her basket and places it on the kitchen table. 'I made you a nice banana cake for morning tea.' She pulls out a chair and plumps herself down, takes in my night attire and adds, 'Brunch, perhaps?'

'That's nice,' I say weakly. There is a part of me that wonders what she thinks of us but there is almost a sense that she doesn't think anything. It's as though she pops in and out of people's houses as a matter of course, sees all sorts of strange behaviour and thinks nothing of it.

'So, Mrs Oldfield, you're from around here originally?' I pull up a chair, still nursing my ear.

'Oh, no, I'm a Melbourne girl. I didn't come to these parts until I was married in '51. So that's fifty-odd years, fairly long time I suppose.'

'What do you know about the olive trees?'

'The olives? They were planted before my time. The old Italian, Frank, put them in – that'd be just before the war, I'd say. They reckon there's exactly one thousand olives there. Probably what killed him in the end, planting all those trees.'

Lauren pours the coffee, passes the mugs around and cuts three large slices of cake for us. It's delicious.

'They say he planted them for the girls, like a dowry in the old days I guess,' says Mrs Oldfield.

'So you knew them well, Isabelle and Rosanna?' asks Lauren, sipping her coffee.

'Different as chalk and cheese, those two. Now Isabelle, she'd already married Jack and moved up the north coast to Elenora when I came to live here. I met her a couple of times, beautiful girl back then. Rosanna was a different sort, bit more rough and ready as they say. Good heart. We both worked at the local hospital, since pulled down, I might add.

'My Bill, God rest him, grew up here and he reckoned the first time he met Rosanna was up at Deakin's waterhole, swinging out on the rope in her underwear. That's convent girls for you. Very strict parents, I believe – wouldn't allow the girls to wear bathing suits or swim at the waterhole. They'd have been horrified if they found out what Rosanna got up to.' She chuckles. 'The family kept pretty much to themselves. Rosanna and the mother went back to Italy after Frank died. Someone told me the mother died too – I don't know when, probably twenty years ago at least.'

'What about Rosanna?' I ask.

'She came back from Italy for a while but then boarded up the house and went away for good. Like so many others around here.' She sighs heavily, as if missing all of them at once. 'Then Jack moved here when he retired.'

'Mrs O, you're something of a cook I gather?' I say, changing the subject.

'I can cook,' she replies cautiously. 'Can't everyone? It's a matter of having to, isn't it?'

'I'm more along the lines of a food *arranger*,' I say. 'I can arrange for food to be available and I can arrange for it to look appetising. But without deliveries and delis, we risk starvation.'

'Or living on toast,' says Lauren.

'The beauty of toast is its availability and predictability,' I say seriously. 'I'm not completely hopeless, I did cook things from time to time – years ago – just not with much success.'

Mrs Oldfield bursts out laughing. 'You'll never starve here. Come with me.' She hoists herself from the table and we follow her out the back door, around to the far side of the house. A path made of flat stones takes us through a small gate flanked on either side by a low hedge. Inside the enclosed area there are raised gardens and several small sheds, one of which has a fenced pen attached.

'Meredith up the hill has goats; you'll probably find the dratted things in your garden at some point. She's been looking after Jack's chooks, but I'm sure she'd be more than happy to drop them home – *if* you want them.' With the air of a prize-proud game-show hostess she takes in the scope of the garden with elegant sweeps of her hand. 'There's every kind of herb here in the garden. That's mint, sage, and the spiky one is rosemary. The freedom has gone to their heads, somewhat – just need reining in. Bit like kids, eh?' She gives me a wink. 'There are still lots of vegies; see this one in the corner with the fluffy leaves? That's asparagus, beautiful. Leeks, parsnips —' She bends over and pulls out a carrot. 'Ta-da! Look at that beauty.'

She hands it to Lauren, who hastily sidesteps, putting her hands up to protect herself from the threatening vegetable.

'It's filthy,' she says in her own defence.

Mrs Oldfield laughs and puts it in her pocket. 'If you get your chooks back, you'll have eggs and fresh chook.' She turns on her heel and heads down the dirt track through a copse of trees, us scurrying behind. 'Did she say French chooks?' whispers Lauren. '*Très exotique*!'

The track crosses a bridge over the creek and leads us out into a large orchard that slopes gently down towards the road. 'There's yer mandarin, oranges, peach, fig, nectarine, pear and even apple – the likes of which no one else has ever managed to grow around here. There was a bit of jealousy among a few of the locals – they'd buy Frank's apples off the stall and plant the seeds, without success as far as I know. We're too far north for apples really. Look, there's nuts, almonds. There's always something in fruit here. The Italian put all these in. He knew a lot about growing things.'

She turns to face her audience. 'It might be a bit more work than you're used to, ladies, but you won't starve.' She strolls off chortling, leaving us standing awkwardly in the orchard.

'So where are these olive trees you're so excited about?' asks Lauren. She follows me up the track and past the house to the back gate. The sun is high in the sky now and the drama of my early-morning discovery seems dissipated by the harsh light. She surveys the olive grove from a safe distance. 'Oh, you'll be right. You do know how to stuff an olive.' We giggle

42

like schoolgirls, still a little embarrassed by our chastisement, our general ineptitude. I can't believe I have actually laughed two days in a row. I can't remember when I last laughed out loud. It seems unnatural and makes me feel a little light-headed and disoriented. As if I wasn't already disoriented enough.

'Are these onions burning?' I lift the frying pan off the stove and tip it back and forth, sending showers of sizzling onions flying. Mrs Oldfield takes the pan from me and replaces it on the heat. I can already see that my cooking style, inspired by television chefs, is rather theatrical compared to Mrs O's more sober approach. We're making a shepherd's pie.

I'm glad of the distraction today. Lauren left this morning. I felt a profound sense of loss as I watched her disappear down the driveway in my car. It was partly her leaving, but if I'm honest it was just as much saying goodbye to my car – a symbol of my success. It's as though I needed to have it taken from me to confirm my sense of failure . . . the clang of the cell door, my freedom gone.

This cooking thing is quite stressful. I can feel myself growing hot all over. Mrs O brought the meat but we had to dig the potatoes and carrots out of the garden. Very messy and labour-intensive. Then the heat, the spitting oil – it's all quite dangerous really, not the frolic TV chefs make it out to be. She's brought me a cookbook she picked up at St Vinnie's, *Cooking for Idiots*. I'm not taking it personally.

Finally it's done. Covered in a snowy layer of mashed potato, the pie is ready to face the heat. We agree on a temperature and into the oven it goes.

'So where's Lauren's dad fit into the picture?' asks Mrs O out of the blue as she squirts detergent into the sink full of hot water.

'Hmm . . . he was American. Still is, I suppose.'

How do I explain Alex, let alone to someone as down to earth as Mrs O? Whenever I'm asked I feel the need to provide some neat explanation that will close the subject. A number of clichéd scenarios present themselves, all of which I've used before. I've never been able to devise a satisfactory explanation for my attraction to Alex – or at least one suitable for public scrutiny. Mature audiences only.

He was the only other delegate at a week-long conference who shunned the endless themed dinners and sat alone in the bar each night. I can only say there was an instant frisson between us. We ran away to Lahaina for three days and nights in an old hotel with a slow-moving ceiling fan that did nothing to cool the room. We drank gin slings on our verandah in the late afternoons and looked out across the bay where young Hawaiian maidens once swam out to the whaling boats. It felt so perfect; like a honeymoon. We were united in our audacity. Perhaps it was arrogance. It was short-lived, anyway. Several months later, in quick succession, I discovered that I was pregnant and he was married.

'Ah – American,' says Joy and, needing no further explanation, reaches for the kettle. 'Cup of tea, love?'

'Thanks. Did my father have a car?' I ask.

'He certainly did. He had an old blue ute. I'm not sure where it'd be. I suppose, with no family at the funeral, someone might have availed themselves of it.' She scalds the teapot and puts in several spoons of tea from a jar on the windowsill. 'Did you know Jack died at the railway station? He was just about to catch the train to Sydney – he used to go a couple of times a week – when he had the stroke right there on the platform. It's better if they go quickly, dear – with a stroke, you know. Especially now the hospital has closed.' She gives an exasperated tut as she gets the milk out of the fridge. 'I'd be checking with Sid at the garage about the car, opposite the station.'

I have a peek in the oven and am pleased to see the pie is safe, the top turning golden. 'How would you feel about taking me into town?'

'Sit down and have your tea, love. All in the fullness of time. Let's do that in the morning.'

It is late afternoon and the air feels dense, heat trapped under the lid of grey cloud. Mrs O rustles around in her basket and reveals a six-pack of 100-watt bulbs. 'They were a special on the shopper docket, so I picked some up.'

She hands me one and I stand on a chair and replace the bulb in the fitting.

'Let there be light!' she cries, and tugs on the string pull.

We sit in silence, drinking our tea in a 100-watt halo. I look around the kitchen. I need to get rid of all Jack's clutter and make this mine. I need a project.

After a while Mrs Oldfield says, 'Would you like me to show you how to bake a cake sometime?'

I didn't want her to leave but was too proud to say so. Now alone, I sit at the window and watch the light being chased from the sky by fearsome dark clouds while huge gusts of wind shake the trees. Corrugated iron clatters. Distant dogs bark. The garden disappears before my eyes. I'm drowning in blackness. I'm paralysed by fear. It's as though every fear I have ever had has come to dance and shriek and jeer at my weakness. Childhood terrors twirl and spin with middle-aged ones. Madman with machete; abandonment; getting old; being buried alive; dying alone. I need a drink. My greatest fear is being needy. Needing people, needing help, needing a drink. My greatest, greatest fear is of giving up, giving in to despair. I'm afraid I will give up like my mother did in her last few years and choose to soften life through a half-full glass of gin, her constant companion. Caught in its sweet embrace, she would lie dozing half the day, cry in her sleep and murmur words in a language I didn't understand.

I could ring a friend, tell them I have the phone on now. Give them the number. It would be nice to have the phone ring. But who? Who do I feel safe to reveal myself to in my current state? I've upsold my move here as a 'lifestyle choice': my business went down the gurgler, but I coped brilliantly. I'm just taking a breather – a sabbatical – doing the country thing for a while. I'm totally in control.

I don't trust myself to make a call. I might cry.

It's as dark in the house as it is outside. I'm in a void, invisible to the world. I used to feel I was pivotal, the core of many lives. People vied for my attention, craved my approval. People sought my advice and paid highly for it. Now the lines of communication are silent, and so am I.

Rain hammers on the roof and drizzles down the window. I feel around for the side table, find the lamp and switch it on. Now I see my misery reflected back at me, rain dissolving my features. I don't even look like me.

I close the curtains quickly, move about the room switching on lights and the television, which floods the room with voices. I notice my hands are trembling as I fumble to open a bottle of wine and pull up a chair to the screen, basking in the light and sound. A gulp of wine sears my throat. The TV emits a long slow whistle and the glittering images of the outside world suddenly reduce themselves to a single dot in the centre of the screen. The only image I see is that of an anxious middle-aged woman in a state of disarray, clutching a glass of wine. Me again.

Distraction is my only escape. I run into the kitchen, spilling half my wine on the way. Switch on the radio. Angelic voices fill the room. A hundred voices, I can see them all in white, faces raised to the heavens as they sing of the sweet chariot comin' for to carry them home. My mother loved this song. She was always happy when she sang along to the radio, especially songs about God, whom she also loved. She did have faith in Him. Suddenly I miss her beyond all reason. I miss her as if she died today instead of thirty years ago. It's not simply my mother I miss. It's something else. I miss the things I never got from her. She never shouted at me, slapped me, cried with me or sang with me. She never let loose in a way that told me she truly loved me – loved me passionately, feared for me unreasonably, felt my pain as her pain. It was as though she had given up on me from the beginning.

I can hear a woman gasping for breath, great choking sobs rising to an animal howl. It's me. I huddle in the corner of the kitchen and wait for the storm to pass, then I creep into my cold little bed and sleep with my clothes on, mouth sour with the taste of wine.

The house is cold and damp when I wake at dawn for the third day in a row. I can't think of a single reason to get out of bed except that I feel so bad lying in it. I haven't finished unpacking my clothes and have to resort to putting on my father's dressing-gown that hangs on a hook behind the door. It's brown, like almost everything he wore – doesn't show the dirt – but softer than it appears.

The desperation of the night before has dissipated. I'm back to feeling tired, worn-down and worn-out. I make tea and drink it, only realising I have done so when I see the cup is empty. I make another cup and take it out to the verandah.

I think about Rosanna swinging on that rope in her underwear. You'd never see my mother in her underwear. Even I didn't until near the end. When that time came I had to sleep with her to keep her warm at night. She was too weak to do anything for herself. I'd help her to the toilet, hold the bowl while she vomited. Every day I thought my father would come. Finally, she asked for him. There was no one else to say goodbye to. I rang him in Mount Isa, begging him to come. He asked to speak to her.

'Come *here* and speak to her,' I hissed. 'She needs to *see* you.'

'I'll speak to him,' my mother called from the bedroom. 'Help me to the phone.'

It took forever to coax her emaciated body from the bed. I could feel my father's impatience radiating from the phone. At her insistence I helped her slip her robe on, the pale pink silk he sent for her birthday the year before. I smoothed her hair back and twisted it into a knot, just the way she liked it.

'He can't see you, you know, Mum,' I said wearily.

She looked gaunt and pale as she sat down in the little chair she kept by the telephone table. Her hand, like a starving bird, flapped at me to leave. Our eyes followed the trajectory of her wedding ring as it flew from her finger and spun across the polished floor. Her face sagged with dismay. Neither of us moved to pick it up. I didn't want the burden of it. She didn't have the strength.

'How are you, Jack? I'm fine, I'm getting there.' She avoided my eye as I left the room. As I closed the door I heard her say in a plaintive voice, 'Please try to find her for me, just this one last time.'

'Who do you want Dad to find for you?' I asked later as I slipped her robe off and helped her back into bed.

'Just a friend, darling. An old friend I haven't seen for a long time. Daddy said he'd do his best to find her. I'd like you to meet her.' She lay back on her pillows and closed her eyes. 'You won't leave me, will you, darling?' she sighed. Yet she was leaving *me*. I felt she was abandoning me, as though she and the cancer were complicit in some way.

And so she waited. I've heard stories about people who hold death at bay until someone arrives or a baby is born, but what if you hold on and on and the person doesn't arrive? What if you have to be fed a drop at a time to keep you alive for a reunion that is never going to take place? What if you hold on until the light has died in your eyes and you don't even have the strength to speak? And no one comes. Even my father did not come to say goodbye to her.

As a child I was instinctively aware that my mother was constantly searching for someone. She would stop suddenly to watch a stranger emerge from a shop or quicken her pace to catch someone walking ahead, always a woman. 'Just someone I thought I knew,' she would say.

Now I know who it was. It was Rosanna. And now I know why she didn't come. She was my father's lover. Perhaps he knew where she was all along. Perhaps he didn't. Perhaps he found her and she wouldn't come. Perhaps it was too late. I may never know.

He came to the funeral alone. During the long hours at my mother's bedside my thoughts often turned to what I would say to him when I finally saw him. It varied from a few barbed remarks to a thirty-minute diatribe on his meanness and his despicable cowardice. My childhood was littered with broken promises from him and in those empty hours I revisited every single one of them, railed against the injustices of his penny-pinching ways and – worst of all – his indifference to our plight. He knew Mum was dying. He knew my youth was being sucked out of me caring for her. I never heard her say a cross word to him. Yet he could not find it in himself to come and spend one hour with her. Why had he even bothered to breeze in and out of our lives all those years? Why didn't he just bugger off for good like other hopeless fathers? Why didn't he have the courage to divorce her and be done with us? (Not that my mother would have ever agreed; she had the moral sensibilities of a bygone era.) In the end I couldn't even be bothered finding out the answers. He probably wouldn't have told me anyway. At the funeral I gave him the key to the flat and left without a word. I took only what belonged to me. I was nineteen years old when I chose to go out into the world as an orphan.

I'm still lounging on the verandah when a car comes creeping slowly up the driveway, avoiding possible stone chips on the BMW's bright metallic gold paintwork. The driver seems to fill the car. He stays in his seat and pushes the door open. A fat globule of saliva lands on the gravel.

'Missus Bennett?' he bellows. I give a slight nod. 'Darryl Leeton.' He doesn't so much shout as boom. When I show no sign of getting up he reluctantly heaves himself out of the driver's seat, gently closes the door and leans against the car. They obviously can't be parted. I'm forced to get up and walk to the top of the steps.

His eyes flick over me from head to foot and back again. He takes in the old brown robe, the man's slippers, the very bad hair thing happening. If only I had a cigarette hanging off my lip to complete the picture. It's not that I don't care what he thinks, I just haven't the strength to try to redeem myself in his eyes. And he's not such a glorious sight himself. He's got the biggest gut I have ever seen. It's securely contained in a stretched-to-capacity T-shirt advertising 'Leeton Earthmovers' gathered like a balloon at the bottom and tucked into a pair of little-boy elastic-topped shorts. I cannot imagine this man making the earth move for any woman.

'How ya goin'?'

'Pretty good. And you?'

'Yar. I'll get to the point. I'm looking for acreage and I might just be interested in your property.'

'Hmm,' I say with a sweet smile. 'Lucky me.'

He raises his eyebrows, folds his arms and reorganises his backside on the car. He glances across the expanse of gleaming bonnet, as though to draw my attention to its golden splendour.

'Nice car,' I volunteer.

'Yer probably used to Sydney prices. Little 30-acre patch like this in't worth much up here.'

I can't decide whether he is deaf or rude. 'What about the olives?' I say loudly.

'Olives!' he snorts. 'What about 'em?'

'Aren't they a business proposition?'

'We don't eat olives around here,' he says witheringly. 'Bloody lot of work to pull 'em out, not everyone wants to take that on. But I've got the equipment, ya see.'

In my old life I'd have had a tart riposte at hand but I don't have the energy. Besides, Darryl clearly isn't the sort to appreciate a camp retort. 'Look, I might well be interested in selling. I haven't had time to think about that option yet. Perhaps you could leave your card and I'll get back to you,' I say in my most reasonable voice.

'Don't yer want to hear me offer?' he says crossly.

'I don't want to be influenced by that.'

He gives a grunt, gets in the car and reverses the entire length of the driveway at high speed. There's a man who knows how to leave in a hurry.

I expect I'll be marked in Duffy's Creek as an eccentric.

The niece of the girl who swam in her undies. People who eat olives. The truth is my mother would be ashamed if she saw the way I looked right now. We might be losing the plot behind closed doors but in public we always look our best.

I still remember some of the clothes my mother made me. Lulled to sleep every night by the soft thudding of her sewing machine, sometimes I would wake to find a new dress had been gently laid on the end of my bed during the night. I would be especially careful not to wake her as I made my breakfast and left for school. She was almost never awake to see me try my new clothes on. It made me sad in a way. Our moments of pleasure never seemed to coincide.

Four

As THE SUMMER slipped into autumn, Jack began to go as often as he could to the farm. He boarded in a house in town with two other Austmine employees: a West Australian called Snow, and Michael, an Irishman, both geologists with an interest in amateur boxing. The three shared a bad-tempered landlady, Mrs Migro, whom they nicknamed Mrs Migraine. With a few gins under her belt of an evening she would thump on their doors, shrilling accusations regarding smoking, drinking, blaspheming and women – none of which were permitted in the rooms or in the house. Michael formed a theory that her husband had run off with a smoking, drinking, blaspheming woman. And now she had it in for all of them. 'Mary, Mother of Jesus, who the fook could blame him!' he muttered with monotonous regularity.

Dinner was immovable at 5.30 p.m., devised – all three men agreed – to sabotage their last half-hour of drinking time before the pub closed. It was an unrelentingly dismal affair of boiled vegetables and overcooked meat – hardly worth missing a beer for.

'Don't go rushing out – I've slaved all afternoon to make

yer pudding,' Mrs Migraine would screech from the kitchen as they sat silently, chewing to the beat of the clock.

'It better not be fooking tapioca again,' Michael murmured into his cauliflower cheese. Pudding was almost always something warm and sloppy they would bolt down, half out of their chairs.

'Just off for our constitutional, Mrs M.' It was Jack's job to keep her sweet. The moment they were out of sight they sprinted down the street, invariably arriving at the pub as the last bell sounded, hurling themselves into the fray at the bar. Later they would sit in the park or by the river, smoking and talking, reliving fights they had heard on the radio. Snow and Michael were good blokes but they bored Jack with their constant jawing about rocks. He wasn't much interested in boxing either, and often ambled off home early to read or sleep. His weekends seemed endless.

Franco had asked if he would come one afternoon and help him put in a new strainer post for the old fence between the orchard and the olive grove where his three cows grazed. It was a two-man job, not that his girls weren't up to it, but the women were still busy preparing the nets for the winter olive harvest.

The warm evenings lingered in early March and Jack enjoyed being outdoors without the sound of the dredge in the background. He had time to appreciate the soft touch of the air on his skin and the pulsing chorus of frogs and crickets. The two men quickly found they liked to work at a similar pace and would stop from time to time and discuss the job or have a break.

They often sat and smoked quietly, watching the light

redefine the landscape as it distilled to gold, creeping ahead of lengthening shadows to its last visible point on the hills that marked the far boundary. One evening, as they sat, Franco gestured towards the hills. 'I want be buried up there. Is where I find my peace, my God. God made this church with His hands. This is my heaven, I rest in the sun, watch over my *oliva* forever.'

'Fair enough,' said Jack as he flicked his cigarette butt into the hole they were digging. 'But you won't get too much sun six foot under, you know.'

Franco was anxious to have urgent maintenance work on the farm completed before winter when the olive harvest would take place and add to the family's already heavy workload. Jack helped him build a new pen for Fiori, the big lazy sow. In late autumn they rebuilt the wooden struts for the vines that were the source of Franco's *vino rosso* – something Jack was reluctantly acquiring a taste for.

These comparatively simple tasks held a level of satisfaction Jack had never experienced in his own work, mostly to do with the scale of the projects. He was surprised at how rewarding it was to complete a job in a single day. It was intensely physical, requiring him to lift, push, pull and pound in nails with a hammer. The outcome was simple and obvious. Yet in many ways these small projects were quite challenging. First, there was no money for materials; they had to either exist on the property or be recovered from the local tip. Then there was the plan. Franco was always convinced there was one right way to do the job and would enter into spirited debate with Jack as to what it was. Jack learned to allow Franco the joy of debate while slowly imposing what appeared to him to be a natural sense of order in the work. Franco clearly had respect for the fact that Jack was a foreman with an engineering degree, even if it had little relevance to the job at hand.

'All right – you the boss!' he would capitulate, hands thrown up in parody of helplessness. Jack was not an easy man to rile and he was amused by the way a recalcitrant nail or a mislaid hammer could set Franco off, muttering furiously, '*Porca Madonna*! *Porca miseria*!' Jack's standard response, 'Keep your hat on, mate', became their private joke.

Many evenings that autumn they worked until dusk laid damp hands on their shoulders and then Jack would feel a surge of anticipation at the evening that lay ahead. It was as though something in him was ripening. It slowly blossomed as they packed up the tools and inspected the work, as Franco clapped him on the back, exclaiming with delight at what they had accomplished. As they walked towards the house, pulled off their boots on the step and pushed through the kitchen door to be embraced by the fragrant harmonies of sizzling onion and garlic, this ripening bud would burst and send a rush of warmth through Jack's body. It was only looking back that he recognised that the feeling was joy. Warm joy.

The first few meals with the family had been a little awkward. Unlike Jack's own family, who were forced to eat in total silence, the Martinos jumped up and down from the table, they passed food and they added helpings to his plate.

Franco insisted he have a glass of *vino d'uva* before the meal, vital for the *digestivo*; then pasta, olives, basil and tomatoes from the garden; rabbit stew; the dense white bread he often saw proving on the shelf above the wood-burning stove; salad with peppery leaves. No slippery pudding but *caffè corretto*, spiked with Franco's precious stock of *grappa*. Jack often had trouble finding his car when he left.

There was talk about food, about what was ripe in the garden and what needed to be done but Jack's role was ambiguous. He sensed there was a contribution he as a guest could and should make but something held him back. Isabelle also remained reserved, shy in his presence. She kept a watchful eye on Jack, which made him wonder what she did with all the information she gathered.

Mrs Martino, at first suspicious of Jack, began to welcome him more when, on Rosanna's advice, he addressed her as Signora Martino and discovered that a simple '*Grazie, Signora*' elicited a shy smile. '*Prego,*' she would reply.

Rosanna seemed mildly amused by Jack. 'Mamma is concerned that my father is corrupting you with his swearing and peasant dialect,' she told him once when Franco was out of the room. 'You have to understand that Mamma is a convent girl from Genova; my father is a *contadino*, a farmer. He thinks that running water in the house is a great luxury.'

'Nothing wrong with being a farmer,' said Jack, affronted on Franco's behalf.

It was in Jack's nature to be curious about what things were made of and how things worked; what size beam might be required to replace a supporting wall or how much cement might be required to fill a particular hole for holding a strainer post. These were topics he and Franco could and would talk about endlessly. He knew women didn't have the same sort of interests but it was the only place he was comfortable. It was Isabelle he wanted to engage with but he couldn't think what to ask her about her work as a dressmaker. Rosanna was a cook at the hospital; he often saw her riding a rickety black bike to the bus stop. He told her how disagreeable the food had been in the army hospital in Alexandria. She laughed, unsympathetic. 'Hospital food is supposed to discourage malingerers.'

'Were you wounded?' asked Isabelle.

'No, I was with the sappers – engineers. We all went down with dysentery. So, when that was done with, we were pretty desperate for some decent tucker.'

When, with a slight sense of desperation, Jack began to ask more searching questions about them it was as though the family had been waiting for someone to share their stories with. It seemed that the Martinos' lives were held together by clusters of stories of the past that somehow safeguarded the promise of the future.

Franco told how his family had farmed the olive and produced some of the best oil in Liguria for three generations. 'The *Taggiasca* – very special tree. A tree that gives to the family for hundreds of years – maybe 600 years! Is a tough tree, strong and tall. It can live through terrible cold and terrible heat – but not with Domenico, not with my *fratello*.'

'His brother,' nodded Rosanna.

'*Si*, my brother. He is a man who cannot read or write,

but ah! He can play the cards for the lira. *Gioco d'azzardo bastardo.*' Franco rocked his head in his hands, seemingly stricken all over again.

'My Uncle Domenico was the youngest brother. He went down to the south, to "seek his fortune" as they used to say,' explained Rosanna. 'Got in with the wrong crowd, so it seems.'

'*Calabrese*! *Siciliano*!' said Franco with disgust. '*Terroni.*'

'Ah yes, it was all very dramatic and my father had to sell the family farm to pay the loan sharks so my uncle didn't end up losing his private parts to a *Siciliano* stiletto.' Rosanna mimed a gruesome twist and slice manoeuvre.

Isabelle looked mortified. 'Rosa, I think you're giving Jack a bad impression of Italian people.'

'He's got a brain, hasn't he? He knows all Italians aren't thieves and Mafia – just some of them.' Rosanna laughed and glanced over at his lap. 'But you better watch yourself, Jack.' He smiled.

'Rosanna! Please . . .' blushed Isabelle. She took up the story. 'We moved from the farm to Genova, and stayed in my grandparents' house. We were to live there until my father found work. Their house was very comfortable compared to where we lived on the farm. I was only four but I remember how impressed I was that they had electricity and a flush toilet.'

Rosanna conveyed the conversation to her mother. '*Si, si, toletta a livello,*' sighed Signora Martino, lifting her hands to the ceiling in mock despair. 'Still no flush!'

'My wife's parents always shouting at me "Get your wife a beautiful house. Get your daughters some pretty dress".

They always angry because they no want Adriana to marry a *contadino* – they think I am a filthy peasant.' Franco smoothed his thick black waves, like an effete hairdresser, and leant forward to confide in Jack. 'For Adriana my beautiful hair, it was . . . *irresistibile*.'

Jack saw Adriana Martino laugh out loud for the first time and he realised that she had once been a beautiful woman. It was from her that Isabelle inherited the honey-coloured hair and grey eyes but Isabelle's were not filled with sadness the way her mother's were. It seemed to Jack that Adriana had faded like a flower that must wither and fall so another may blossom.

'The cane farmers from Queensland came to many big cities in Italy looking for workers for the cane fields,' explained Rosanna. 'They were prepared to pay the passage on the ship and guarantee work, so Papa signed up and sailed off into the sunset.'

Isabelle leant towards Jack across the table. 'Rosanna was only two years old; she doesn't remember how terrible it was when Papa left on the ship. I was five and remember all too clearly. I cried and cried – the ship was so huge and crowded with people I was sure that it would sink at any moment and Papa would be lost.'

To Jack's great discomfort, tears welled in Franco's eyes as he described the moments when the ship pulled away from the port: the sight of Adriana and his little girls waving from the dock – the unbearable pain in his heart. Overwhelmed by grief and loneliness, he turned away only to be confronted by a vast ocean he was about to cross, taking him further and further from the family that made him feel whole.

'Queensland very hot. Very hot,' said Franco, shaking his head in disbelief. 'We go to work when the moon is full – three in the morning. Come home when the sun she's full. Sleep, eat, back to fields in afternoon. Is hard life, sleeping on ground, no soft bed – mattresses with coconut hair. Rats, mosquitoes and always our hands, blisters, infected.'

Franco had made friends on the ship – Luigi, Alberto and Sergio, Italians from the north who became part of his canecutting gang and like family. Sergio was counting the days until he had the money he wanted to take home but Luigi and Alberto were excited about the opportunities in this new country. They delighted in the distances from one place to another, and were intoxicated by its vastness and the freedom it offered. Franco was torn, but in the end Mussolini made up his mind for him; he wasn't going home to fight for fascism.

Franco knew that olives wouldn't grow where sugarcane did and he knew his daughters couldn't survive in a town where the tide of anti-Italian feeling was rising and the 'olive peril' had become the new underclass. It was one of the happiest days of his life when he packed up his newly purchased second-hand truck and headed south to Melbourne to collect his family from the ship, almost three years since he had last seen them.

'*We* were the ones who brought the olive trees with us. We are, in fact, the heroines of the olive,' said Rosanna as she helped her mother clear the table for the next course.

'How so?' asked Jack, fearing a joke at his expense.

Rosanna leant on the back of her chair opposite Jack and announced dramatically, 'We stole our inheritance back!'

'It wasn't really *stealing*,' said Isabelle firmly.

'Uncle Domenico drove us up to the farm in his new American car – which he won in a card game,' she added, with a glance in her father's direction. 'He heard that the new owners were going to Genova for a wedding.' Rosanna mimed tiptoeing into the olive groves. 'Mamma, Bella, our two cousins and myself. We did a little midnight pruning, you might say – *prugna secca*, Mamma.'

'Ah! *Si, si*!' chimed Signora Martino. She came and stood beside Rosanna, tugging excitedly at her dress. 'On ship. Water every day. Sew here,' she said, pointing out the seams to Jack.

'All our olives have been propagated over time from those cuttings we smuggled in; that's why some of the trees are much older than others.'

'Beautiful family,' beamed Franco. 'Beautiful *Taggiasca*.'

Jack was not a man who cared to talk for the sake of it but it seemed as though his own history began to take shape around that table. The expectation that he also had stories forced him to cast his mind back to the defining moments in his life, to work out what he had – however unwittingly – invested in and what was worthwhile about it. He was thirty-four years old and had, as yet, done very little thinking about what sort of shadow he cast.

He found an audience in the Martinos when he began to talk about his experiences in the Outback working the mines. In his first job as a driller's offsider he spent a lot of time on top of the drilling towers replacing rods and watching the changing light of the desert. He struggled for words to describe the dramatic beauty of the place, the different times of the day when the sun and shadows played with light on the canvases of ghost gums, the vivid colours, the contrast of smoky-green spinifex against red soil. As he talked about the desert he remembered how free he felt out there. But it hadn't stopped him wanting to go underground.

Jack tried to convey the atmosphere waiting at the brace, 300 men all going underground blast-hole drilling. The murmured discussions, the sense of purpose and camaraderie as the shift bosses moved quietly through the crowd allocating jobs. Someone would crack a joke, then a ripple of laughter followed. There was the sense that they were different from other people with their underground world. He described how it felt to go down in a cage cramped with forty men, the smell of the mine, the sulphides and occasional blasts of heat, the pervading cold dampness. He shared his sense of wonder at the sheer scale of the mines, at finding trains and massive equipment operating under the ground.

Jack told stories about the men he worked with, mostly Hungarians, Ukrainians and Poles. Then there were the Germans, ex-Luftwaffe, who marched to the mines in high boots. There were those who took pride in their work and others who took pride in dodging it, *and* dodging the foreman. He told them about the pub at Mount Isa where you had to bring your own glass and line it up ready for the flow of beer that would often only last an hour; how his workmates would share their lunch with him when they saw the soggy mess of beetroot sandwiches his landlady gave him every day; and about the chess games that were played in shifts over days and nights, a game that crossed all borders and required no linguistic abilities to win.

Rosanna and Isabelle translated these stories so their mother could understand. 'But what of his family?' Adriana wanted to know.

Jack found it hard to explain that things were different with them. His family didn't make him feel whole. If he had been brutally honest, he would have said they actually made him feel empty, but he wasn't one to share his feelings on these matters. It would have seemed disloyal to talk about his father's sense of rough justice, learnt from his own childhood spent in an orphanage. He bullied his sons mercilessly and goaded his wife with insults and threats.

'He never knew a mother's love,' his mother would tell them in an effort to excuse his behaviour. He never knew an employer's love either, it seemed to Jack when he grew old enough to become more sceptical about his father's version of events. Every new job represented a new start, his father relieved to be free of the unreasonable tyranny of his last boss. Every job ended abruptly. Boilermakers were in demand, but for some reason his father could never seem to find two jobs in the same town. Another job, another town, another house, another school. By the time Jack left home, they had edged their way through Victoria and South Australia and halfway back again.

After the first couple of schools, Jack and his brother Henry could scarcely be bothered making new friends. By high school Jack was marked as a loner by teachers and students alike. It didn't concern him. He realised early on that as long as he took out the school's mathematics prize at the end of each year he could remain relatively undisturbed, both at school and at home, a member of his own private club. The first time he won the prize – much to his surprise – he saw the shift in attitudes around him and understood that it was his talisman, guaranteeing safe passage. There was something muscular about maths that won him the grudging respect of more physical students. It served him well as an engineer, but later he thought he'd happily trade his mathematical prowess for better social skills, for a First in small talk.

Although the old man had mellowed with the years, Jack could sense the anger and resentment simmering quietly below the surface calm. After a lifetime of unhappiness his mother lived in a state of constant nervous anxiety. Sensitive to perceived slights and prone to sulking, she seemed to believe her survival depended on total order and predictability. The mysterious appearance of crumbs on her sparkling bench or an unexpected phone call could send her into a spin. Jack couldn't begin to explain to the Martinos why he and his brother had nothing to say to each other any more. Only perhaps that neither wished to be reminded of the years they spent together, imprisoned by childhood and the shared dread of the next town.

After dinner the women would clear up while the men sat by the fire. Franco taught Jack to play scopa. Jack taught Franco to play euchre. Rosanna had recently bought a small radio, brown and plump as a pudding. She was clearly thrilled with it. When the chores were done the sisters would place it on the kitchen table and huddle in front of it while Isabelle, who had been top of her Pitman's class, took down the lyrics of the latest songs in shorthand. From time to time Franco would call for the volume to be turned up, thinking he recognised an Italian song, only to be disappointed. Not to be put off, he would comment, 'That chap has beautiful voice, I think must be Italian anyway.'

The after-dinner conversation always returned to Franco's obsession: the farm and the future of the olives. Despite evidence to the contrary, he was convinced that he would make his fortune from the olive. Each week he sold his excess produce at the market – they took his tomatoes, corn, carrots and summer fruits – but no one wanted the olives. Now he believed his fortune lay in the oil.

'The Australian thinks olive oil goes in the ears!' he laughed. 'Our oil will not be yellow like corn ears, but green like the river.'

He and Jack talked about the olive press. Jack drew up plans of the stone mill and press, based on sketches Franco had brought from Italy. They would pore over this drawing, discussing materials, weights and techniques. Franco's mill would make pure olive oil and once people tasted it everything would change for the family. People would understand the gift of the olive and they would see he was a hero, not a fool.

In later years Jack could close his eyes and enter that vibrant room again and again. He could feel its warmth, smell the rich infusion of herbs and tomatoes, hear Rosanna humming as she moved about the kitchen and see Isabelle glance up from setting out the glasses on the white cloth to smile at him. He would look back on this time as the happiest of his life. A time when he felt loved.

Five

I'M ASLEEP ON the couch when Mrs O arrives mid-morning to take me into town. I don't ever recall napping on the couch in the daytime before. She doesn't seem fazed, and makes me a cup of tea while I get changed. I'd be furious if I was doing someone a favour and found them not only not ready, but snoozing on the couch. What did I do to deserve this guardian angel?

She's a confident driver, zooming along in her little car.

'Mrs O?'

'Call me Joy, dear.'

She hoots with laughter when I ask if that's her real name.

'We don't change our names around here, love,' she says. Just so I know.

'Joy, if I was looking for work around here . . .'

'What sort of work can you do?'

'I have a marketing degree . . . corporate communications is my area.'

'Telecommuting is all the go now, dear,' she says helpfully. 'Do you have a web site?'

'No. Do you?'

'Noooo! I don't even have a computer. But I wouldn't mind one of those notebooks – *very* dinky. Can't think what I'd use it for, though.'

'I need work. Any work at all.'

She says she'll think about it. She buzzes through town and pulls up with a jolt outside the service station. 'There's Sid,' she says with a nod in his general direction. 'I'll wait here.'

As soon as I enter the workshop a dog begins to trail me, sniffing my legs. It's a short-haired mutt, black and brown with begging eyes. I cautiously offer my hand and receive a soggy lick.

Sid emerges from a back room, looking like a grubby Teletubby in yellow overalls that have been hacked off at the shoulder. His upper arms are blue with tattoos; he's had a few changes of heart, by the look. I know the feeling. He has a wicked-looking scar down his left cheek. This is one tough Tinky-Winky.

'Yer right?'

I explain who I am and why I'm here. Under his hostile gaze I hear myself stuttering slightly. Stuttering! What fresh hell is this?

Just when he looks as though he has no intention whatsoever of cooperating he pulls a filthy rag from the pocket of his overalls and wipes his hands. He goes into his office, pushes aside the greasy jumble of tools and papers, opens a cupboard and takes a set of keys off one of the hooks. 'Ute's out the back. The dog goes with it,' he calls over his shoulder.

'Dog?' I yelp.

Sid comes out of the office and throws me the keys. 'Used to stay in the back of the ute when Jack went down to the big smoke. Took me three days to convince the bastard to get out. I've been stuck with it ever since.' He waits for me to leave. Hands on hips. Conversation over.

A battered blue ute is parked out the back of the workshop. I try the key. Hello, my new car. It is not like any car I ever thought I would own, but actually I am grateful to have a car right now. At the sound of the engine the dog comes skittering out and leaps into the tray. As we pull out of the driveway beside the service station Joy waves madly and gives me a double thumbs up as though I have just accomplished something truly amazing.

I feel a little self-conscious as I cruise down the main street with the dog running back and forth yapping excitedly in the tray but there is hardly anyone around and no one pays any attention. I stop and buy groceries at the Superette, two bottles of wine at the bottle shop next door (bottom shelf, but not at the cask stage yet) and go back to the Superette for dog food. Forgot I owned a dog.

As I drive up to the house the dog yelps with excitement, leaps out of the tray and heads straight to a bowl on the verandah to snuffle around for food. It scoots around the garden, pokes its head in here and there, sniffs at this and that and shoots off down towards the orchard. If I knew its name I'd probably call it back. Or perhaps not.

I must have chronic fatigue or something even worse because I'm completely exhausted by what amounts to one hour out in the big wide world of Duffy's Creek. Tempting as it is, I cannot spend the rest of my life lying on the couch.

I need to be busy. Busy, busy busy.

I make a cup of tea and a tomato sandwich and sit down on the couch. For the first time I really focus on the room. There are a few pictures on the walls, amateur landscapes in watercolour, and a big polished *chiffonier* full of glasses and crockery. Some stacks of books stand against the wall. There's a stone fireplace made by someone who didn't entirely have the hang of it. The floor is a dark timber, not in great shape, and there's a large rug rolled up in the corner. The curtains are yellowing lacy jobs, windows cloudy with dirt. Now that we have cleared the top layer of debris another one seems to have emerged. I get up and take a closer look at the paintings. Dear God, his name is on every one of them. Talk about the secret life of Jack Bennett. It has to be the ultimate irony that a mining engineer should take up landscape painting in later life. Who is this Jack?

I'm starting to understand that this house is an archaeological site. When I look around I can see the patch of worn lino where my grandmother would have stood at the sink. There are burnished brass hooks on the back of the kitchen door where my grandfather probably hung his jacket in the winter. When I open the back door I can see the groove in the doorstep where the family dragged off their boots a thousand times. *My* family. I close my eyes and try to imagine them in this room as they prepared a meal, sat at the table and ate and talked together – in Italian?

The dog is back. Tilting its head, looking expectant. What is this blasted dog's name, I wonder. 'Dog?' His tail thumps on the floor.

For two days no one comes, no one calls. It's just Dog and

me. I make myself busy. I move the furniture, polish, clear out virtually every box in the house. I take down the curtains and clean the windows, roll out the rug on the living-room floor; it's the milky blue of opal and gives the room a real lift.

I clear out the bedroom that has the double bed, all the while resisting the temptation to compare it with my former white, sky-filled room. Finally there is only the bed with its plain wooden bedhead, a chest of drawers and the wardrobe; it's quite pleasant. French doors open onto the back verandah and garden. The walls are whitewashed. I take down the faded pictures of Naples and Rome and replace them with two of my own large prints of Picasso's line drawings. I make the bed with my mother's sheets and a dark blue satin quilt that was in the chest.

That night as I lie on the cool white sheets the smell of lavender lingers. A bright patch of moonlight falls across the bed. I get up and open the doors to let the moon in and find Dog stretched out on the verandah. The garden is lit with a vivid fluorescence. The warm night resonates with a chorus of clicking, thrumming and twittering, a delicate undulating sea of sound. I leave the door open and climb back into bed; soon I hear soft shufflings as Dog migrates across the threshold.

It is odd to think that my grandparents once lay in this bed, on the same mattress by the feel of it. I wonder what they talked about, what they worried about. I wonder if they made love in the light of the moon. I sleep soundly that night, for the first time in months – a deep, dreamless sleep. I drift off to the percussion of tiny feet running up and down in the roof space and wake to the cries of the kookaburras.

Apart from the birds, the mornings are so quiet here. I miss the hum of distant traffic, the sound of the lift arriving on our floor, even the 'bing' of next-door's microwave. For me these are the sounds of people with purpose, people with places to go. I feel as though I am marooned. It's as though no one can reach me. No one even knows I exist.

Again, I try to keep busy. Polish, clean, clear. The curtains are gone and the furniture glows as the sun sends prying fingers through clear glass. The living room has come to life with the blue rug, a bowl of tiny cream gardenias from the garden on the side table and an exquisite blue, white and gold coffee set out on a tray on the *chiffonier*.

I discover Jack has records and a record player. The rich sounds of Ella Fitzgerald melt like butter through the house. My steps slow. I find myself humming. The phone rings.

'Adrienne? How are you, Sweets?'

'Fine, Diane. I'm fine.'

'Now look, I know things are a bit tough at the mo. Remember, everything happens for a reason. This was meant to be, Girl, for whatever reason, it was meant to be.'

I *hate* that hippyshit. 'Thanks for the wise words, Di. So, what's been happening?' There's no stopping her then – she comes out with all the industry gossip I've been hungry to hear. A major client has moved agencies; an embargo was breached on a critical press announcement – riveting stuff.

'There's a marcoms position coming up with Dalkeith, Gregg & Smith, high-level account exec,' reports Diane. 'Top consultancy – I'm sure they'd be paying over the hundred-and-fifty-thou mark to start. You interested?'

A hot sweat moves the length of my body and wraps

73

itself around my face like cling wrap. 'Maybe,' I say as coolly as I can. 'Do you think they'd be interested?'

'Oh, they'd be lucky to have you! I'll make some discreet enquiries. So how's country life? Must be divine! Do you have frogs? I looove frogs – I've got a gorgeous froggy screensaver.'

'Frogs . . . I guess there are frogs. Di, have you seen Charles?'

'Speaking of frogs . . . Are you sure you want to know?'

'I'm a big girl.'

'Charles will always find a new groove, Adrienne. He's picked up a CEO position with a US agency.'

'Hmm,' I sniff. 'They'll find out the hard way.' I hate the bitter edge to my voice.

As soon as I put down the phone I turn off the record player and pace the floor. I'm out of the loop. I need email and I need it now. A US agency! That could have been me. That bloody well *should* have been me! Charles has 'moved on', despite the mess he made of my business. He was the one man I really thought I could rely on; a family man with kids in the best bloody schools in Sydney, an impeccable business background. Solid. We were equally ambitious, committed to acquiring smaller agencies to build the company into the biggest corporate communications group in the country. He had the MBA, the contacts, the credibility. He had a board-table manner that was practically irresistible. The business took off. I gave him an executive title and a slice of the action. It was hard to see then but he was a broad brushstroke man. When it came to the due diligence, he slipped up. Badly. Details were his weakness; details and a dangerous belief in his own bullshit. He took risks he had no right to take, risks that ended up costing me my business. The thing I'm truly pissed off about is that *I* believed his bullshit and let him convince me to sign the personal guarantees that ended up costing me my home.

If Charles can do it, I can do it. I need to be connected with the real world. I go out to the shed and unpack one of my many boxes marked 'Office' and find my laptop. I take it inside, open it up and slide my fingers over the keys. It feels good. Damn. The cable with the phone jack is missing. I unpack the whole box – still don't find it. But I'm on a roll now. This is going to happen. There's a little computer shop in town that's bound to have the cable. I grab my bag and jump in the ute. Dog just makes it into the tray before I spit gravel all the way down the drive.

I park right outside. With my new sense of purpose I'm in a jovial, chatty mood, but the guy behind the counter seems depressed. Perhaps it's the minimal nature of my purchase. I get the impression that if people are going to come blundering into his shop and disturb his meditative tinkering, they better have a bloody good reason.

Wordlessly he gets the cable, puts it in a bag and enters the sale on the cash register. I remain cheerfully patient while he laboriously writes out a docket and then enters the item in an exercise book.

When all the paperwork is taken care of and I turn to leave he suddenly gets chatty. 'Looks like rain.' He raises his eyebrows to the skies. He's right. Huge cumulus clouds are forming pyramids in the sky. I dash into the butcher's.

'How are yer, my lovely?' he says, wiping his meaty hands on his apron.

'I'm simply divine, thank you. I need some mince, please.'

'And what would you be making tonight, Princess?'

'Shepherd's pie, actually.'

'Lovely.' He gives me a slow wink. 'I'll bet yer quite a cook.'

'The best,' I lie, winking back.

I quickly pop into the tiny post office to send a card to Diane for her birthday next week. I find one with a fat green frog on it. Several people come through the door as I'm scribbling a message on the card. The woman behind the counter greets each by name, almost without looking up. By the time I finish I'm third in line.

'What you having tonight, Mavis?' the woman asks as she pounds an account with not one but three different stamps.

'Well, I always do sweet and sour veal chops on Friday. Ces likes his sweet and sour.'

I want to get home before it rains and am now itching with impatience. If I hadn't already written on the card, I'd drop it and run.

'How about you, Mel?' she says as she enters the details in the computer.

The man in front of me ponders for a moment. 'Friday, eh? Sausages, I reckon.'

'I'm having shepherd's pie,' I volunteer, to speed things up. All three look at me and look away again. No one says a word. I feel quite unreasonably left out. Finally, it's my turn at the counter. 'Yeah, good idea,' says the woman belatedly with a smile. 'Yer can't beat a good shepherd's pie.'

By the time I have finished my other shopping the light

has vanished and the sky has darkened to a dusky grape. I let Dog into the cab with me as fistfuls of rain are flung on the roof. It buckets down. The wipers simply rearrange the water pouring down the windscreen and I have to drive at 10 kilometres an hour all the way home. Thunder rolls over us like a barrel. The roadside trees shudder, the tops of the big gums dance madly in the wind. Branches and twigs ping off the windscreen. I feel the panic tight in my chest; I can hardly breathe.

I get to the top of the driveway and creep up the drive, which is sheltered by trees on both sides. The creek that runs beside is swollen and running fast. As I near the dip where the driveway turns I see that there *is* no dip – the water has broken the bank and has reached the high ground. Even Dog looks worried. I slowly drive into the water and hear it swishing around the doors as I ease the ute through. Suddenly, water starts to leak in through the bottom of the doors, swilling around my feet. There are blinding white flashes as lightning cracks overhead. Dog barks madly. It's chaotic. The ute gasps and dies. I give it several tries but the engine won't turn over.

I take off my shoes. I love these shoes. Bought on my last junket to Milan, they are the most comfortable shoes I have ever owned – although there's not much in the way of competition. I put them in the carrier bag from the computer shop and stuff the bag down my shirt. Hanging my handbag around my neck, I wind down the window and very inelegantly clamber out, feet first. It's like being at sea in a gale, knee-deep in water, wind and rain tearing at my clothes and hair. It's cold.

'Dog! *C'mon*!' My voice is shrill as the wind. Dog doesn't move. He sits and shivers. I hurl a few threats his way and a couple of expletives he might not have heard before. No go. I throw myself back in through the window. I manage to coax him across to the driver's seat with me and command him to stay. I climb back out the window with my hand firmly on his collar. Gravity and Dog join forces – it's as though he's fused to the upholstery, it's impossible to lift him.

I take the plastic bag out of my shirt, stuff it down the front of my pants and wrap my shirt around the idiot dog. Rain slaps at my body with great wet sheets. Now, clad only in a bra and pants, I wrap my arms around Dog and lift. Suddenly he demagnetises and practically throws himself into my arms. He's heavier than anticipated and I stumble backwards, dropping him as my feet slip from under me and we both slide sideways into the creek. Water closes over my head and, gagging on the earthy taste in my mouth, I roll on the bottom, arms flailing wildly for something solid to hold onto. My knees hit the creek bed. I begin to get my balance and come up for breath. I find I can stand waist-deep in water in a shallow part of the creek. Still wearing my shirt, Dog has struck out for the high ground, front paws churning like a paddle steamer. The force of the water rushes against me, carrying sticks and branches twisting with the current. As I wade slowly towards the bank my precious carrier bag dislodges itself and one shoe spins away with the tide. Furious, I hurl the other one after it and crawl up the bank with my handbag still around my neck and the phone cable between my teeth.

Nothing, I tell myself as I stagger back to the house,

nothing will stop me from getting online today. I burst in the door and flick on the light switch. No response. Flick, flick, flick. I run to check the phone. Silence.

'Shit! Shit! Shit! Shit! *Shit*!' I rage around the room looking for something to vent my frustration on, something to kick, something to smash. I pick up the tray holding the blue and gold coffee set and in one motion hurl the lot against the wall. Once the damage is done I feel calmer. Not in control, but calmer.

I calmly light some candles, run a hot bath and peel off my clothes. Calmly, I salt three fat leeches feeding off my thighs. Calmly, I tip the entire bottle of *Jardin de l'Olivier* bath oil I have been hoarding into the bath. I lie in warm oily water doing deep-breathing exercises I learnt at an executive stress management workshop. Stress? Pah! They wouldn't know the meaning of the word.

I get into my pyjamas and dressing-gown, pour the filthy water out of my handbag and throw my ruined Palm in the bin. God knows what happened to the mince. I let the whining bloody troublemaking dog inside and we sit in the living room grimly eyeballing each other for quite some time.

He tires first, gets up and flops down on the rug in front of the fireplace with a wet and windy sigh and gazes at me with the bored expectancy of a palace pet. There's kindling, wood and newspaper. Why not? Perhaps I should rephrase that – why? Why do people light fires? It looks so simple and yet it's so extraordinarily difficult, dirty, messy and smoky – plus you get burned. It's dangerous. It torments you with a tiny hopeful flame, then a frisky little blaze. Then it dies. I try again. And again. And again. I'm not angry, I am determined. I *will* light this fire if it takes me all night. Finally, I give up. I lie beside the dog and contemplate my miserable ineptitude and bawl sooty tears. Dog looks concerned.

Suddenly, a crackling sound. There's a hint of warmth and the smell of wood smoke. I sit up and see a perky little fire. Almost as though it started itself, it has eaten through the twigs and nibbles vigorously at a log. I long to take control, prod it with something, show it who is in charge. But I wait. Finally, we have a blazing crackly fire – heat! I am so excited I dance a victory lap of the living room and jump up and down on the sofa, bellowing 'I am invincible . . . I am wommaaan!' Dog sighs and looks away. I think my mood swings are getting him down.

I take my place by the fire. It's 7 p.m. I wonder what the rest of the world is doing right now. What are normal people who lead normal lives doing on this rainy Friday night? I know what they're doing. They're chugging champagne at the Summit bar, eating freshly shucked oysters at Lombards, raking over the wins and losses of the week, criticising movies as if they actually knew something about them. They're in noisy bars shouting 'Where are you now?' into their mobiles, getting belligerent at dinner parties, talking about ideas, flirting, laughing, shopping, eating, drinking, joking . . . without me.

I don't recall it ever raining so much. Or was it just that I didn't notice?

Saturday mints a fresh new day. The world washed clean. A fat kookaburra sits on the verandah railing, watching the lawn intently for worm activity. Tiny swallows practise their stunt flying around the garden. Little clouds of insects jitterbug in the air. I put on some old clothes, tuck my pants into my socks as an anti-leech strategy and put on some gumboots I find in the shed. The driveway is now clear and the ute starts first time. I park it beside the house.

My dog and I take a stroll in the olive grove. The trees seem reasonably intact despite the storm, although there are plenty of broken branches lying about. Groups of wallabies, nibbling the grass, sit up still and quiet when they see us. Dog is remarkably restrained, or too lazy, to chase them. They scatter as we approach, bouncing away towards the hills. I need to buy some sturdy walking shoes; I'd like to explore the hills and see what the valley looks like from up there.

We make our way up and down the rows, inspecting the troops. These olive trees are taller than any I've seen and more twisted and gnarled too. Their uppermost branches stretch towards one another to form a glittering cathedral of silver and green.

Dog stops and listens. After a moment he starts to bark. A car horn beeps from the direction of the house. We tramp back to find a little green car parked outside and a young woman in an ill-fitting maroon suit standing on the verandah, peering into the house.

'Can I help you?' I say, sounding a little waspish.

She leaps back from the window. 'Oh, there you are – the door was open so I knew you were about. Natasha Jones, my card . . .' Her hand is outstretched.

I glance at the card. Real estate agent. She lifts her

sunglasses for a moment and smiles at me with her eyes. Part of her sales training, no doubt.

'Yes?'

'I have a buyer who is very interested in this property. He has asked me to act on his behalf – arms-length and all that – and I wondered if you had a moment to chat.'

'No. I don't, actually.'

'Perhaps another time?' she says, smarmy now. She's trying not to sound huffy. She's got far too much make-up on. No one wears eye shadow any more, let alone blue.

'I can't imagine that a man with a car that big and shiny would consider living in a house like this.'

'Oh, he wouldn't live in it,' she says, in an ill-considered moment of breathtaking honesty. 'He'd knock out the walls and use it to store his machinery. He wants to build up on the hill. He's showed me the plans, it's huge – it even has colonnades.'

'He must be very sure of himself to have plans.'

She shrugs. 'I guess.'

'You probably shouldn't have told me that. Tell him I'm not selling,' I say impulsively. Foolishly. If I could get that job Diane mentioned I'd sell this place in a minute and convert the money to a deposit on a new apartment. I just need to know I have the job.

She bites her lip. 'His offer is very generous. I really think you should hear it.'

Despite myself, I turn away and walk to the front door.

'Please,' she calls, a little note of panic in her voice. 'My client doesn't like people saying no to him.'

'Who does?' I say with a shrug and a smile. 'When I'm

ready to sell I'll put it out to the market – he can make his offer then.'

I step inside, shut the door and wait there until I hear her drive away. Jeez, I'd like to know what his offer is. I find the lights are on again. The phone's on too. Within minutes I can be online, connected to the world! All in the fullness of time, as Joy would say – tea first.

Before the kettle has even boiled I get a call. It's someone called Leonie phoning on behalf of the Duffy's Creek Business Women's Network. She has heard about me, she says. She would like to invite me to be the guest speaker at their next meeting. Perhaps I could talk about corporate communication – or whatever, she suggests. I'd be happy to, I hear myself say charmingly.

On checking emails I have 263 unread messages. I skim through my in-box looking for something beyond the spam and subscriber mail. There are three. One is from Diane, saying that the marcoms job looks promising. She gives me a contact number to call and organise an interview. There's one from my friend Sarah in London, asking how I am. How is it that she and Diane are the only decent friends I've got? And one from Lauren:

Are u sure Benz has to go? 2 cool 4 words. Can you just pay my next month's rent? Lu

I hit Reply.

Hi Lauren, Please call Mr Arnold, he's the administrator in charge of closing down the company. Call him

immediately *and ask him where he wants the car delivered. His number is on the paperwork I gave you. Otherwise he will be on my case. I'll see what I can do about the rent. Possible job on distant horizon.*
A xx

I trawl around the usual web sites to see what's happening, check out the credentials of DGS Communications and read the profile of the contact Diane gave me. There was a time that I would read and write these sorts of communications every day, spout forth my theories about viral marketing and vertical communication. Reading this now, I have a dazzling insight. It's a collection of carefully selected meaningless words crafted into a document that is purely cosmetic. All lipstick, no kiss. It dawns on me that this is not a productive insight at this point. I need to get myself back on track before that interview. I read it again. It's a well-written, well-crafted, professional competency statement. Good. I feel better already. I ring and make the appointment. Step one of my escape plan in place.

Six

THAT GLORIOUS AUTUMN swiftly became a winter bitter with winds and driving rains. Jack had still not spent a single moment completely alone with Isabelle. If it were a conspiracy, he knew by now that she was part of it. She was as elusive as his dreams.

Although she spent many hours in the olive grove, Isabelle was careful to protect herself with long sleeves and wide hats, and her pale skin gave the appearance of refined fragility. Jack longed to stroke the creamy smoothness of her slender neck. In so many ways she seemed untouchable, intriguing.

When they sat side by side at the dinner table he imagined he could feel the warmth of her body radiate across the space between them. When their eyes met, she would hold his gaze for a moment and then glance away, as if afraid to reveal her most intimate thoughts. He longed to know what those thoughts might be.

Over time Jack came to think of Rosanna as something of a rival for Isabelle's affections. She had an intimacy with Isabelle he would have happily slain a dozen dragons to achieve. The older sister would often slip her hand into Rosanna's or put a protective arm around her shoulders – as if *she* needed protection. Rosanna seemed largely unaware of these affections and would shrug her off as if discarding a garment that had suddenly become too hot or heavy. It was the way their bodies melded softly together in a love borne of complete trust that Jack craved for himself.

On several occasions he had overheard them talking through the window of the room they shared and had been surprised to hear Isabelle chattering and laughing out loud in a way she never did in his presence. There were no secrets between the sisters and he wondered what they said about him in those languid moments before sleep.

That winter Isabelle became his obsession. At first he enjoyed the sensations he felt when she was close to him; the breathlessness, the bracing pulse of sexual anticipation that made him feel alert and invincible like a hunter. Later he felt hunted. Sensations thudded through his body like voltage, leaving him dizzy and weakened in their wake. Even so, the farm was the only place he wanted to be. His own work was a distraction and he was aware that he was not taking care – mistakes were being made. He also knew that, within weeks, his role in the current project would be coming to an end and the company would send him off to God-knows-where. Most likely up the north coast where Michael had been transferred several weeks before.

Jack waited for his moment. He waited without any distinct thought of what that moment might hold or how it might redefine the terrain of his relationship with Isabelle. He waited for that moment of communion between two people, that moment of madness and clarity that scars or heals. He simply knew that he had to wait.

Jack's opportunity came not far from the location of their first meeting, although the day was very different from the white heat of that afternoon. High winds and torrential rain had swept over Duffy's Creek for three endless days. The dredge operation had been brought to a standstill, leaving Jack no choice but to attend to outstanding paperwork. The streets were deserted as Jack parked his car outside the municipal buildings. He knew that Isabelle went often to Mrs Mack's Fabrics and Haberdashery to buy sewing supplies. Brides and debutantes would meet her at the shop to select fabrics, beads and lace, and Mrs Mack would order special fabrics to be brought up from Sydney. The shop was less than a block from the council offices.

As he left the council building Jack drove past Mrs Mack's as he had done a dozen times before, just on the off-chance he would catch a glimpse of Isabelle. He almost couldn't believe his eyes. There she was, standing in the rain outside the shop, sheltering under a flapping raincoat. He stopped the car, threw open the passenger's door and called her name. In a moment she was beside him. Wet and slightly breathless, she had a faint blush rising on her cheeks from her dash through the rain. Rain hammered on the roof of the car. They smiled at one another and she shivered.

Jack switched off the ignition. He reached into the back seat for the rug he kept there and laid it gently around her shoulders. Without a word he leant down and peeled off her shoes, removed his tweed jacket and wrapped it around her feet as carefully as if he were swaddling a newborn. As he straightened up he caught sight of her expression, a look so tender he felt giddy with sheer bravado. He gently tilted her chin towards him and kissed her sweet lips.

For the next month Jack wore the look of a man who couldn't believe his luck. Although in no way keeping pace with his imagination, his relationship with Isabelle had become more rewarding. She met his eye more often, returning his hungry looks with a shy smile, and there was the occasional flutter of kisses in the shadows and tender moments alone that only she could orchestrate.

Isabelle accepted Jack's proposal without surprise. 'We will be married in the spring,' she said firmly. Jack was impatient and would have been married that week had it been his choice, but the timing was important to the bride-to-be. Isabelle would not consider an engagement of less than three months. 'And you must speak to Papa,' she smiled winningly. 'You're so good with him.' She laid her hand gently on Jack's wrist and tapped her ring finger. 'Then we must visit the jeweller and choose a ring to formalise our engagement.' He nodded with uncharacteristic eagerness, momentarily bedevilled by the warm softness of her body as it brushed against his own.

It was fortunate for Jack that Franco was ready to give up his dream of handsome Italian sons-in-law because he welcomed Jack's proposal in a way he might not have in earlier days. Jack had a university education; a practical education as an engineer; he was young and strong and he was a Catholic. From Franco's jaded perspective Jack was a good man in a place where good men were hard to find.

Over the next weeks there was an air of industrious festivity in the house. Signora Martino seemed less sad than usual, busy helping Isabelle with the sewing of the gown and the creation of the *bomboniere*, wrought from tulle and ribbon. Occasionally Jack glimpsed a flash of white and heard the rustle of satin as Isabelle swept the dress out of sight.

Isabelle seemed possessed of a new kind of confidence. She was a butterfly emerging from her chrysalis. Previously reluctant to speak Italian in his presence – despite the limitations of her mother's English – she now regularly spoke rapidly to her mother in a low voice as they discussed the various arrangements for the wedding.

Invitations were sent to Franco's friends Luigi and Alberto, now living in Wollongong, as well as to his cousin Rocco, a barber who followed Franco across the world and found work in Sydney. Jack invited his parents and brother. His brother didn't even reply.

'Now I will have a son,' Franco declared proudly more than once, as though his daughters were rendered superfluous by his new acquisition.

'Gain a son, lose a daughter,' commented Rosanna, perhaps a little too flippantly for Franco to take note.

Three weeks before the wedding, which was to take place at Our Lady of Sorrows Church, Jack was given notice that he was to be transferred, as suspected, to the new site, 250 miles to the northeast.

Jack thought Isabelle might be resistant and spoke to her about it at the first opportunity. He could see that whatever reservations she may have had, Austmine's offer of a subsidised loan with which to buy a house of their own overrode them. 'A wife must go where her husband goes,' she said primly. Jack wondered if she would have acquiesced so gracefully had it been Broken Hill.

Several days later, Rosanna took him aside. 'Papa won't be happy about this – don't expect congratulations. He's over the moon about you helping him build his olive press. Try to let him down gently.'

Jack nodded but there was a moment when he saw a flicker in her eyes and understood just how clueless she thought him.

'It's my work – at least it's not Broken Hill,' he said, sounding more defensive than he intended.

Not knowing how to start the conversation with Franco, Jack let another week slip by. It was Saturday morning. Jack had arrived early to help prepare the garden for the wedding feast. He and Franco took their coffee and cigarettes out to sit in a bright lick of sun on the front steps.

'Franco . . . you remember I told you Austmine moved me from Mount Isa to Duffy's Creek to get the operation up at the lake started,' began Jack as he sat down.

Franco nodded. He lifted his face to the sun and gently blew a feather of smoke into the bright sky.

'My job there is coming to an end. They're going to send me up to Elenora. Up on the north coast.'

Franco shrugged. 'Say to them you can't go'. He sipped his coffee and gazed up into the sky as if the matter was settled.

Jack laughed. 'And then what? I *have* to go – this is my job.'

Franco drained his coffee and crushed his cigarette butt underfoot. He stood up and stretched. 'Then you leave job. We build press, we sell the oil. Is simple.'

Jack stood. He was suddenly conscious of how much taller he was than Franco and aware of a curious tension building between them. 'It's not that simple, Franco. How would we live? *Where* would we live? This is your farm. These are your olives. I can help you, but they're not mine.'

Franco's face darkened. 'When your children grow they have the farm. They buy more land.' He gestured in a wide circle around the horizon. 'They plant more olives. Thousands of olives. We lay down seeds – that's all. You stay with the family.' He turned to walk away. Jack caught his arm.

'Franco – this is your dream, not mine. It might never happen. I have a job that is certain. After we are married, Isabelle and I will be leaving here. We'll be moving to Elenora.'

'I say *no*!' Franco's eyes were as sharp and black as quartz. 'You don't take Isabella away. She stay with her mother. Is final!' he thundered.

The silence inside the house was palpable. The women's chores were forgotten as they waited still and quiet, listening. Jack stood his ground as he had stood before his own father on many occasions. He had seen enough fights in his time to know that his expression must remain neutral. He held a theory that men were often spurred into action by the reflection of their own anger. In the mines he had seen men killed over less.

'Isabelle's place is with her husband,' Jack said quietly. He saw an anger rising up in Franco beyond anything he had witnessed. Jack gave a slow shrug. These were not his rules; it was simply the way things were.

Suddenly Franco turned and walked into the house. A furious stream of invective broke the silence inside. Jack could hear Signora Martino pleading with him, Rosanna shouting him down. He heard the same phrase over and over from Franco – '*Brutta figura*! *Brutta figura*!' – and Jack understood that he had brought shame upon the family.

Jack felt as though he had been slapped awake from a warm and peaceful slumber. Suddenly it seemed the world was falling down around them. The whole time Isabelle stayed quietly in the background, and it occurred to him that this was the final test of his worthiness; she had always known this was the way it would be if they left the farm.

In the space of a few moments Jack's status with the Martinos slipped from golden son to gangster, and he had no idea how to recover the situation. It was Rosanna who stepped in to limit the damage. She strode side by side with her father up and down the grove and Jack could hear their voices raised in battle as she fought for her sister's freedom.

Although Franco grudgingly accepted the inevitability of the situation, over the next few weeks he was moody and Jack did not feel welcome at the farm. The wedding plans were now discussed in hushed tones and the hem of the bride's gown was stained with her mother's quiet tears. Even the serene Madonna, whose image presided over every meal, looked a little unsettled at the turn of events.

Jack headed north to find a cottage for the newlyweds. He imagined roses around the door but had strict instructions from Isabelle about indoor bathrooms and electric ovens. He found it good to get away. Guilt sent out its little shoots but he cut them back mercilessly before they found fertile ground. They would visit Duffy's Creek. Franco would come around. Jack had other things to think about.

Gusts of spring rain occasionally redeemed by bouts of brilliant sunshine provided plenty of weather talk for the wedding guests as they gathered in front of the church. Standing at the altar, Jack watched Isabelle, a sugar-spun confection in white, float up the aisle towards him and felt suddenly humbled by her beauty. She appeared in that moment as almost angel-like, and he could hardly believe she was his. But beside her, Franco's bleak expression of resignation imposed a shadow over even that tremulous moment.

The couple emerged from the church to clear skies and a storm of rice and, hearing Isabelle laugh out loud, Jack felt his spirits lift. Even his parents looked happy. His mother stepped out from the group and kissed him on the cheek. 'She's lovely, dear,' and then under her breath, as if taking him into her confidence, 'so lucky she's not dark like the other one.' She caught a glimpse of his irritation. 'For the kiddies' sake, I mean. Your father and I don't mind, of course.' Jack began to wish the day were over.

The reception feast was held at the farm. Trestle tables and metal folding chairs had been borrowed from the town hall and set up under the trees. They were covered in cloths so white as to dazzle the eye.

Franco had slaughtered Petalo, the fattest piglet, earlier

in the year to provide *salame* and *prosciutto* for the family and he selected the very best from his tiny cellar to serve to his guests. He cooked chicken, goat and spare ribs on a slab of flat rock over the fire. There were bowls of olives and baskets of bread with oven-roasted potatoes, parsnips, aubergines, tomatoes and onions, stuffed *zucchine*, salads of rocket, basil, soft lettuces and tomatoes from the garden, all accompanied by Franco's own *vino rosso*.

The guests slowly took their places at the table, seeming a little uncertain of what was required of them. Jack's appetite vanished as he noticed his mother's disdainful glance over the laden table and heard her comment to his father that she wasn't hungry.

'Mum, sit beside me, here,' he said brusquely. He pulled out a chair for her. She plumped herself down sulkily. His father ignored her but sat down beside her. 'What if it rains?' she said in a stage whisper.

'We'll get wet,' said Jack, and turned away before he had to deal with the tears that would surely follow.

It was odd to have his wife on one side of him and his mother on the other. Franco and Adriana sat beside Isabelle with Rosanna. At one end of the table sat Michael, Jack's best man, and Snow. Both had already discarded their jackets, their ties a little askew like schoolboy truants. Opposite them were Dot and Marge Roland, the plump, pink-cheeked, elderly sisters from the neighbouring farm. Marge, the flirtatious one, dimpled coyly when she noticed Jack's gaze upon her.

Mrs Mack from the haberdashery and her husband sat next to them. Mrs Mack looked as proud as the mother of the bride. 'What a day!' she exclaimed from time to time, addressing the table in general. 'Isn't the bride divine?' All the while she built a pyramid of food on her husband's plate; finally satisfied, she laid his napkin on his lap. Jack thought for a dreadful moment she was going to cut up his food for him too, but Mr Mack came to life like a clockwork toy once his plate was full and silently put his back into the job of clearing it.

Luigi and Alberto were as excited as children. Luigi had brought Lorraine, his Australian girlfriend. She wore a white dress clinched hard at the waist, her blonde hair in a salon coiffure. She fingered the brittle flicked-up ends and looked bored.

At the other end of the table sat Rocco and his wife, Erminia, who spoke no English. Their son, Joseph, was a handsome boy with thick black curls worn a little long for Jack's thinking. This must be the fellow whose twenty-first birthday the Martinos had attended in Sydney some months ago, Jack thought. The table became noisier and noisier as the stack of green bottles under the tree grew higher.

Rosanna and her mother cleared the table and carried the dishes inside to the kitchen. Erminia helped. She and Signora Martino hadn't stopped talking since the moment they sat down. Jack had never seen his mother-in-law so animated. He was relieved to see her sorrowful expression of the last few weeks transformed, at least for today.

The wind had spent itself and a gentle breeze now wove its way through the trees. Feeling a little drunk, Jack leaned back in his chair. He noticed young Joseph's attention was drawn towards the house and he turned to see the women returning across the lawn, his mother-in-law proudly bearing the tiered wedding cake. The light spun on Rosanna's emerald-green satin dress as it lifted and flattened against her body, caressed by the breeze. Her lips were blood-red, her hair loose and wild, and her eyes black as olives. She looked gypsy-dangerous.

The cake was placed in the centre of the table to exclamations of delight and a sprinkle of applause. But Jack noticed Joseph's eyes were only on Rosanna. He licked his lips.

'*Evviva gli sposi*!' cried Alberto, as he raised his glass.

'Hurrah for the newlyweds!' translated Rosanna. The Italian contingent clapped and cheered madly, building momentum as the other guests followed their lead.

'*Bacio*! *Bacio*!' shouted Luigi drunkenly. Lorraine nudged him to be quiet.

Isabelle took Jack's hand as she stood and drew him to his feet. For a moment he was transfixed by the image of the plastic bride and groom on the top of the cake. He had a strange sense of being just a groom, any groom . . . that he could just as easily be sitting on the other side of the table, watching another man stand and kiss Isabelle.

The cake was cut and served. Franco made a short speech, very different, Jack imagined, from the one he might have made several months ago. The wedding party seemed subdued afterwards. Alberto, sensing the time was right, took up his guitar and Rosanna leapt to her feet. 'Yes, Papa, let's dance.'

'First the newlyweds,' said Franco, not looking up as he rolled a cigarette.

Jack led Isabelle out onto the lawn and took her in his

arms. Everything and everyone around him fell away as his wife's soft body relaxed against his, her cheek resting on Jack's shoulder. Rocco and Erminia, lighter on their feet than Jack could have ever guessed, led the way for the other guests.

Jack's mother, looking a little flushed, danced rather awkwardly with Snow. His father never danced. Joseph lost no time partnering Rosanna, and the Roland sisters waltzed together while Mrs Mack and her husband swooped about the lawn like a couple of professionals on show.

The evening was still, the sky as smooth and pale as a moonstone. Reluctant for the day to end, the guests languished over coffee and cigarettes. Alberto sang softly as he idly strummed his guitar. Luigi and Lorraine could be heard in the distance having a blazing row. Rosanna and Joseph had disappeared. It was time for Jack and Isabelle to leave.

Franco stood smoking a cigarette at the back gate, his gaze tilted towards the hills. Jack wandered over and leant on the gate. He could see the faint outline of a sickle moon almost transparent against the sky.

'I am thinking,' said Franco softly after some time, 'I am remembering my wife's mother. She say her daughter and granddaughters going to Australia, it was like a death in the family. I was young. Now I understand. This is my punishment.' He opened the gate and walked into the field beyond. Jack watched as he slowly walked the length of the grove. He stopped now and then to lay his hand on a branch or limb with reverence and affection, as if greeting old friends, as if saying goodbye. He touched each tree with love and with sorrow.

Seven

I GATHER UP the coffee set I smashed so childishly on the night of the storm and take the pieces out into the morning sun on the front verandah. Bringing out a chair and small table, I lay out the pieces on some newspaper. It's not all smashed, but it's no longer complete. Forever flawed by my anger. It takes me more than an hour to assemble and glue together two cups. I would never have believed I had the patience.

Just as I decide to have a break and take Dog for a walk there is the sound of a truck coming up the driveway. Dear God, let it not be Leeton again. The truck, which has a small tractor on the back, pulls up in front of the house and a man jumps down from the cab. Looking past the battered aku-bra, the hair that needs a decent cut, a two-day growth and generally sweaty appearance, he's quite good-looking – in a hewn sort of way. He is, however, the antithesis of everything I find attractive in a man – not that I'm looking for one. I can already glean his idea of entertainment is watching the rugby with a slab of beer for company; he loves country music and eats petrol-station food. (For the record, my ideal man flies business class, wears Armani and knows his pinot noir from his shiraz. Plus, he always smells good.)

His name is Joe Oldfield. He tips his hat and I find myself a little breathless.

'Mum suggested you needed some mowing done.' He gestures towards the lawn.

'I'm not sure . . . what sort of costs are involved?' I move down the steps, trying to remember if I brushed my mop this morning but willing myself not to check.

'I'll do it for nothing this time. A welcome-home gift.'

'Hmm . . . the old loss-leader marketing strategy. You just want to show me how good the place looks and then I'll think I can't live without you – it – the mowing,' I stammer, all hot and bothered.

'It's a gift, really.' He smiles.

'Can I think about it?'

'Look, if you decide within the next two minutes I'll throw in a free set of steak knives.' He folds his arms and waits. 'The thing is, it's too high for your lawnmower, especially Jack's old one. If I whip around and slash the lawn now, you'll be able to handle it yourself next time.'

'Me? Mow the lawn?'

He throws his head back and laughs. 'What about if, instead of the steak knives, I throw in my Introduction to Lawnmowing seminar?'

'Oh, you deal-maker, you. How can I refuse?' I dimple against my will.

I'd like to say that I turn out to be an excellent student but the truth is that lawnmowing makes cooking look easy. It's noisy, dangerous and dirty and the actual starting of

Jack's old mower requires a level of hand–brain–eye–foot coordination that proves completely beyond me.

Joe simply puts a foot on the mower and with one deft flick of the wrist the thing snarls into life. I have trouble working out which foot to plant on the machine and the starter cord, so taut and responsive in Joe's hand, is utterly lifeless in mine. The man's patience is highly commendable but in the end even he sees it is hopeless. He throws a couple of ramps down from his truck, backs his tractor off and in fifteen minutes the lawn looks like a lawn. He drives his tractor back onto the truck and secures it on the tray.

'I wish I had a beer to offer you, after that hot work,' I call out to him.

'I don't normally drink beer quite this early in the day. A cup of tea'd hit the spot, though, if it's not too much trouble.'

He sits on the front steps and waits while I make the tea. When I come back Dog has his head in Joe's lap, having his ears rubbed. I put the cups down and sit on the top step. My hair looks fine – I checked. Not that it matters.

'It's beautiful here,' he says. 'It's none of my business, but I hope you're not going to sell out to Leeton. He'll carve the whole place up, pull out the trees – it'd be a bloody shame. There's a business in olives these days.'

'So are you a contender?'

'You're a very suspicious woman, aren't you?' He sounds hurt.

'Not at all, I just like to know what people's agendas are.'

'Well, I don't have an agenda. I'm not motivated by any

of the things you might imagine. I am a free man. I just know that you don't plant olives for yourself, you plant them for your grandchildren, and whether you like it or not, that's you.' He throws back the last of his tea and stands up abruptly. 'How about you don't assume anything about me and I won't assume anything about you?'

Before I can thank him he stalks to his truck, reverses out and drives away. My, people come and go quickly around here – is it me?

The heady aroma of freshly mown grass is quite intoxicating; I pad around the damp lawn barefoot, just for fun. Enough of that. It's 11.15 on a Monday morning. Without the demands of work, time seems to stretch and gape. What the hell should I be doing?

I need to write my CV. There's plenty of time, though, the interview's not until Friday. I could unpack some more of my stuff. Finish gluing up the coffee set. Joe's eyes were a rather distracting shade of green. Deep and dangerous. One could easily drown in there. Then there is the smooth creamy skin of his forearms to think about. I decide to visit Joy.

Joy, I discover, lives in a shed. It's a shed out the back of the house she used to live in, now occupied by Joe's brother, his wife and four children. She doesn't seem at all apologetic or embarrassed about the fact that she lives in a shed, and doesn't even appear to think it odd, or that I might think it odd. It's like a studio apartment. Her bed, a small table and chairs, a two-seater floral sofa, a couple of occasional tables and a little improvised kitchen are all in one room. Her windows look out across the paddocks and one side has a tilting door that opens onto a carefully tended vegetable garden. It reeks of quiet contentment. I'm envious.

She makes me tea and, while we're chatting, whips up a batch of scones and slips them into her tiny bench-top oven. She throws a fresh cloth on the table and sets out the cups and saucers, side plates, napkins and homemade fig jam.

'Soooo,' I say casually. 'Joe came and mowed the lawns today. At your request, I understand.'

'It was in need of doing, dear. Don't want you to have an altercation with a red-bellied black, do we?' she says briskly. 'Joe's a good boy. Knew Jack quite well, you know.' She sits down and pours the tea.

'Well, any friend of Jack's is a friend of mine.' I give a brittle laugh.

'Now, you're being a little bit sarcastic there, aren't you?' Her cup clinks sharply on the saucer as she puts it down and looks at me over the top of her glasses. She gives me the same disappointed look my mother used to employ when I had 'spoilt things'.

I feel seriously chastised. 'Sorry. Sorry, Joy. This is a very confusing time for me. I'm not really myself at the moment.'

'People are only trying to help, you know, dear.'

'I know. Tell me about Joe.'

'Anything Joe wants you to know he'll tell you himself,' she says firmly.

I try again. 'Tell me about Jack.'

'I can't imagine I could tell you anything about Jack that

you don't already know.'

'I hadn't seen him for thirty years.'

'Thirty years! Good Lord!' She thinks for a moment and then says quietly, 'Do you mind my asking if there was a particular reason why you didn't see him? I half assumed he saw you when he went down to Sydney so often. Did you have a falling out?'

Now it's my turn to be cagey. 'It's complicated.' Truthfully, it *is* complicated, but it is also as simple as I forgot about him. Having cut him out of my life, I did, eventually, sort of forget about him. I have a great capacity for neatly cutting people out of my life and, not for the first time, I regret it. This time I cut to the bone. I have come to realise in the last few days that I've missed out on the opportunity to get to know Jack in a role beyond that of my absent father. I have forfeited the right to even say that I knew him. I wish it were otherwise.

Joy leans her elbows on the table and taps her fingers on her lips as though arranging her words in exactly the right order. I can see she was pretty once, when the grey curls were blonde, the skin peachy and not yet mapped by a thousand small worries. She has the sweet smile of a pretty child.

'Jack had his fair share of altercations with people but he was a fair-minded man,' she begins. 'He was a bit change-able. He could be generous one day and like a bear with a sore head the next. I suppose you'd say he didn't suffer fools.' She slides her hand over mine. 'He loved that farm, dear. He'd be thrilled you've come home.'

I haven't the heart to tell her I'm not 'home' in the real sense of the word. When the solicitors, who went to some trouble to track me down, wrote to tell me that Jack had died and left me the farm I thought it truly was a gift from someone in heaven. I had heard stories of the farm. My mother always promised to take me there but, as with so many things, I suspect she had no intention of doing so. She could appear willing but possessed a sort of passive resistance that made her mysteriously immovable. She never mentioned olives. Still, she never mentioned she had a sister. No wonder we never came here – too many secrets. But here it was, being delivered to me at a time when I was sliding slowly down the cliff face of my aspirations towards the murky waters of bankruptcy. Caught up in my money troubles, I barely gave a moment's thought to my father's death when I heard about my inheritance. Any flicker of regret was snuffed out by my old bitterness. The truth is that I was online Googling real estate prices in Duffy's Creek within minutes. Bloody Leeton's right, it's worth bugger-all.

I get a call from Diane. She hears a little tension in my voice, tells me I need to listen to my body. As I lie in bed waiting for sleep to come, I listen. I can't imagine my body telling me anything I want to hear. All I hear is the sound of the blood rushing through my veins, like a torrent in my ears. Or perhaps I'm just drowning in my own self-absorption.

In the morning I get a call from Sarah in London; it's midnight there and she's just arrived home from work. She's worried about me. I'm worried about her, working until midnight. Next, I get a call from Lauren to tell me I'll have to get my act together if I'm serious about the job. She thinks I am definitely losing the plot; I could have told her that Mr Arnold had cancelled her mobile phone service. She's right, I could have.

I get a call from Joy. I can hardly think straight with all these calls. If I am really desperate for work, she says, there is a lady by the name of Deirdre who does house cleaning locally. Deirdre doesn't like to clean on her own and her cleaning buddy has moved to Queensland.

'I'm helping her out at the moment but I've got the tennis ladies' Christmas luncheon, highlight of my social calendar. I wondered if you'd fill in for me – give it a go? It's not till Wednesday week,' she says.

How could I refuse? If all else fails, what alternative do I have? But first things first. The real world awaits my triumphant return. I hope. I get my best grey suit dry-cleaned and touch up my grey roots ready for Friday's interview with DGS.

The 7 a.m. express from Duffy's Creek station to Central; all around me people are either reading or asleep. I had a wakeful night but am way too hyped to snooze. I re-read the material printed from the DGS web site and watch the paddocks slide past my window, silently psyching myself up to dazzle.

Even in such a short time the city has changed. It smells different. An unhappy amalgamation of a million infinitesimal odours. The place is frantic. People rush past, their faces tight with worry, mobiles clamped to their ears. A man scurries past carrying a huge stack of legal documents festive with fluttering pink ribbons, his face a study of self-importance. Is that the road map to world peace in his arms? More likely documentation of an ugly divorce – or an ugly bankruptcy. It suddenly all seems so farcical.

The offices of DGS are quietly swish, not unlike my old offices. Lushly polished antique furniture is juxtaposed with contemporary interior design and bold 'out there' colours. We're creative heavyweights but, hey, we're funky and up-beat too.

I am ushered into the boardroom, my coffee is delivered promptly, a mini-plunger on a stainless-steel tray, *accoutrements* by Alessi – the client treatment. If only they knew it's this job or scrubbing toilets with Deirdre.

I meet two of the directors, Warwick and Warren. They seem quite excited, or at least enthusiastic. Hard to know if it's me, or if they're just high on life.

Warwick is about my age, handsome in a corpulent self-satisfied way. He's the more conservative of the two with his Hong Kong tailoring, initials monogrammed on the breast pocket of his crisp white shirt and a golf-course tan.

Warren is ten years younger, leggy as a foal and given to running his hands frantically through his hair like a tortured artist. Throughout the meeting he leans forward open-handed, earnest and conspiratorial, then hurls himself back in his chair, ankle across knee, hands laced behind his head, as if he has been to a workshop on how to confuse people with contradictory body language. I perform admirably, I think. Warwick doesn't mind a little gossip and clearly would like to know more of what went down when I went down. I demonstrate my professional integrity by steering away from that and manage to not even mention Charles. I make them laugh. Tempt them with pithy insights. We part with warm handshakes and assurances. Meaningful eye contact is made and I don't stutter once.

I meet Diane for lunch at Café Uno. I'm touched out of all proportion when the staff recognise me and greet me like a long-lost friend; or at least a long-lost customer.

Diane thinks I look well. Relaxed, she says. Just shows how deceiving looks can be. She, on the other hand, is 'stressed to the max'. She's under so much pressure at work she feels in desperate need of a holiday. She's now stressed about whether to have, say, two weeks at the Hyatt Coolum where she could be pampered back to life, or ten days at the 'adults only' Club Med in the Maldives from which she would most likely return exhausted but satisfied. Would I like to come? she wonders.

'Is that because you want me to make that onerous decision for you? Diane, I can't possibly think about a holiday until I get a job. I don't think you really understand that I am literally broke.' I stir my coffee aggressively and bang the spoon on the saucer. 'The joke is this – I thought we were doing fantastically! Charles didn't do his homework when the company bought those three agencies. He told me he had but he hadn't. He was conned and when he realised – without even bloody consulting me – he made the decision to trade our way out of trouble and just got us deeper in the shit. Correction: got *me* deeper in the shit. I was the one who was liable. He didn't lose his fucking house.' I can hear how bitter and whingeing I sound.

'Adrienne, you've got to move on,' she says kindly.

'Di, I don't *want* to move on, and – for the record – I *hate* that expression. I want to be severely *pissed off* until further notice.'

We sit in an uncompanionable silence for several minutes. I feel no remorse; Diane is the sort of woman who dives into conversations without checking the depth all too often. She's bound to get hurt.

'So,' I say, still a little tight-lipped, 'the upshot is that at the moment I need DGS more than they need me.'

'You're the media queen, Adrienne,' Diane says brightly. 'That's why DGS want you. Those corporates will flock in when they know you're enthroned there.' She orders another latte. 'I'm thinking of getting some Siamese cats for my new apartment. It looks sensational but it's very static. I'm keen for you to see it, it's every shade of *crème de cacao*.'

'Brown, you mean?' I say, irritated all over again. 'What about a frog for the bathtub? I've got them up the drainpipes – I could bring you one next time. What colour would you like? Small, medium or large?'

She smiles but I know I've bruised her feelings.

All the way home on the train I fret that my only attraction to DGS is as a Trojan horse to take them into the boardrooms of my old clients. I'm not sure whether to be hurt or flattered. I know it's a business decision for them. No point being a girl about it.

The train journey is depressing. I see some of the same people, heads slumped on chests, trying to find their way back into the dreams they had this morning. One by one the phones come out. 'I'm on the train' ripples through the carriage like a Mexican wave. Who cares? Well, obviously someone does. I don't have anyone to call. I'm suddenly filled with foreboding at the thought of the empty house that awaits me.

The man next to me looks as though he's come from a building site in grimy steel-capped boots. He stares angrily out the window, occasionally taking a swig from a bottle in a brown paper bag. High-school kids sit in the aisles on enormous backpacks. Shaggy-haired boys, and girls with hooped earrings chew gum and munch chips at the same time. They can hardly take their eyes off each other: even when they're not looking, they're looking. It's tiring to watch. I feel old and fragile as if the rhythm of the train is rocking me apart.

I had forgotten Dog was waiting for me in the ute at the station. He's delighted to see me. I've never had someone hopelessly devoted to me before. It's rather nice. I let him sit in the cab on the way home. He sits right beside me and gets hair down one side of my suit.

The house is somehow welcoming – peaceful – and the garden is cool and shady in the late afternoon; the smooth green lawn a welcome-home gift. I make tea and toast and fall into bed before eight.

I wake feeling very flat. I have played my last card; if it doesn't come good I've nowhere else to go. Gloomy, trapped and restless is the theme for the day.

On the front verandah I discover I have another welcome-home gift, a pair of sturdy elastic-sided boots. Mysteriously, they fit perfectly. A note taped to the left sole invites me to dinner and includes a detailed map and instructions. It's from Joe Oldfield, Mr Don't Assume himself. Perhaps a chiko roll washed down with a tinny? I assume nothing. Nevertheless I'm suddenly feeling a little more cheerful. I have a bit of a romp on the lawn with Dog; he's clearly relieved by my girlish high spirits.

What on earth does one wear with a pair of elastic-sided boots? In the end I decide on a pair of black pure-wool pants teamed with a cream suede jacket that has just a whiff of Western in its styling. I am getting a little tired of being hopelessly overdressed everywhere I go.

The map takes me to the other side of Duffy's Creek and along a winding road around the perimeter of a steep hill. It's like a different land, almost mystical, with quite incredible views across the deep valley to more steep hills. The further I get from town, the more dilapidated houses, the more falling-down fences and off-the-hinge gates I see. Finally, I reach Joe's gate.

Inside the gate is an open barn where his truck is parked. I park the ute beside it as instructed in the note and give him a toot. His property is on the high side of the road with a steep path, no wider than a track, heading up the hill. Within moments I hear the throaty sounds of a motorbike.

It hardly needs saying that motorbikes are not my thing, but I soon find myself sitting high on the back of this rasping piece of machinery, my arms clamped around a man I barely know, as the bike hares up an almost vertical track like a frisky mountain goat. The track takes us through dense bushland, rainforest I suppose, which clears gradually as we go higher, then just as it seems we are heading skyward we leap over a ridge onto the plateau at the top and emerge into the late afternoon sun.

The hilltop has been mostly cleared of trees and there is a cabin – God knows how he got that up here, there must be another track – and some rather primitive-looking shelters; poles supporting a corrugated-iron roof. It's like having several pavilions: one is an eating area with a gas stove, mismatched chairs and a big old table. It's set with a white cloth, plates, cutlery, wineglasses and even candles. Another pavilion has some bits of furniture, chairs and a hammock. The shower is a bag hanging from a tree. I don't even want to know about the toilet but he insists on showing me – self-composting, apparently. Clearly it's a source of great pride for him.

'I can see you're not wildly impressed,' he says, amused. 'But I do have one more rabbit in my hat. Come with me.' He takes my arm and we walk across the plateau to the other side.

The view from the top of the mountain is something else. I can see all the way to a silver ribbon of sea in one direction and as I turn towards the hinterland there are valleys and farms, orchards and vineyards until the hills start to rise again and then, as far as the eye can see, undulating blue bush.

'Your place is directly across there to the southwest. Now, have a look down the hill just below us.'

I do as I'm told, determined not to open my mouth until I work out what the hell it is I'm supposed to see there. Finally, he puts me out of my misery.

'There're eighteen wild olive trees growing on this hillside

111

alone. *Taggiasca* olives – progeny of your grove – sown by the birds. They're growing on quite a few properties around here now and there's a local guy going around harvesting them. He sends them to a mill down in Victoria somewhere. He's winning medals with his oil.'

Olive, olives, olives – is that all this man wants to talk about?

We sit down at the table and he opens a bottle of not-too-shabby pinot noir. He's a little older than I first thought, maybe forty-five. It's hard to tell; his body is lean but the weather has left its mark on his skin. His shirt and jeans are clean, if a little frayed here and there. The hair is boyishly long and fine as a baby's and appears to have been washed and brushed for the occasion. I can see a sprinkling of grey pushing in at the temples.

'So, is that what you wanted to talk to me about?' I say. My chest feels tight and my words sound more abrupt than I intended.

'I think we have lots of things we could talk about,' he says calmly as he pours the wine.

'So you do have an agenda,' I reply, suddenly feeling thoroughly uncooperative.

'I think you're looking for something.'

'In all the wrong places?'

'I just thought you seemed a little lost, that's all.'

'I *was* lost, but now I'm found. I'm expecting a job offer and I'll be heading back into the real world.' I hear how smug and dismissive I sound, all too late.

'Great. Maybe you're right – maybe we don't have any-thing to talk about.'

His calm resignation has the opposite effect on me. 'Just because you've found peace and harmony mowing lawns and living on a mountaintop doesn't make you bloody Mohammed,' I say crossly. 'This sort of existence would *not* work for me. I want my old life back.' The backs of my eyes throb. I can feel my chin quivering. He sits still and quiet. But I can't stop.

'I never, *never* in my wildest dreams thought I would hit fifty with nothing but a trail of failures behind me.' I'm horrified to hear the truth pouring from my mouth. 'This isn't the real world, Joe. This is La-La Land. You're a runaway. Just like Jack.' There is a sense of satisfaction at having found the source of my anger. Just like Jack.

He takes a sip of wine and leans back in his chair, seemingly unaware of the gravity of the insult. 'In my old life I was a builder. I always thought that being a builder was a worthy trade – practical – and I think I was pretty darn good at it.'

He looks at me as though he thinks I'm going to challenge him on that. 'I thought my job was to work with materials, timber and steel, terrain, drainage. Things I could handle. People talk about their dream home but actually they think you're going to build them a dream life. I can't tell you how many times I have stood in beautiful homes watching two people tear each other's hearts out over the choice of tiles. They think a house will make them happy the same way that people think money will make them happy. But the richer they are, the more choices they have and the harder they are to please. They start to believe that nothing is good enough for them. They dedicate themselves to proving it. To themselves? To the world? I don't know.'

He gets up and checks inside the oven. The fragrant aroma of rosemary and roasting lamb wafts over me. He pours us both more wine and sits down. 'I was married, couple of kids, house in the suburbs. My wife had this same expectation that the more stuff you throw in the void the fuller you will feel. Ditto the kids – bloody frantic for the latest toy and gismo. I was killing myself to make everyone happy. I'd wake up in the night and think I was suffocating. My wife despised me. My customers were driving me insane. So, you're right to a point, I did run away. I had a heart attack at forty-two. I ended up having to come home to Mum.'

'Well, everything happens for a reason, so I'm told,' I say, wearily resistant to taking on his stuff when I have so much of my own. But I suddenly realise that it is not as though I really loved my old life – I'm not even sure that I was happy. It's simply that it was *my* life. 'I just feel so disoriented. I feel as though someone has taken away my script, my soundtrack – even the backdrops – to my life. I don't know what my role is, who I'm supposed to be any more.'

'Isn't there a freedom in that? You can be anyone you want.'

'People don't change,' I say finally. 'Anyway, I haven't got the energy or the courage to reinvent myself. It's too late to start afresh.'

He looks at me as though he doesn't believe a word. As though he can foresee everything I will come to know. He looks as though he's waiting for me to understand, to know what he knows. I've never felt further away from it. But he lets me off lightly. We eat lamb roast with baked vegetables from his garden. We talk of other things, of life. We talk until the moon moves from one side of the mountain to the other.

I don't like the way he looks after me so tenderly. The way he laughs at my jokes. I don't like the way, half-asleep on the back of the bike, my hands slide under his shirt of their own accord. I don't like the way his flesh feels as smooth and warm as summer mango and he smells almost as sweet. I don't like the way he lifts me from the bike and whispers 'Stay.' But I am strong. I get into my ute and drive home slowly. The last thing I need in my life is a dreamer.

Eight

THREE MONTHS LATER, Jack stood at the gate to the olive grove once more. This time there was no one in the grove. Franco was dead. Jack thought then that he would give almost anything to have that day back again, to walk the grove with Franco, to have the chance to change his mind and stay. At the time it didn't even cross his mind.

Jack had been at work when the telegram came. He had come home to find Isabelle faint with grief and shock. It told them all they needed to know in that odd, faltering language of telegrams: *Come home stop father dead stop heart stop Rosanna stop*. Jack felt as though he had killed Franco with his own hands. He had stolen the princess and now the king was dead, the kingdom in ruins. He felt nauseous with guilt. They had planned to visit in a month's time to celebrate Franco's sixtieth birthday. And now he was gone. There was a tightness in Jack's chest and a pain in his heart that made it difficult to breathe. He felt the brutal hand of grief crushing him, squeezing the life out of him.

During the long, almost silent, drive back to the farm he found himself calculating his losses. When he had claimed

Isabelle all for himself he only knew he wanted to possess her in body and spirit. He was convinced that making love to her would slake his thirst for her and he would regain the clarity of mind he had lost over the last few months. He had imagined her yielding herself to him, her body melting into his. His fantasies didn't take into account the awkwardness of an inexperienced lover and her natural modesty – the lack of which he so deplored in Rosanna. His transit to heaven was hampered by earthbound fumbling and embarrassed apologies.

They never spoke of it. Isabelle understood her role and played her part. She succumbed to him as her husband but there was never a moment when she gave herself to him. She accepted his affections but there was something missing, something he didn't want to even begin to face. It seemed as though his beautiful butterfly had quietly folded herself back into her chrysalis.

She was, he realised, a loner just like him in many ways. She never complained about him being away on field trips overnight or even for several days. When he arrived home she would look up from her sewing or tapestry with a smile. 'Ah – there you are,' she would say, as if she had just that moment wondered where on earth he had got to. She would tilt her cheek to receive his kiss and it seemed as though she was pleased to see him.

He bought her an electric Singer sewing machine to replace her treadle. She would sew most afternoons and always cleaned and oiled it before she put it away. As he came up the side path of the cottage he would hear its metallic trembling stop and start and he expected there would be a new cushion or curtain or some other such frippery in the house. Now and then he would catch a glimpse of a tiny gown, decorated with satin ribbons or embroidered rosebuds. Isabelle folded these briskly and put them away in a camphor chest.

Gradually it seemed that, apart from a battered copy of *Peele's Mining Handbook* and several other books about metallurgy propped on the bookshelves, there was almost nothing of Jack's old life in the house. She had asked him, very reasonably, to remove his boots and clothes in the laundry on the back porch before he entered the house each evening, and he did. She asked him, also reasonably, not to bring the men he worked with, particularly Michael, to the house, so he didn't. Although she attended church daily she requested only that he attend Sunday mass with her, which he did. Life was quiet but he wasn't unhappy. It had a predictable rhythm he rather enjoyed. Their solitary ways seemed well suited, although he thought from time to time that they were perhaps too alike; it closed them off to one another somehow.

Isabelle sat quietly beside him in the car. Although the funeral wasn't until the next day she was already dressed in black. Her face was pale and tight, eyes red-rimmed. When they stopped in a small town for a cup of tea and a devon sandwich he could sense the curious looks.

They arrived at the farm late that afternoon. Rocco sat on the verandah, smoking moodily, his face impassive. He hugged Jack, kissed Isabelle on both cheeks and led them into the house. As she stepped over the threshold, Isabelle collapsed, a reedy wail rising from her throat. Jack caught her just in time and lifted her to the couch, taken aback by such an uncharacteristic display of emotion. It took a moment for his eyes to adjust to the dimness of the room – the curtains were drawn, the only lighting a dozen small candles. He began to make out the figures beside the casket, which was on a low table in the centre of the living room. Signora Martino rose from her knees and came to sit beside Isabelle, the rosary in her hand. She wrapped her arms around her daughter and rocked her as they wept together.

Erminia knelt beside the coffin, praying and weeping. Rosanna came towards Jack from the kitchen. He could see Rocco and Erminia's son Joseph leaning against the kitchen bench eating an apple. Rosanna stopped before Jack and looked up into his eyes. Neither of them spoke; he felt quite rigid as she put her arms around him and hugged him. She stayed there for a long time, her head on his chest, listening to his heart. He could feel the warmth of her body. It took all his strength to lift his arms and return her embrace.

Jack was familiar with death. He'd seen it when he served in Egypt during the war. He'd seen children dead in the street, he'd seen men die who had barely begun their lives. In the mines he'd seen death snatch silently, but more often grotesquely – his memory stored jagged screams as scar tissue. But when he looked at Franco's face – smooth and peaceful, the familiar rugged lines that mapped his face now faint – it was a loss beyond anything he had ever experienced.

Jack had not spent a great deal of time in church until he met Isabelle. Now he found himself sitting on a hard pew thinking about God. His mother believed in a God who notated wrongdoings in big black books, a grand man with grand plans in which each and every person played their tiny part. For a moment Jack was so overcome by the sheer preposterousness of it all he was tempted to leap to his feet and share his outrage with the congregation. Trapped and restless, he shuffled his feet and twitched the muscles in his back. The sermon offered him no comfort. It annoyed him the way Father O'Hara talked more about God than about Franco.

The little church with its white picket fence and backyard of headstones sat on a scruffy block, half a mile out of town. The land had been bequeathed to the church by the Simmonds family, who had spawned so many children and grandchildren that their name prevailed on every school roll and committee minutes in the district. The well-to-do faction of the family still owned the farmland surrounding the church and made up much of the congregation.

The church had a simple functionality Jack approved of, however. The pews and pulpit were built in red cedar, a soft, fragrant timber that was once common in the area but was now all gone. There were several dozen people there, which surprised him. He knew that when the Martinos first attended, several of the congregation had made complaints to the Father. Call themselves Christians, Jack thought bitterly.

It was an odd congregation that day, almost a reunion for his wedding guests: there was Mr and Mrs Mack; Snow; Rocco, Erminia and Joseph; Alberto and Luigi; but no Lorraine. And some people he wouldn't have expected were there: Nobby, the town clerk; two nuns from the convent school; and a German who was something of a recluse.

Jack had met the German briefly once when scavenging the tip with Franco. An inhospitable man, everyone called him Hans but Franco had said that was not his name. His name was Friedrich. He and Franco had been friends but once the war began their friendship had made the locals suspicious. They were arrested on the same winter's night and held in the lock-up at the police station in Tindall until transport could be arranged to an internment camp in Hay. Father O'Hara had intervened and pleaded Franco's case on behalf of his family and he was home within a week. It was two years before Friedrich came home, though, and since then, despite speaking four languages, Friedrich spoke to no one, not even his old friend. Today he sat alone, his eyes closed as if in private communion.

Across the aisle were Dot and Marge, rosy-cheeked but tearful in their best finery. It was the same finery he had seen them wear to milk their goats, as it happened, early last summer when Franco had first taken him up the back paddock to meet them. As the two men climbed the hill they could hear the women's distant warbling floating in the stillness. 'Doraaa! Nessieee! Staaarlight! Petuuuniaaa!'

Behind their neat pink weatherboard cottage was the goat shed. The basic timber and corrugated-iron structure was transformed by several dozen candles propped in jam jars placed on ledges and in crevices around the shed. The sisters sat squat on low milking stools. One wore a red dress and a cream shawl around her shoulders; a satin hat with a small veil completed the ensemble. The other was in jade green with ruffles down the front. She'd added pearls and a red cloche hat. The trilling of an operatic soprano could be heard from a large wooden radiogram against one wall.

'*Buona sera, Signore Martino*!' called the sister in red. 'Where are our darling girls? We haven't seen them for weeks! Who is *this* you've brought to see us?' Keeping one hand on the goat's udder, she reached out and gave Jack a damp handshake with the other. 'Dot,' she said. 'And this is my sister, Marge.' Marge stopped milking for a moment and blew him a kiss.

'Can we offer you a sherry?' Dot gestured to the half-empty flagon sitting at her feet.

Jack laughed. He picked it up and took a swig. Its warm sweetness seemed to seep into every part of his mouth, it seared his throat and warmed his gut. He gave a delicate cough that set both women almost toppling off their stools with laughter.

'Just let me finish with Lilac and I will show you the *caprino*,' said Dot. 'They smell divine, don't they, Sister?'

'Divine,' smiled Marge, giving Jack a wink.

Using Lilac for support, Dot hoisted herself off the stool, dusted her skirts, adjusted the tilt of her hat and led the two men to the laundry behind the house.

'Is always the same,' whispered Franco. 'Beautiful.'

There was no room for Jack in the laundry. He was relieved – the acrid, intimate odour of goat cheese emanated from the room. He leant on the doorframe and watched the candle-lit shed across the yard become a cavern of flickering lights as the night engulfed it.

But now, in the church, Marge gave him a sad smile across the aisle and he acknowledged her with a nod. For

Jack, the place to dwell on Franco's life was not in this church. He longed to escape its stifling atmosphere and the pinch and scratch of his best tweed suit.

As the service ended Luigi, Alberto, Rocco, Joseph, Snow and Jack stepped forward to bear the coffin. As the men lifted the casket to their shoulders Friedrich stood and came towards them. Jack saw the strain in the German's face, the regret pooled in his eyes, and Jack fully understood what he wanted. Friedrich had left it too late to make amends with Franco. Jack's face felt hard and unyielding, his heart numb. He would not give up his place. He looked straight ahead and led the pallbearers down the aisle and out into the small cemetery behind the church.

Jack was shocked at the sight of the gaping hole in the ground. He wanted to crawl into it like a wounded animal. Around him he saw the faces of his wife, her sister and mother, distorted with sorrow, exhausted by grief. He felt helpless and angry.

Late that afternoon Jack stood at the gate for a long time. To step onto the hallowed ground of the olive grove filled him with foreboding. As the wind picked up he could see flapping scraps of black cloth tied to every tree. He opened the gate and walked slowly through the grove just as he had watched Franco do. He wished he had learnt more about the olives from Franco when he had the chance. He had vague thoughts about carrying on the work – building the olive mill. Jack ran his hands over the rough terrain of bark, trying to feel what Franco felt, trying to understand the hold these trees had over Franco. But in the end they were just trees. He wasn't even particularly fond of olives.

He climbed the hill on the far side of the grove. From there he could see the entire farm. A lazy plume of wood-smoke drifted from the house chimney. The sun was low and the paddocks were now in shadow but on the hill he stood bathed in the last rays of sun. Then he realised there *was* something he could do for Franco. It seemed so right he practically ran back down the hill and through the grove. He slowed to a walk as he saw Rosanna leaning on the gate, watching him.

They faced each other.

'He was trying to move one of those millstones when he had the heart attack,' said Rosanna without emotion.

'Did he say anything – at the end?' he surprised himself by asking.

'About you?'

'No. Anything.'

She paused for a moment. 'There is no translation.' She turned and walked away.

All the mourners had gone home and dinner was sub-dued. No one seemed to want to meet Jack's eye and yet he somehow felt they were looking to him for guidance. As soon as the meal was over he excused himself, began to fab-ricate a story about something he had to pick up; then he saw they were waiting for him to go, and left. He felt Rosan-na's eyes follow him.

He threw a shovel and several ropes on the back of the truck and roared off into the night.

Jack flicked off his lights and cruised, almost silently, down the last part of the road. Rather than take the drive-way used by the hearse, he opened the gate into the paddock beside the church and drove around to the back of the cemetery where he couldn't be seen from the road.

By torchlight he carefully examined the way the earth had been left, its shape and gradient, the gravedigger's trademark shaping of each corner of the plot. He stood for a moment to observe the layout of the various wreaths and bouquets. One made to resemble a clock with the hands set at eleven – the time of Franco's death – had been placed in the centre, a bouquet of lilies to the left, beside a white floral cross. An extravagant arrangement of mixed blooms lay at the feet, a wreath at the head. He laid them out in the same formation on the neighbouring plot, just to be sure. He threw his jacket into the cab of the truck, pulled his shovel off the tray and set to work.

A waning moon offered barely enough light. He would have to come back at dawn to put everything to rights. It took much longer than he had anticipated to open the grave. He hitched the ropes around the handles of the casket and, using the truck as a counterweight, hauled the box to the surface. Inch by inch he dragged it to the truck and used his last vestiges of energy to winch it onto the bed of the vehicle. He had the uneasy feeling of being watched. God? Franco? Or just his Sunday-school conscience?

Leaving the grave in disarray he drove back to the farm, bumping along the rough hilly track that ran along the eastern perimeter of the property until he came to the point where the track dipped down and ran along the back of the grove. Here, he turned off the dirt track and urged the truck up the steep incline of grass. Near the top of the hill was a long, flat ridge, protected from winds but touched by the dying breath of each day's sun. The ridge was home to generations of flowering wattles. Each year its flare of golden blossom lit up the cold winter days. Jack could think of no better place for Franco than high above the olives, the wind at his back, the sun setting at his feet.

Driven on by the fear of an unforgiving dawn a mere hour or two away, Jack lowered Franco's casket off the truck and pushed it under the low branches of the wattles. He swung the truck around and headed back to the church. He was almost there when he suddenly realised that there wouldn't be enough soil to fill the grave without the coffin. He slammed on the brakes and came to a shuddering halt, pounded the steering wheel with his fists, furious at making such a stupid mistake. He recalled that nearby was a pile of gravel dumped by a road gang – he had passed it dozens of times. He turned the truck around and drove with his head half out the window, eyes desperately scanning the roadside. Finally his lights illuminated a dark heap among the roadside grass. The gravel was heavy on his shovel and the crash of metal on stone made his head throb.

First light found him on his knees, clothes encrusted with earth and almost weeping with exhaustion. He carefully brushed the soil over the top of the gravel grave and replaced each wreath and bouquet.

By the time the church bells tolled for Sunday mass he had scrubbed himself clean under the icy stream of the yard tap and slept for an hour in Franco's armchair.

The women declined his offer to drive them to mass, clearly not happy that he had no plans to attend. Until she started up the truck and backed it out, Jack was not even aware that Rosanna could drive. It was only later he realised that it was a special mass dedicated to Franco.

When they had gone he made himself bacon and eggs, three rounds of toast and several mugs of strong tea. He put his shovel on his shoulder and walked up through the grove. The sun warmed his back, his boots glistened with morning dew and he could hear a thousand birds calling. He felt at peace. He felt as if Franco walked beside him.

Nine

AN OFFER IS made to my great relief and, after an appropriate period of restraint, I email Warren and accept the position. I will start mid-January, after the holiday season. As I press Send I know that all my problems are solved; my future is secure. I feel good.

Lauren is happy for me. 'How much are they paying you?' she asks over the phone.

'Why do you need to know?'

'I'm just wondering if you're going to get a decent apartment,' she bleats.

'Perhaps I'll just commute for a while. I rather like the train.'

'Yeah, right.'

'I'll sort something out,' I say airily.

'I might not be around anyway. I've had a job offer.'

'From whom?'

'Well,' she's says coyly, 'Sarah rang me to see how I was doing. I told her about you abandoning me with no money and the uni fees and everything . . .' She expects to hear me protest but I accept that as an accurate description of the situation. 'I applied for a job with her London company as a marketing assistant – and got it. I'll be working right in Knightsbridge!'

'What? This has all happened very fast,' I venture, dismayed.

'Ah, friends in high places, you see.'

'*My* friends in high places. What about the airfare? What about your marketing degree? Why didn't you even tell me?' I finish on a shrill note. Jesus! Sarah didn't offer *me* a job!

'It's only come together in the last few days. I'll defer for a year and Diane's lending me enough for a one-way fare.'

London, one way. Who's abandoning who here? I know I'm going to say the wrong thing seconds before I do. It's as though I'm watching myself from a distance, a middle-aged woman with bare feet and in a brown dressing-gown, gripping the telephone with both hands. 'Lu, I cannot deal with you going away right now. It's not a good time. Everybody giving us hand-outs . . . you're not going,' I suddenly snap.

'Giving *me* hand-outs? It's got nothing to do with you! I didn't tell you before 'cause I knew you'd kick up a stink. I'm taking this job and there's nothing you can do about it.'

'There *is* something I can do about it. I can tell Diane and Sarah to butt out.'

'Why? Why would you do that?'

'Because I forbid you to go.'

'Forbid me? Why?' she demands once more.

Silence. Just the hum of the line between us. The ground beneath us seems to be shifting, sliding away. She knows the answer.

'Everything's always about *you*, isn't it? You're just selfish, Adrienne. Incredibly selfish. You always were, and you always will be.'

'I beg your pardon! I've worked my *derriere* off the last twenty years so you could have the best of bloody everything and now I'm in the shit all you can do is whine about losing your bloody mobile phone.'

'You haven't worked your so-called *derriere* off for me – that was for you! It made *you* feel important. Your business was like your brilliant eldest child who had to be protected from any disruption by the "little nuisance". It was like a perfect older sister I couldn't possibly compete with. I was a drain on resources, an impediment to your glamorous existence. I've always felt – been made to feel – that I was the biggest mistake you've ever made.'

'What rubbish! I've never tried to hide the fact that you were an accident – it's the truth – half the people born in the world are conceived by accident.'

'I didn't say *accident*. I said *mistake*,' she replies coldly. 'But the difference between those people and me is that mostly their parents actually care about them. They hang around netball courts on freezing mornings, they go to see their child in the school play – every performance! Where were you, Adrienne? Where were you when I needed a mum? And what about you pretending you were an orphan? It's a joke really – *I* was the orphan.'

'I don't think you really understand what I've been through the last year —' I cling stubbornly to the script I've learnt off by heart.

'I don't think *you* really understand what I've been

through the last nineteen years. You know, I was actually glad in a way when the business died because I thought —' She stops and gives a heavy sigh. 'You're so convinced you've lost *everything* —'

She falters mid-sentence. There is silence for a moment, then the line goes dead.

In the days after my fight with Lauren a sort of lethargy overtakes me and slows me down. I seem to wander through the next week getting almost nothing done, half expecting a placating call from her. How ridiculous for her to be in competition with the source of everything she has ever owned, her education, her holidays – the lot! She is *the* most self-absorbed, unreasonable child. It's impossible to please her.

My thoughts turn, selfishly perhaps, to my own future. Now the job is in place, I need to tie up the many loose ends around here. It takes me a week to dig out the letter from Goldsmith & Son, Jack's solicitors. When I ring them they insist I make an appointment to collect my father's documents.

Their offices are in a red-brick building in the main street of Duffy's Creek, above the printing office. The tiny reception area smells sad. A stain on the carpet the size and shape of a large dog is the focal point of the room. The elderly receptionist gives me a sorrowful look.

Mr Goldsmith Senior and his son have tiny offices located opposite one another across a narrow hallway. Both have metre-high piles of manila folders teetering around the room and stacks of papers slewed across their desks. Mr Goldsmith Senior is unnaturally affable. As he shows me in, I see him glance across the hall to Mr Goldsmith Junior, who immediately materialises at my side. There almost isn't room to sit down but finally we uncover a visitor's chair and the meeting can commence. Mr Goldsmith Senior settles himself, rearranging files in an exasperated way as if they had got themselves in such a silly old pickle.

Son of Goldsmith is in his mid-fifties, thin of hair and thick of waist, so conservatively dressed that he seems like a man from an earlier era. He takes his place as though on sentry duty beside his father's desk. I'm flattered they consider me too hot for one solicitor to handle. Arms folded, the son nods his head encouragingly as I explain the purpose of my visit. His pants cuff has caught halfway up his shin on what appears to be a garter holding his socks up. Very Mr Bean. I have to avert my gaze so as not to be distracted by it.

'Mr Bennett's bank accounts I *can't* help you with – you'd need to see Mr *Finley* at the bank. You'll need to provide the *death* certificate to access his accounts, which we'll give you today, but I can't imagine there'd be too much there . . .' says Goldsmith Senior ponderously. Goldsmith Junior shakes his head sadly to indicate just how strongly he concurs with his father on this one. Obviously my father was not one of the shakers and movers of this town. 'Now, Jack didn't make a will *as such*. Mr Bennett, in fact, gave us an envelope for you *quite a while* before his untimely death and signed the property over to you at that point. When we wrote to you it was simply to discharge our duty and deliver it to you personally as the beneficiary.'

I half expect him to say that the envelope is here

somewhere and we should all pitch in and start looking. I glance around the room and notice an entire column of files propped in the corner all marked Leeton Earthmovers – a vexatious litigant if ever I saw one.

But Mr Goldsmith slides an envelope across the desk with my name on the front. 'Perhaps you would like to look at the papers *now*, in case there is anything you would like to *discuss* with us.'

Against my better judgement I open the envelope and take out a deed document, the death certificate and a sealed envelope with my name on the front. I read the deed carefully, fold it up and replace it in the envelope. 'No, I don't think there is anything I need to discuss,' I say brightly. 'It all looks *perfectly* in order, thank you.'

They both look disappointed. 'If you do decide to *sell*, we would be very happy to handle the sale and conveyancing aspects of the transaction.'

'I'll keep that in mind, should I decide to sell.' I get up to leave and shake both their hands. 'Can you tell me which bank Mr Finley's with?'

They smile in unison; now *I'm* the joke. 'We only have one bank in this town, Miss Bennett. Right next door.'

I pop into the bank and it seems Mr Finley is expecting me too, for he has the paperwork prepared for me to sign and another envelope with Jack's bank statements for the past year. I tear it open in the car, hoping it will reveal a six-figure balance, but sadly not. It's only four figures – better than nothing, but not enough to make a difference.

When I get home I put the letter from my father on the mantelpiece, where I can keep an eye on it. What could he possibly have to say to me after all these years? I'm not ready to find out.

Dog is happy to see me. *Dog*! What am I going to do with him when I move back to the city? I can't be responsible for him. He was just foisted on me, really. I don't even know his name, for God's sake.

Leonie calls to confirm my talk to the local women's network tomorrow night. I'm looking forward to it, I assure her. I have a couple of topics to run by her. What does she think about 'Talking business in the global village' or perhaps 'Horizontal communication in a vertical organisation'?

'Both sound interesting . . .' she says unconvincingly.

'How many businesswomen are you expecting?' I ask.

'Well, there were going to be twelve but it looks like there'll only be six.'

'Six!'

'Yes, I'm sorry about that. There's been a little split in the group over our sponsorship deal with the Miss Duffy's Creek pageant and the network has broken into several factions . . . I won't go into it – it's been awful, really, just awful. But there'll be some terrifically keen businesswomen there. Jenny runs the takeaway; Annabelle Challis has the gift shop; and Cecilia Simmonds – she's one of the top saleswomen for Supperware – she usually gives us a bit of a demo of the new products. And, of course, myself – you've probably seen my salon in town, the Chit-Chat and Chop? Now, what shall I put in the minutes as your subject?'

'What about "How to get a free plug in your local paper"?'

'Oh, that sounds wonderful! The girls will be tickled pink.'

The venue, Martha's Restaurant, is the local cream-tea coach stop. This evening there is a sign on the door saying 'Closed for Private Function'. Martha herself greets me, wearing a powder-blue tracksuit and a pair of pink fluffy slippers. In her late seventies, with a few too many cream teas under her waistband, her claim to fame is that in her early life she was something of an aviator; a barnstorming babe, by the look of her. She flew the Outback for the Flying Doctor Service and then became a stunt pilot. The theme of the restaurant could loosely be described as 'antics of the air'. The walls are crowded with pictures of her, a mere slip of a girl, in various open cockpits wearing leather headgear and goggles. In later shots she starts to look more glamorous in colourful (sometimes even sequined) jumpsuits, posing with other (presumably) luminaries of the air. Her suits are preserved on dejected-looking mannequins propped in the corners. A dusty parachute cascades from the ceiling. You can follow the whole story of her life because every item has a terse caption like 'Martha with Reverend John Flynn, Alice Springs 1947' produced on one of those little machines that impress letters onto strips of plastic.

We sit at one of the long tables. The six members face one another, with me the odd one out at the end of the table. I am, of course, hopelessly overdressed in a black tailored suit and white silk shirt.

Leonie gives me a friendly little wave. She's easily

recognisable as a hairdresser, her hair a colourful brawl that does not inspire confidence. No one explains the format of the evening as I sit through an interminable hour of minutes and general business. Martha ducks in and out of the room at intervals, then shouts from another room, 'Okay, it's ready – all hands on deck.' The meeting is abandoned as the group seriously bustles. Cecilia sets the table while the others ferry plates of steaming sweet and sour pork with rice to the table. Finally, Martha emerges hot and bothered from the kitchen and pours us each a half-glass of warm riesling.

'Thank you, Martha,' twinkle the group like polite schoolchildren.

'The cheesecake is defrosting,' says Martha with a wink. Wicked.

Finally, it's my turn. The secret to free publicity, I explain, is the angle. The secret to angles is brutal opportunism. I ask each of them to give me a two-minute run-down on their business and then we 'blue sky' and come up with angles. They love it. Soon we're laughing and dreaming up more and more outrageous ideas. The one who really doesn't get it is Cecilia, the Supperware queen. She's one of those brawny saleswomen, bedecked in gold, who have spent forty years knocking down doors and selling their wares. Her stance is to go direct, cut out the middleman. Why faff about when you can just bully till they buy?

'Pah,' she says. 'Marketing's just another word for selling – what's the difference, anyway?'

'With selling, people know what you're up to,' explains Leonie. 'Marketing comes around the back and bites them on the bum – and convinces them it's an experience worth repeating!' We all shriek with laughter. Half a glass of sweet wine and we're like kids on cordial. Then the sugar hit arrives. I don't know how big the mother ship was but the waxy cream wedge that docks on my plate direct from Planet Cholesterol probably weighs half a kilo. Naturally, the meeting sidetracks to a discussion on who wants to lose some weight (almost everyone) and when they are going to start (tomorrow).

Cecilia announces she has an item for the agenda. She wants the Duffy's Creek Women's Business Network to start a campaign to lobby the government to bring back national service. 'The reason the youth of today are off their brains with drugs and alcohol is because they have not had the discipline of army service,' she declares. She's so belligerent you would have to be one brave businesswoman to go up against her. Everyone looks appropriately concerned and there are murmurs of concurrence around the table. Within minutes, Jenny, the owner of the 'Quik Chik' takeaway (whose greasy pallor is no doubt a side-effect of toiling over vats of boiling oil), yawns discreetly and glances at her watch. Cecilia eyeballs me.

'I'd love to enter into a spirited debate on this . . . um . . . fascinating topic, but unfortunately I have to get up very early in the morning, and I need my beauty sleep, heh heh . . .' I slip out of my chair and pick up my bag.

Leonie makes a short speech to thank me for my presentation and hands me a very nice blue silk carnation in a tube. Annabelle of the gift shop takes it upon herself to see me to the door. She presses her business card into my hand.

'I'd love you to drop in and see me, I'm an old friend of your aunt's,' she murmurs. She opens the door and I'm finally released into the cool of the night. If I didn't have a job lined up in Sydney, this evening would have depressed me beyond measure but I giggle all the way home.

I'm still chuckling as I walk in the door, pick up the phone and call Sarah in London, forgetting that I'm semi–pissed off with her. I tell her the story of my evening, every little detail. 'I think they like me – they've invited me to come to their Christmas do next week – the male strip show called the Bilberries at the footy club!' The line reverberates with our screeching.

'So, are you going to go? Probably just what you need.'

I yelp with laughter but the line is silent. 'What *do* you mean, "what I need"?'

'Friends, fun, a bit of frivolity – wouldn't do you any harm right now, Adrienne.'

I sigh. 'The thing is, I actually liked them, even Cecilia the Conqueror. There's something touching about their naïvety, something that's more honest than I'm used to. They just say what they think.'

'So, do you see a place for yourself there, helping the business network?'

'Sarah, it's not a *business network*, it's a *jumble sale* – I'm out of my league. And you're out of your mind.'

'Just asking, just exploring the options.'

'There is only one option and I have taken it.'

The line goes silent and we both know why.

'You haven't said anything about Lauren coming over.'

'No, I haven't,' I sigh. 'I don't want this to be an issue

between us. I was hoping to ignore it . . . hoping it would just die a natural death when it dawned on everyone that I was not happy about it.'

'I thought you'd be thrilled for her.'

'I thought I would be too.'

'She's very excited about having Christmas in London.'

Christmas in London? Christmas is barely a week away. I'm sinking to my knees as I say in as casual a tone as I can muster, 'When does she arrive?'

'In the morning,' Sarah says. 'I'll get her to call.'

I mumble something about the lateness of the hour and get myself off the phone. Lauren's gone. My girl's gone. To the other side of the world, without seeing me, without a word. She had that ticket when she called me. I know she did. I am so angry with her. *So* angry. Not sad – just bloody angry.

I lie awake half the night, thinking not of Lauren's Christmas in London but my Christmas in Duffy's Creek. My mind darts from place to place. Where can I go? Who would have me? The thought of being alone at Christmas terrifies me out of all proportion, it always has. I need to be somewhere with people. I get out of bed at 4 a.m. and throw Jack's dressing-gown around my shoulders. I wonder how many Christmases Jack spent here alone.

I walk past the letter on the mantelpiece. I don't know why I'm so fearful of its contents. I pick it up and put it down again. Walking on by, I slip my boots on, much to Dog's pleasure, and walk around the lawn in the muddy dawn light. I follow the path through to the vegetable garden. So much work has gone into building these gardens – I would love to see them put to rights. Taking the track through the trees to the orchard, we stand and admire the apple tree. I get the feeling Francesco Martino garnered more local respect for this apple tree than for a thousand olives.

The mystery surrounding Rosanna and her whereabouts nags at me. In fact, I would like to know more about Franco and Adriana too. I had no idea I was named after my grandmother. It has occurred to me that for me to have inherited the farm, Rosanna must surely be dead. Over the next couple of days I manage to dig out the card Annabelle Challis gave me and I drive into town.

The summer heat and lack of rain these last few weeks have scoured the road and added a thick layer of fine dust that coats the roadside grasses and dulls the landscape. I've been letting Dog sit in the cab with me lately; don't want him eating my dust. He seems grateful.

Annabelle runs the Lavender Gallery, a shop full of New-Age knick-knacks and dust collectors. There's wooden spoons with tea-towel capes and little faces painted on them, teddy bears in tutus, dangly crystal things – it's a treasure trove. Annabelle herself is quite fetching in a purple tie-dyed kaftan with matching hair wrap.

'What perfect timing! I'm expecting a tour bus in an hour and it will be very hectic in here. I'm burning bergamot to help them relax and stimulate spending.' The laughter rolls out of her. 'Now, sit here, perhaps you'd like a reading. Although, I think there is already someone tall, dark and handsome in your life – am I right?'

'Did your crystal ball tell you that?' I try to match her playful tone but we both hear the false note.

'What can I do for you, my dear?'

'You mentioned that you were a friend of Rosanna's. I'm wondering if you know where she is.'

'We were in the same class at Mother of Mercy Convent, you know. We were great friends; there was her and me, Charlotte Furnell and Marcia Simmonds. Charlotte was a lovely woman, she died four or five years ago. Marcia's still around, she runs the annual Duffy's Creek flower show – done it for years . . .'

'And Rosanna?'

'Could be anywhere – she was the wild one. I heard she moved to Adelaide and was working in a hotel as a cook. But even that information is probably twenty or thirty years out of date.' She notes my disappointment. 'I wish I could be of more help. I'll consult my angels and see if I can't come up with something – some little whisper for you, my dear.'

I thank her and make an effort to be charming.

'If you find Rosanna, tell her Annabelle sends her love and laughter. A thousand dancing blessings,' she warbles, chins wobbling, as I leave. 'Take care, take care!'

'I do appreciate you filling in for me with the cleaning job. Can't let the tennis girls down. We've had Chrissie lunch every year for the last thirty-five years. We went thirty-four years and didn't lose a single person, then last year we lost three. I suppose we'll all just drop off one by one from here on . . .' says Joy over the phone.

'Good to hear you're in a party mood, Joy. I'm happy to do it for you. Out of interest, what does it pay?'

'It's probably a little less than you're used to – it's $8 an hour.'

'Each?'

'Of course each, silly goose,' she laughs. I like to make Joy laugh.

I discover that one of the reasons Joy's cleaning partner Deirdre can't work alone is that she doesn't drive. It takes me twenty minutes to get to her neat little brick house on the edge of town; she's waiting at the letterbox with a bucket full of Amfam products and some sort of high-tech mop. She slings them in the back of the ute and jumps in beside me. She's a stringy little woman, middle-aged, wearing a *Baywatch* T-shirt, the last pair of stone-washed stretch jeans left in the country and a pair of ugh boots. Her face has a crinkly parchment quality to it and the hair is as lank and stringy as any I've seen.

The other reason she needs a buddy is that Deirdre likes to talk. I recall a crack Jack made about one of my mother's friends; he said her skin must be too tight because every time she sat down her mouth opened. Deirdre is nattering before she even bends her knees.

'Left me fiancé Walter at home. He doesn't like me being away for too long,' she confides. 'Jealous type.' She rolls her eyes and sighs theatrically. 'Even when I'm off doing me cleaning he gets in a panic, thinks I'm seeing some other bloke. Honestly. Can't complain; I'm a lucky girl. Thinks I'm the sexiest thing alive. Can't keep his hands off me.'

'That's great,' I say stiffly. 'You are indeed lucky.'

'How old do yer think I am?' she says, reading my mind.

'Ah . . .'

'Forty-eight,' she says jubilantly. 'You?'

'Forty-nine,' I say a trifle sulkily. She's got to be lying.

'How do yer keep yer trim figure there?'

'I had a personal trainer for a long time, actually. How about you?'

'Me? I don't need a personal trainer. Coke gives me the sugar; ciggies keep me slim; cleaning keeps me fit. Saving up for me wedding dress. Like to see a picture?' She pulls out a much-folded clipping from a magazine and props it on the dash in front of me.

'Isn't that Catherine Zeta-something?'

'Yep.' She winds down the window and lights a cigarette. 'Walter can't wait to see me in that dress,' she smirks. 'Can't wait to see me out of it, more like, ha, ha.'

The house we are to clean belongs to the Simmonds family – not Cecilia of Supperware fame, thank goodness, but one of many Simmonds families. A beautiful old country home, the grounds are groomed like parkland; the redolence of old money. I feel intimidated somehow, embarrassed about the ute and my servant status. I'm tempted to loop the circular driveway and drive on out. Deirdre, however, hops out of the car virtually before I've stopped. She grabs the stuff out of the back and charges up the steps. The front door is open and she walks straight in, calling, 'Yoo-hoo, Margaret! Where are you, darl?'

Dropping her bucket, she opens a cupboard in the hall and pulls out the vacuum cleaner. 'You have a bit of a vac around, I'll do the dusting, then we can tackle the kitchen and bathroom together,' she instructs as she marches off down the hall. I *hate* bossy women. I start the vacuuming.

The house is beautifully cared for. An antique circular table in the hall holds a glass bowl of pale yellow roses. Glossy polished floors flow through the house, occasionally interrupted by soft, lush rugs. There's a veritable library of books, walls filled with wonderful art works. I feel bitterness seeping through my veins. What am I doing cleaning someone else's house? I'm only just coming to terms with cleaning my own. It is utterly humiliating.

Margaret eventually glides into the house and introduces herself. She shakes my hand firmly. My guess is she's a little older than me (and no doubt mature enough to admit it, should the subject crop up). She's tall and elegant, even in an old shirt, grubby riding breeches and straw-flecked socks.

'Deirdre tells me you've stepped in to help out; that's very kind of you. We've lost our housekeeper recently and I spend so much time in the stables at the moment I need all the help I can get. Are you a horse person, Adrienne?'

I rear back in fright. 'Definitely not!'

She laughs. 'Well, either you are or you aren't. When you're done, come out to the stables.'

Two hours later I am prepared to mount the most dangerous bloody stallion in order to gallop off into the sunset and escape Deirdre's incessant, deluded, self-absorbed stream of consciousness. It just pours out – nothing is held back. She over-shares on every single topic, virtually all of which are about her, Walter or cleaning (on which she is the world's greatest authority). Special subject: stain removal. Occasionally she runs out of things to tell me about herself and asks me a personal question like what star sign I am or do I shave my legs or wax them. My monosyllabic replies naturally turn the conversation to *her* star sign or *her* favoured depilatory method. I follow instructions mindlessly; the sooner it's done, the sooner I'm gone.

We go to the stables to collect our princely sum of $16 each. Margaret has the grace to look embarrassed as she counts out the coins into my hand.

'Fancy a ride, Deirdre?'

'Jeez, Margaret, don't know if you've got anything spirited enough to handle me,' Deirdre snorts. The woman is a parody of herself. Next thing I know she's got her bony bum in a saddle and is bouncing up and down like a pro. 'I'll just warm him up and take him for a spin, shall I darl?'

'Go, girl!' calls Margaret. 'Sure you wouldn't like a try, Adrienne?'

Maybe I'm more competitive than I thought, or maybe I'm just bloody sick of being treated as though I'm an idiot. 'Sure, why not.'

'Good on you,' she says. Oh, shut up, I think.

It's a long way to the ground when you're up on a horse. The ascent is extremely undignified but I can imagine the descent could be a lot worse. It's a big, warm, live, unpredictable animal. Actually, it's terrifying. I had the idea that I would be trotting around the paddock on my own but am vastly relieved when Margaret leads the horse. It's like learning to drive. She's shouting instructions to me and again I'm doing as I'm told. Surprisingly, it seems to work – the horse turns this way and that, almost like a car. The best bit is that when I get off I do it quite, well, professionally.

'Well done! Good on you,' says Margaret. I beam like a teacher's pet. 'Will you be coming with Deirdre next week?'

'Um, no, Joy will be back on deck by then.'

'If you want to do more riding you might like to come and help me in the stables and I'll give you some lessons in return.'

I agree to think about it and am taken aback when, as Deirdre leads her spirited mount in, Margaret throws her arm around my shoulders and proclaims me a natural rider.

'Who would have thought, eh?' Deirdre chortles. I don't know what she means by that.

The ride, unfortunately, has a stimulating effect on Deirdre and she talks non-stop all the way home. The sheer quantity of it makes me hot.

'Oh, look, yer bloomin' – me too.' I ignore her. 'Some women hate 'em. I love 'em. Like being on a battery charger, let's you know you're alive. Walter calls me his little firecracker.'

Hot flushes as a spectator sport – that's new. The subject of hot flushes naturally segues into other private women's matters. So engrossed is she in giving me a blow-by-blow account of her hysterectomy – you'd think she'd performed the operation herself – that when we get back to her house I have to lean over and throw open her door in order to make it abundantly clear that it is time for her to exit stage left.

Never again. On the way home I stop at the bottle shop and blow my entire pay on a decent bottle of wine.

Joy rings to invite me to the Duffy's Creek Christmas Eve party. I was hoping it was Lauren. She still hasn't called.

'I hear you went well with Deirdre,' she says.

'Deirdre. Yes,' I reply coolly.

Joy laughs. 'She's a bit of a handful, I know, but she's got a good heart.'

'She gave me the status on virtually every other organ in her body, but I don't recall her mentioning her heart. She's completely mad.'

'That's true. I thought you'd like Margaret, though.'

'And did you think Margaret would get me on a horse, by any chance?'

'Never crossed my mind, dear. Pick you up at six then?'

The party is in Bramley Park, which is in the centre of town. It's got a little rotunda and meanders along beside the river. The gathering is a Rotary do-gooders thing to raise money for some youth project.

The evening is quite beautiful, the air sultry, the sky clear and blue. For once I'm perfectly dressed in a white cotton sleeveless top, purple silk sarong and sandals. Coloured lights have been strung from tree to tree. There are stalls set under the trees selling sausages and steak sandwiches, buttered corncobs and baked potatoes. A local winery has tastings, and schoolchildren roam around selling tickets for the chocolate wheel.

There is a table of prizes provided by local businesses. It's got the look of unsaleable items – an imitation Tiffany lamp; a stampeding elephant carved in wood. There is a small stage decorated with a sleigh and Santa painted on plywood with an improvised dance floor in front. The atmosphere is timeless: there is the sense that although people have done this every year since God knows when, the novelty will never wear off.

Santa arrives on the back of the fire truck and throws sweets out to the crowd; almost no one can resist the scramble. He looks uncannily like my friend from the garage, Tinky Winky – which is a bit of a worry. I for one will not be sitting on his knee.

I'm surprised at how many people I know. There's the pink-slippered aviator Martha, taking unfair advantage of the wine tasting. She looks quite glamorous in a vivid floral frock, and I see she's wearing shoes tonight. Leonie and a gaggle of hairdressers with equally bedevilled hair-dos are here, and I can see the Goldsmith solicitor boys trailing about with their families in tow. The sorrowful receptionist appears to be one of their wives. She doesn't look any happier tonight. Margaret Simmonds gives me a friendly wave and on the other side of the park I can hear Annabelle Challis's distinctive fat-lady laugh. I manage to narrowly avoid Deirdre – thank God – walking arm-in-arm with Walter, who is as round as she is lean. They're sporting matching black jeans and crimson cowboy shirts.

And everywhere I look I see Joe Oldfield. And every time I sneak a look at him, he catches me. I can tell he finds me amusing. I'm annoyed that he's here. I can't relax now. I'm all tense and jittery.

Darkness slowly descends; our faces glow red and orange in the lights. People settle down on their rugs and open up eskies. Hark! The herald angels sing. A motley crew of children wearing back-to-front white shirts mumble their way through the old favourites. A local band – The Bush Brats – takes over the stage, a couple of guys on drums and guitar and two girls singing country pop. They're surprisingly good. People start to get up and dance. The girls sing about someone who's something of dreamer and something of a fool and right on cue Joe appears at my side.

'May I have this dance?'

'No.'

He laughs out loud. 'Come here, you.' Slipping his arm around my waist, he pulls me to the dance floor. He holds me close as if I might make a run for it, but as it happens this gal ain't going nowhere.

Ten

WITH CHRISTMAS ONLY weeks away, it was decided that Jack, who needed to go back to work, would drive home alone and return to the farm for Christmas.

By the time he returned the mood had shifted. The three women, each in her own way, had changed – as if they had become distillations of themselves, undiluted as it were by the influence of men.

He arrived on a day thick with heat to see Rosanna and Isabelle wandering languidly up to the house, deep in conversation, hair wet and tangled from swimming in the river. It was as though he didn't exist; had never existed. His relationship with Isabelle suddenly seemed very fragile. There was something he wanted from her, something visceral. Something she was reluctant to entrust him with. Deep in his heart he knew that Isabelle was not in love with him.

'We've made some decisions while you've been away,' Rosanna said as they sat down to dinner.

Jack felt his gut tighten. 'Yes?'

'Mamma wants to go home to Genova,' Isabelle said, looking at him steadily.

'All of you?' Jack's voice sounded thin and strained.

'Don't be daft!' snorted Rosanna. 'Isabelle's married – in case you've forgotten.'

Jack felt no relief. 'What? Sell the farm?'

The women looked at each other guiltily. 'No,' said Rosanna. 'We can't sell it. Papa's blood, sweat and tears are on that ground, not to mention *our* sweat and tears. In any case,' she continued more cheerfully, 'Mamma might decide that Italy is not what it's cracked up to be and want to come back. I'm going with her,' she said through a mouthful of food. She spoke briefly to her mother in Italian.

Signora Martino now spoke directly to Jack in a way she never had when Franco was alive, her voice full of emotion. When she finished, Rosanna translated. 'Her parents are getting old, our grandfather is almost blind now and our grandmother hasn't been well. They want to see Mamma – they're paying the passage for us. My aunt has been helping care for them but Mamma feels she should be there.' She abruptly turned her attention to her meal, clearly feeling no further obligation to explain anything to him.

Jack looked at Isabelle, not knowing what sort of response to expect, but her face was unreadable. The decision was made. Rosanna was the boss around here now, so it seemed.

Driving north after Christmas, Isabelle was silent. She sat pale and hunched in a blanket of grey misery. Jack longed to reach out and break the surface of her stillness. He felt helpless in the face of it.

Within a week of Rosanna and her mother's departure, colourful postcards from exotic ports began to arrive that would brighten Isabelle's day. Finally, a letter came to say the travellers had arrived in Genova. Increasingly Isabelle seemed to live by or through these letters that arrived every week. Not privileged to read them, Jack was offered titbits across the table while he ate his dinner.

'Rosanna and Mamma have been to visit my father's village. She said it makes Duffy's Creek look very cosmopolitan, and our house the height of luxury,' Isabelle laughed. 'Rosa says that Mamma never stops talking. Listen: "You wouldn't recognise our mother who art in Italy, she has become so extroverted. She haggles at the markets, scolds tradesmen, talks to everyone in the street. She knows *everyone*. When we meet people who haven't seen her for twenty years they're all bawling and hugging – it's hilarious! They all ask about kangaroos and crocodiles and why I am not married yet at the ripe old age of twenty-five. Little do they know."'

'What does she mean – little do they know?' asked Jack.

'Rosanna says she'll never marry.'

'How can she know that?' Jack felt disturbed somehow.

'She knows her own mind, I suppose,' said Isabelle, folding up the letter with a sigh.

They had been married almost a year by the time Isabelle told him what the doctor had said. She was shy about matters of the body – shy or modest, he wasn't sure if there was a difference – and he had yet to see her naked. He hadn't thought much about children but it had never occurred to him that they wouldn't have any. It was just a natural part of life.

He suggested she see another doctor, which she did. Later there was an appointment with a specialist. Soon he could read it in her face when she started to bleed each month.

Every morning she had a letter ready for him to post to Rosanna. He wondered what on earth she filled them with – their life was so quiet, there seemed little to report. He was grateful to Rosanna for her dedication – her letters were like oxygen to Isabelle, whose moods he was finding increasingly difficult to read. Some days she was calm and serene, just as she always had been, but at other times she looked dishevelled when he got home, as if she had been asleep – although she always denied that she had. There was an indefinable tension between them. It was as though she had drawn an invisible circle around herself that kept on expanding, the gap between them ever widening. She rocked herself to sleep at night; eyes closed tight, arms wrapped around herself. He finally asked her why she did that. Her lips set tight. He never knew when he was about to cross the line but her silence told him when he had.

She made little effort to make friends in Elenora; she was either too busy or too tired, so she said. There was a plump bottle blonde called Christine who lived a few doors up with whom she was friendly for a while. Although Jack found the woman's mannerisms irritating – she fancied herself to be theatrical – he encouraged Isabelle in the friendship.

Before Isabelle married, she and Rosanna had taken the

bus every Saturday afternoon to the picture palace in Tindall. For some reason he couldn't fathom, she was reluctant to go with him now, but would, on occasion, go alone. She had met Christine at the Thursday matinee; they had taken the same bus home and discovered they were neighbours. They began to go together every Thursday and on good days he would sometimes hear Isabelle hum the songs from *Singin' in the Rain* – which she had seen several times – in the next room and the quiet tapping of her slippers as she did a little turn around the kitchen.

Quite abruptly, it seemed, Christine's name wasn't mentioned any more. 'What's happened to your new friend?' Jack asked over dinner one night. 'I thought there was talk of her and her husband coming over for cards.'

'She's a bit of a busybody,' said Isabelle dismissively.

'Really? What did she busy her body about?'

'Just nosy. Asking personal questions, that sort of thing.'

'And you don't want her coming here, spying on you,' Jack joked, but he saw by the way Isabelle glanced away that he had struck a chord.

'We've got nothing to hide, Isabelle. There's nothing *mysterious* going on here,' he said teasingly.

Isabelle stood up and clattered the dishes as she cleared the table. 'There are things you don't understand, Jack.' She stacked the dishes in the sink and turned on the taps. Jack felt they were on the brink of something. He got up and crossed the kitchen. Her back was stiff and unyielding as he put an arm around her shoulders and turned off the taps.

'Enlighten me,' he said.

She closed her eyes and slowly shook her head. A tear slid down her cheek.

Finally a letter arrived from Rosanna that lifted Isabelle out of the fog she had been trapped in. She greeted Jack at the door waving the envelope, as jubilant as if she had won the lottery. Rosanna was coming home.

Isabelle began immediately to make plans to travel down to Duffy's Creek to meet Rosanna when she arrived in a month's time. She was suddenly a different woman, busy and industrious, and had thrown off the lethargy that had slowed her down for so long. There was a sort of intensity in her that was quite new, a sense of purpose.

'Look at this lovely cotton shirting I found at the sales.' She skipped about the back verandah and held it against herself as Jack pulled off his boots on the step. He never knew what to say about fabric.

'I don't think I've seen you in, ah, turquoise?'

'It's for Rosanna, silly,' she laughed. 'Look, here's the pattern. It's B, the shirt-waister.' She held up the packet of patterns and he squinted politely at a drawing of a woman wearing a dress.

'Hmm, dinky,' he said, and hung his hat and jacket on the hook at the back door.

'Rosa said she's put on some weight, so I'm making everything one size larger.'

'Everything?'

She looked guarded. 'I'm buying all the fabrics in the sales.'

'It's not the money . . .' he said. And it wasn't the money;

it was the nervous energy with which Isabelle was attacking this project, spinning around like a willy-willy that would eventually fall to the earth as dust. At least that's how it seemed to him.

With his trips to the farm Jack had had more than his fair share of time off work, and could not ask for more. After New Year he and Michael would be away for at least a week with a couple of surveyors looking at a possible new mine purchase on the north coast. He suggested to Isabelle that she might like to stay on at the farm with Rosanna, perhaps even until the end of January.

He was struck by the childlike way she eagerly took up his suggestion. He could see that she had not given thought to anything past getting back to the farm. Everything else she was leaving up to him and Rosanna.

Driving south, Jack couldn't decide whether he was looking forward to Rosanna's return or not. At first he was relieved to see his wife happy and excited, to see her emerge from a malaise for which there had seemed no cure apart, perhaps, from a baby of their own. It was something he had no control over. But now he felt a finger of jealousy prodding at him, needling him. He knew it was laughable to be jealous of his sister-in-law. It wasn't as though he wanted himself and Isabelle to be a pair of cooing doves, but there was something about the sisters' familiarity with each other, something he now felt he might not achieve even if he were married to Isabelle for forty years. She seemed to always drift just beyond his reach.

Isabelle had planned that they arrive at the farm the day before Rosanna's return in order to ready the house for her homecoming. They left at sunrise and before they met the main highway had to stop several times to wait for herds of cows crossing the road for the morning milking.

The day was gloomy, with slow drizzle that irritated Jack because of the need to turn the windscreen wipers on and off. He was concerned that, without humans about, mice and rats might have burrowed their way into the house over the winter months and would have almost certainly taken over the sheds. He felt a surge of disgust at the thick odour of rat that he knew would pervade the buildings that he would have to clear out.

Not that Isabelle would take things easy. Her trademark white gloves and creamy complexion gave people the impression of someone who'd had a privileged upbringing. He remembered his shock at seeing her on her knees in the propagating shed and her embarrassment at being caught dirty-handed. But he knew that once they reached the farm she would set to work in her methodical way. She had no time for modern mops and cleaning powders; everything was done exactly how her mother had taught her. Linen was washed, starched, ironed and folded precisely the way her mother did – towels folded three times widthways and twice again. It was more than habit – it was a mark of respect, a silent tribute in every movement.

The grey sky finally gave way to blue and Jack's spirits lifted as they turned into the driveway leading up to the house. It had rained heavily for some days, judging by the sleek swiftness of the creek as it passed the bend in the driveway. The

Prefect's shock absorbers were stretched to the limit splashing in and out of deep puddles. As they tipped from side to side Isabelle held onto the dashboard, laughing as though on a fun-fair ride. Sunlight played through the leaves, bouncing scraps of light around the car. Jack wound down the window and the joyous calls of the bellbirds made them both smile.

The house smelled empty and forgotten, but at least the tang of mouse wasn't present. Isabelle and Jack moved around the rooms silently. For Jack it was like the set of a play he had seen long ago. Without the players and the props of everyday life there was a strange unfamiliarity. The carving on the sideboard, the pattern on the couch, black patches of worn linoleum – details he had never noticed before seemed to leap out at him.

He left the house and waded through the thick grass of the lawn to the back gate. With one hand on the latch he stopped, mesmerised at the sight of the grove. Lush from the summer rains, the trees shimmered and danced in the sun. He pushed through the gate and stood before a single tree. For the first time he could really see the signs of maturity in the tree, in the thickening of the branches and in the tiny green olives that decorated every branch. He knelt on the ground and began to wrench out handfuls of grass from around the base of the trunk. When it was clear he smoothed the earth with his hands and sat back on his haunches. He was about to move on and clear another when he stopped himself. He touched the trunk, tentatively at first, slowly becoming aware of the delicate textures and scaly patterns of its hard skin. He'd felt this sense of awe before but only with rock. Now he saw the same depth of beauty in this living tree. He wondered why he had never observed it before and was humbled by its presence.

Despite the long drive he felt a renewed energy and, abandoning his plan to clear more grass, strode through the grove, stopping from time to time to pull off the last scraps of black fabric still clinging to the trunks. The mourning was over.

Jack carried the vine-leaf table and chairs out from the shed and placed them exactly as they had been when he first sat under the grapevine with Franco, waiting to catch a glimpse of Isabelle. Now she came to the door, glanced at the sky and went back inside. For a fleeting moment he was possessed by the strangest sensation of having become someone else, or perhaps it was of being an imposter in his own life. It was a moment of disorientation but one of clarity as well. He realised that at some point over the previous year of his marriage he had mistaken feeling comfortable for feeling happy. He had confused being looked after with being cared for. He had relinquished his freedom for a state of comfortable limbo.

Isabelle moved from room to room, busy with her preparations, seemingly unaware of his presence. By nightfall the house was clean, the debris of dust and dead insects vanquished. Isabelle prepared a simple meal. New potatoes and asparagus were abundant in the garden and even the rabbits couldn't keep up with the fennel and coriander that had gone to seed.

Jack noticed that although his wife had made up her parents' bed for them, she had also made up both Rosanna's bed and her old bed with the sheets they had embroidered as children. Although tired after the long drive, he could hardly take his eyes off Isabelle as she finished her meal and languidly stretched her arms above her head, smothering a yawn. Her honeyed hair was a little dishevelled, and she wore an old white shirt. Slightly torn, it drooped at one shoulder and exposed the outline of her breasts, unwittingly wanton. He felt that old weakness coming over him, so overwhelming that he had to try to calm himself in order not to alarm her. He stood and took her gently by the hand, slipped his arm around her waist and guided her firmly inside to the cool sheets of the marital bed.

Two days later Jack was once more in their bed when he woke disoriented in the early hours of the morning. The room was lit by a patch of moonlight. He could feel something was different and remembered that Rosanna was sleeping in the next room. A moment later he became aware he was alone. He sat up, swung his legs over the side of the bed and padded out into the hallway. The other bedroom was darker, but he could see by the huddled silhouettes that both beds were occupied.

Jack returned to his room, trying to work out what the implications were, if any, of Isabelle going back to sleep in her childhood bed. He wasn't unhappy about it, but he wasn't happy about it either. He felt as though he was back standing outside the circle looking in, just like before.

Standing on the platform with Isabelle waiting for Rosanna's train the day before, he had found himself becoming more restless by the minute. He told Isabelle he was going to the men's room and went to the kiosk for a pack of cigarettes. He felt the distant rumble of the train and found himself, for no reason he could think of, walking in the other direction, out of the building. He stood on the pavement and smoked his cigarette without really noticing. He had to make himself go back into the cavern of the station. Walking briskly onto the platform, his expression implied that something out of his control had delayed his return.

As people spilled from the train his eye was caught by a woman wearing a cream blouse and dark slacks, her hair partially obscured by a scarlet silk scarf flung carelessly over her head and shoulders, eyes hidden by large dark glasses of the sort recently made fashionable by Audrey Hepburn. She moved unhurriedly through the crowd towards them and he took in the spilling curves and the swing of her hips. Beside him Isabelle gave a yelp and dashed towards her. There was a split second between Jack's awareness that his expression betrayed his thoughts and the realisation that the woman was Rosanna.

On Christmas Eve, Rosanna and Isabelle spent their first afternoon together cooking, as Jack knew they would. He wandered through the grove, stopping now and then to remove a broken branch or two, and walked up the hill to sit under the wattles for a while with Franco.

In some ways he was looking forward to the job up north, just living with a couple of blokes and the basics, although eating out of tins was not as appetising as it once had been;

his palate had been spoiled by too much good Italian food. But having a beer or two and a yarn without having to take his boots off had its own sort of appeal. Isabelle would have company here with Rosanna; they would look after each other. They spent all their time nattering to each other anyway. He had overhead Rosanna telling Isabelle some story (she had taken the precaution of speaking in Italian so it clearly wasn't for his ears), and he suspected from Isabelle's gasps of shocked delight that it was about a lover – a shipboard romance, perhaps? He found himself curious. There was something odd going on. He wouldn't ask. Rosanna had been uncharacteristically evasive when he asked her why she had made the decision to return to Australia.

Jack roused himself and spent some time clearing the area around Franco's grave, pulling out some lantana plotting to take over the fertile patch that had served the wattles for so long. That job complete, he set off along the ridge skirting the upper boundary of the farm to the barbwire fence that separated the Martinos' property from the Roland sisters'. Looking at the fence, he cursed Marigold and Petunia and friends. The blasted goats had forced their heads through to eat the grass on the other side and used the fence as a ladder to pluck the lower leaves off a stand of kurrajongs that marked the boundary. Yet he felt a little guilty – Franco had had an innate sense of responsibility to the sisters, simply because they were female and his neighbours. Jack had not given their welfare a moment's thought since the funeral. He followed the fence until he found the makeshift gate and let himself through. It was too early for the milking and he wondered if the sisters were dolling themselves up in readiness.

He knocked at the front door and waited. The curtains were drawn and it seemed possible that no one was home but the old Ford truck was parked in the garage, so they couldn't be far away. Finally, the front door opened. It was so dark inside he could hardly make out who stood behind the screen door.

'Yes?' The voice sounded slurred.

Jack peered in at her. 'Ah . . . Miss Roland?'

'Yes, what is it?' She made no move to open the screen.

'It's Jack, Jack Bennett.'

She opened the door slightly and looked carefully at him. 'Jack?' she repeated, and her voice softened. 'Of course, how are the girls? We miss them. Would they like to come up and feed the kids?'

Jack recognised now that this was Dot, but not Dot as he remembered her.

'The girls are well. Rosanna is home. We wondered if you and Marge would like to come down for a drink after the milking? A Christmas drink.'

'Milking? Marge isn't well. I'm not sure that she'll be up to a drink – she can't get up . . .' Dot began to weep softly.

Jack stepped backwards, anxious to be away from the sour odour leaching from the house, from the sight of her – helpless, shapeless, all the pretences fallen away. He suddenly thought of his mother, weeping silently as she swept up broken crockery, his father walking the night somewhere beyond the shouting and the slamming of the front door. How he had longed for his mother to tuck her hair back behind her ears, take out her compact and pat her mottled cheeks with the little skin-coloured pad, slide her cherry-red lipstick expertly around her lips – to paint her face happy.

'I've tried to get her up . . .' said Dot.

'Another time then,' Jack replied as he walked backwards down the steps.

Dot raised her voice to reach him as he turned to walk away. 'He was so proud of you, you know. Like his own boy, he said.'

His own boy. He walked down the hill with the words gnawing at his mind. He had the feeling that Franco was dogging his footsteps, disappointed at his cowardice. He threw open the back door and shouted, 'Isabelle! Rosanna!'

Rosanna came hurrying out. 'What is it? Bella is resting.' He told her of his conversation with Dot and before he had finished she was tearing off her apron and scribbling a note to Isabelle. It was only later that he recalled how drawn and pale Rosanna looked.

The driveway up to the Roland house was clay and rock and Jack found it quite unbelievable that the two old girls managed to negotiate it in their truck. It would be a mudslide in the wet.

Before he had even switched off the ignition Rosanna jumped from the truck and ran to the back door. Pushing it open, she called into the house, '*Zia* Dorothy, where are you?'

It was growing dark and Rosanna switched on the lights as she moved through the house. Following her, Jack was shocked at the state of the place. There were scraps of food on sticky, encrusted dishes on every surface and also stacked carelessly, brown and greasy, in the kitchen sink. Out of the corner of his eye he caught the flicker of a marauding mouse.

He stood awkwardly in the hall and waited to be summoned. Rosanna was talking quietly in the bedroom. He could hear a woman's muffled sobbing. Feeling like an intruder, Jack turned to leave just as Rosanna came out of the room. Without looking at him, she went to the telephone, wound the handle once and asked the operator to put her through to Doctor Kilby. Her words 'Death certificate' had a chilling finality, punctuated by the slam of the screen door as Jack left the house.

He opened the gate and walked across to the barn. The goats had already gathered, playing about like schoolchildren given an unexpected early mark. They butted each other affectionately and nibbled experimentally on sacks and pieces of cardboard stacked in the barn.

Suddenly, he heard the gate creak open and he turned to see Rosanna striding towards him. The light was too low to make out her expression but he could read the purpose in her movements. In a moment she was standing squarely in front of him, and without a word she gave him a whack across the side of his head with the heel of her hand.

'How could you leave her alone? What is the matter with you?' she shouted. 'Don't you care for anyone but yourself? *Egoista*! *Bastardo*!'

They faced each other in fury, but Jack's anger quickly seeped away – there was a relief in being punished. He saw she was crying and only just caught her wrist in time as her hand flew up to clout him on the other side of the head. He felt the pain he saw in her eyes.

'Go home. Take care of your wife. I'll stay here tonight. Tomorrow you can come back and take Marge down to the undertakers – they'll never get up that driveway.' She dismissed him with a wave of her hand. He walked back to the truck without a word.

As he pulled up in front of the house he could see Isabelle's face, ghostly, at the window. She came to the door.

'Where's Rosa?' she asked anxiously.

'She's staying the night with Dot.' She looked so pale he hesitated. 'Marge isn't very well.'

'What's happened to her? Should I go up there?'

'No, Rosanna wants you to stay here. I have to go back in the morning. Isabelle, I'm sorry, but Marge has died.'

Isabelle's hands seemed to spring to her belly of their own accord. 'Oh no, oh no, oh no . . .' she wailed. 'Everyone is dying . . . everyone is dying.'

Jack took her gently by the shoulders. 'Isabelle, people die. We're all going to die.' He couldn't think of anything else to add, so he put his arm around her and gave her a sympathetic squeeze. 'Sit down, love. I'll get you a little brandy.'

She covered her face with her hands, shoulders heaving with each sob. He steered her towards an armchair and went into the kitchen to search through the top cupboards where the liquor was always kept.

When he returned a few minutes later with the brandy in a coffee cup, the chair was empty. He wandered down the hall and put his head around the bedroom door, expecting to find her lying on the bed. But no. He was alone in the house. He stood on the front verandah, the little blue and gold cup still in his hand, staring into the blackness. He put the cup down, went to his car, opened his workbag and pulled out a torch. He stumbled into the night, calling her name, the beam of the light jumping and bouncing ahead of him. He leapt the gate and stopped dead. She had gone up to Dot and Marge's, of that he was sure, but because the two properties met along the length of the farm's western boundary, it was possible to access the neighbouring property almost anywhere along the fence line.

'Isabelle!' His voice searched the hills and came back to him empty. Frantic now, he ran through the grove, flicking his torch beam in every direction. Several times he tripped and fell but was on his feet again in seconds, running, shouting her name to the night, the olive trees silent witnesses to the crack in his voice.

Finally he reached the fence line. Panting, he strode the line, flashing his torch across the field. The goats glanced up, startled, eyes reflecting pin spots of light.

He crossed the fence and could now see the lights of the Roland house ahead. He fell heavily on the front step and limped to the door. As soon as Rosanna opened the door he knew Isabelle hadn't arrived.

'What now?' she said, and then he saw his fear reflected in her eyes. 'Let me just get *Zia* Dorothy settled.' Her voice was calm.

She returned minutes later and handed him another torch while she pulled on a borrowed cream cardigan. Side by side they walked silently back towards the farm. Once they crossed the fence they separated. Soon Rosanna's torchlight disappeared and there was only the echo of her voice across the valley like a song in the night. 'Bella, Bellaaa.'

Jack swung his torch back and forth through the trees until he heard Rosanna's howl, 'Jack! *Jaaack*!' He followed her voice to the beam of the torch urgently strafing the grove.

He lifted his unconscious wife carefully off the ground and carried her home. It was only when he placed her on the bed that he realised his shirt-sleeves were soaked with blood.

Eleven

I WAKE ON Christmas morning alone in a strange bed. Stretching out, I touch the other side, and the sheet is cool. I hear Joe rummaging around in the kitchen. I smell toast, coffee and bacon. Throwing on my sarong and shirt, I wander out. He turns and smiles.

'Hey, Merry Christmas.' He wraps an arm around my shoulder and kisses me on the forehead. He smells soapy and fresh. 'I've got a surprise planned for you.'

'How could you *plan* a surprise when you didn't know I'd be here?'

'Oh, well . . . you know, just in the hope that you were.' He grins. 'Or else I would have had to come and get you.' He pulls out a chair from the little kitchen table and shovels books, newspapers and piles of drawings together. Looking around the cabin for a spot to sling them, he finally drops them in an armchair.

'Eat up, I'm just going to take the esky down to the truck.'

He darts out the door and moments later I hear the bike buzz off down the hill. I've barely finished my toast when he's back for me.

'What about my clothes?'

'Very nice, I just *lurve* that shade of purple, darrrling,' he purrs.

'I mean, are they suitable?'

'Sure, whatever – it's very relaxed. Just you and me, babe.'

Going down the hill on the back of the bike with my skirt flapping, I feel I should be riding side-saddle. He stops beside the truck and lets me off, scoots around the back and rides the bike straight up a ramp he's attached to the tray.

'Isn't that a canoe?' I say, peering warily into the back of the truck.

'It is indeedy.' He ties down the bike, pulls in the ramp, flips up the tailgate and jumps off. He opens the passenger's door and ushers me into the cab.

'Where are we going in a canoe?' I shout above the roar of the engine.

'Remember *The Wind in the Willows*?'

'Hmm.'

'We're going to mess about in boats.' He looks as happy as a ten-year-old. 'We'll drop the bike off downriver and then we'll go upriver, past your place, put the canoe in and then we'll just drift on down, snacking on cold chicken and champagne and soaking up the sun.'

'What if we fall in?' I bleat, sounding like a uncooperative child.

'It's not the Zambezi; it's just a lazy ol' creek. Trust me.'

It takes us over an hour to drop off the bike and find the place upriver to launch the canoe but once we're in, it's really okay. The canoe is quite wide and flat, like an Indian one. The creek is slow, sleek and green and the bank not so far away. Joe sits in the back, paddling with a single paddle like a brave and I sit facing him at the other end like Pocahontas, with the esky and a canvas holdall in the middle between us.

We drift along for a while, seduced into silence by the gentle ebb of the river, the play of light on the water and the rhythm of the paddle pulling us forward.

'Why are you alone on Christmas Day?' I ask.

He looks at a point somewhere over my head. The silence changes tack.

'When my heart broke it was more than a physical thing. I had stuffed up everything in my life. I lost my family, my kids – the only things worth having. Worse still, I was stuck with a problem – me. I've had to get to like my own company.' He pauses and looks at me. 'Anyhow, I'm not really alone, I'm with you. Tonight I'll see Mum and my brother's family. Tomorrow arvo I'll go down to Sydney and see my kids. How about you? You said the other night you'd lost your business – did you go bust?'

'I didn't quite go bankrupt. For months the company was like a semitrailer teetering on a cliff edge – waiting to see if I'd go over or hang on.'

'And?'

'A liquidator was appointed – the dreaded Mr Arnold – he took on the role of gravity. In the end the company just melted away. The creditors were paid off but I was personally liable for around one point four million. My apartment fetched one point two and a half, I cashed up my share portfolio and that was it. I walked away from the wreck, literally with the clothes on my back.'

'Of which there were quite a few, I imagine.' He smiles.

'All last season's, sadly.'

'At least you walked away.'

'It's only a metaphor. People don't die of financial disorders.' I think about that for a moment. 'There was a time when I thought I might die of despair, though.'

'You don't have nothing – you have the farm.'

'That was my secret stash. If I'd been made bankrupt they could have taken that too. Let's just say I was quietly resistant to that option.'

'What about your daughter – Lauren? What's her story?'

'She's left the country, as of this week. London.'

'You missing her?'

'Yes and no. We had a spat. She told me I was selfish.' I sound flippant but feel my carefree mood start to crumble. 'Perhaps I'm more like my father than I care to admit.'

'Jack could be a bit of a moody bugger, but I never found him to be selfish – the opposite in fact. Which reminds me, there's something on your farm I must show you sometime.'

'He's left me a letter. I haven't opened it yet.'

'Oh? Why not?'

'I know that's what he wants me to do. He's going to have the last word.'

Joe roars with laughter. 'You're as stubborn as he was. There's a good picnic spot just up here; I'll pull in as close as I can but you might get your feet a wee bit wet getting off.'

He paddles hard towards a small beachhead and says 'Hold on tight!' as we breach the bank. He steps out and pulls the canoe further onto the dark sand. He offers his back. 'Jump on, I'll bet it's a while since you had a piggy-back.' It is indeedy.

The spot is like a little dell, a secluded patch of grass surrounded by large trees that create stippled shade. The sort of place a French impressionist might have set up to paint friends enjoying a picnic under parasols and wide-brimmed straw hats. There's a small patch of pebbled sandy beach, almost hidden from the river by large white rocks big enough to lie on.

'We're actually on your property right now,' says Joe. He points out a track through the bush that leads to the farm. Opening the holdall, he spreads out a rug and some cushions. The esky holds champagne and glasses, chicken, ham, tomatoes, olives, cheese and bread. We spread the rug and cushions in the dappled shade of a tree, set out the picnic and pop open the champagne.

'Merry Christmas!' we say in unison, clinking glasses.

Joe settles himself comfortably, props a cushion behind his back and leans against the trunk of a tree. He stretches out his legs, crosses his ankles and takes a sip of his champagne as if performing a ritual. 'I don't want to mislead you – I am more a beer man than a bubbly boy at heart.'

'I don't want you to mislead me either,' I say.

'Come over here,' he says and pats his thigh. I lie down and rest my head on his lap. He gently traces a finger around my jaw as though calculating its dimensions and brushes my hair back from my face.

'While I was recovering in hospital I was seriously depressed. Hardly anyone came to see me apart from a couple of blokes I'd worked with, my brother Sammy, and Mum when she could. I felt as though my life had been a complete waste of time. Then one day they put me in a wheelchair and stuck me outside under a tree in the hospital grounds. It was a big old oak tree and there was almost total shade under it. I was cold and uncomfortable, even though the day was sunny and warm. It seemed like the sun was shining for everyone but me. I sat there for ages – felt like hours – sort of blindly staring into space, just waiting for it to be over. Then there was this sort of thread of wind that ruffled through the tree and a drop of sun fell onto my face. I felt as though I was being lit, like a candle. I could feel the warmth. It was glorious. I realised that this is how happiness comes – in little unexpected spoonfuls. It probably sounds overly romantic but it gave me hope. That little trickle of sunlight gave me the strength to get myself going again.'

'I know you think that relates to me somehow.' My eyes prickle unexpectedly.

'Does everything have to relate to you?' he says kindly.

'Of course it does,' I reply, only half joking. I sit up and stare at the river flowing past. My flippancy is a diversion. I envy him his epiphany. Deep down I'm shallow. I want my life to be comfortable again, and as soon as possible. I envy him his certainty. I envy his acceptance of happiness in small dollops; they just don't seem enough for me.

'I know I can be happy,' I sigh. 'I just don't know what I need to make me happy.'

'At the risk of sparking Mohammed accusations, I think happiness is something that comes to you, not something you can pursue as a lifestyle, like getting fit. The more you look for it the harder it is to find – like love.'

'Well, I'm not looking for love,' I say quickly.

'Hmm, you better watch out,' he murmurs as he wraps his arms around me and plants tiny kisses on my neck. 'That might just creep up on you too.'

When I wake in my own bed the next morning I am not alone. Joe sleeps beside me, his face as serene as a child's. He seems to fill my little white room with his presence and his salty sweat. With his spoonfuls of sweetness and light.

When your heart has been broken in five places you can only offer a piece at a time. There are countless ways to betray someone and I have somehow suffered every one of them, been let down on every count. My love life has been a rugged descent into the depths of disillusionment – and it's not as though I had illusions in the first place. I may be stuck, but it's safe and comfortable. The way I feel about Joe right now terrifies me. I don't want to be responsible for his happiness and I'm desperately afraid to entrust him with mine.

The phone rings and I slip out of bed quietly so not to wake him, sure that it's going to be Lauren. It's Diane, full of Christmas cheer.

'Did you have a nice day yesterday? What did you do?' she asks.

'I messed about in boats.'

'Really? I'd like to hear more about that. I've got lots of yummy food, I thought I'd drive up and make us lunch – what do you think?'

'I'll be here with bells on.'

'How festive! See you about eleven.'

I make tea and take two mugs back to bed. Joe's awake, stretching and yawning. He has this way of smiling every time he sees me as though just the sight of me makes him smile. I've never had that effect on anyone before – apart from Dog.

He sits up and takes the mug of tea from me. 'This is nice. Nice room. Nice woman.'

'You don't know me that well; this isn't really me,' I say as I slip back in beside him.

'I'd like to, and that's what counts.'

'If you stay this morning you'll meet Diane – she's arriving at eleven.'

'Do you want me to?'

'Maybe. Let's see how we go.'

'Yeah, it could all be over by eleven.' He grins at me and sips his tea.

'Dog has been rather neglected these last few days. Perhaps we could take him for a walk up the hill after breakfast?' I suggest to placate him.

'You know Dog's real name is —'

'No! Don't tell me.'

'A walk up the hill with Dog sounds good,' he says, feigning nervousness.

Dog is delighted to see us pull on our boots at the front door, still eating our toast. The day is clear and bright, yesterday's humidity has dissipated overnight and the air feels fresh. It's been several weeks now since all the rain and the grass is not as lush as it was – it's easier to walk through the grove. Joe offers to come and slash the whole grove; apparently the trees don't care for all the grass around them. As we walk, Joe talks about the trees and how the rootstock was smuggled into Australia by my grandmother and her two young daughters in the seams of their clothes and the linings of their suitcases.

'Jack and your grandfather had plans to build an olive press together. You can see the two big millstones in that shed out the back – that was the propagation shed. The old man died before he saw his oil flow, unfortunately. Both old boys did.'

He throws a stick for Dog, who lollops after it but then lies down to chew it. 'If I had the money I probably would think about buying this place from you. It would be a tragedy to have this grove ripped out. I am interested in olives in the long term but short term – hey, I'm pretty darn happy slashing paddocks.'

'I don't really believe that mowing grass is enough for you.'

'Depends what you're after,' Joe replies. 'I find it satisfying. I can see where I've been. It's continuous. I have time to think. I hate to disappoint you, but that does it for me right now. I don't need a title to tell me who I am.'

'Well, I don't think cutting grass or growing olives will do it for me. I'm not going to take on the family burden – the proverbial millstones.'

The sun is hot on my back as we walk the length of the grove and start to climb the hills beyond. It's a long climb but not difficult. The gradient isn't too steep so it comes as some surprise as we near the top to turn around and take in the extent of the view. Off to our left we can see the river winding covertly through the bushland that borders the grove. The grove itself, laid out to a grid, is unexpectedly satisfying to the eye with its rigid lines contrasted against the random nature of the bush. The faded red corrugated-iron roof of the house is all but swallowed up by the trees surrounding it. I can see the meandering driveway with the creek a dark ribbon beside it. It's in fact a little tributary of the river.

'There's something I want you to see,' says Joe, taking my hand. We climb higher and reach a small area where the ground flattens out. It's quite sheltered and populated by wattles. He leads me to a spot among the trees, crouches down and pulls away the grass to reveal a headstone. I kneel beside him and read:

Francesco Luciano Martino
1891–1951
Here He Rests in Peace

'What on earth is he doing up here?'

'Jack brought him here. Had the headstone made years later. No one else knows he's here.'

'No one else knows? He was buried somewhere else and Jack dug him up? Good God! Why?'

'Wanted him to be here, on his land.' Joe gestures across the valley. 'He loved him, I guess.'

'Well, that's a problem. I can't sell the place with him

up here.' I sit down in the grass. What a strange thing for Jack to do. What a strange man that father of mine was. 'He must have trusted you to have told you,' I say, giving him a sideways glance.

'More fool him, eh?' says Joe as he folds his arms behind his head and lies back, gazing up at the sky.

I lie beside him and watch a single cloud drift across the blue.

'Can *I* trust you?'

'Trust needs time, my love. Give it time.'

When next I look, he's fast asleep.

Diane's gleaming silver Audi noses its way up the drive and pulls up beside the steps. She steps out of the car perfectly attired for poolside champers and canapés and runs an appraising eye over me.

'Hmm, you're obviously eating well – you look terrific,' she drawls as she gives me a peck on the cheek. She flicks open the boot of the car. It brims with David Jones carrier bags. 'I had a little shopathon – I know how difficult it is to find food in the bush.'

We each take a handful of bags and carry them inside, followed closely by Dog, who catches the scent of delicatessen on the breeze. Diane squats down and rubs Dog behind the ears, murmuring sweet nothings.

'Whosealovelyfellowyesyouarealovelydoggiewoggie. What's your name? A dog, Adrienne! I never took you for a dog person.' Me neither.

I'm glad Joe decided not to stay; she talks non-stop

over lunch. I want to quietly enjoy the food and flavours of Persian fetta, pheasant pâté, five types of lettuce, smoked salmon, fresh baguette, mangoes and mascarpone, but it's yadda yadda yadda. I'm all of a tizz, drink too much chardonnay and have to go and lie down in my room.

When I emerge, Diane (who has also drunk too much) has decided to stay the night. I try to get her to come for a walk to clear our heads. She demurs, she hasn't brought the right shoes – God knows why not, she's got about a hundred pairs.

In the end it's just me and faithful Dog walking in the silence of the grove. The only sounds are the sighing of the wind in the trees and the calls of the birds as they hurry to wherever home is tonight. The last of the golden light is spirited away by the shadows as the day fades before my eyes.

'So, Adrienne, I'm thinking there might be a man on the scene?' says Diane, opening another bottle of wine to accompany the leftovers from lunch. We arrange them artistically on the kitchen table. 'You've got a smug look about you.'

'There could be,' I say with a coy smile as I sit down.

'So what *did* you do yesterday?' she asks, breaking up the last baguette.

'Mmm . . . we talked, drank champagne, swam in the creek . . .'

'Sounds divine to me,' coos Diane. 'Do I get to meet him?'

'Probably not, we're not at that stage yet.'

She's quieter now, more relaxed. The tension she transmitted earlier in the day seems to have eased. We sit companionably and nibble on our leftovers.

'I think we need to talk about Lauren,' Diane says suddenly.

'Yes?' My voice is suddenly hoarse. I have, with some difficulty, managed to avoid that subject all day.

'I gather you two had words – she left in such a hurry. Talk about here today, gone tomorrow. I was surprised you didn't come down to see her off.'

I can feel that telltale burning at the back of my eyes. 'It was very generous of you to lend her the airfare, Di. It's just . . . I just wasn't ready for it.'

'If you love somebody, set them free,' she says sweetly.

I feel like whacking her over the head with the last of the baguette. Her attempts at philosophical commentary run the full gamut from bumper sticker to karaoke. She doesn't have children; she has no bloody idea how betrayed I feel. And never will. I don't even want to talk about it.

'I'll keep that in mind, Di.' The chill in my voice lowers us into awkward silence.

'So, the big new job starts soon?' she gushes. 'Excited?'

'I *was* excited about getting the job, but now . . . I don't know if I've got the energy. I've become quite lazy. I'll miss my naps —'

'What a cop-out! Do I sense a few confidence issues here? This is going to put you back on your feet, Adrienne.'

'I know I've got to start somewhere, I think my resistance is working for someone else. It's not something I've ever aspired to.'

'Well, I have a little proposal to put to you. I do have a spare room in my new apartment and, although I'm not actively looking for a roomie, I thought it might be a starting point *pour toi, mon ami*,' says Diane. 'I know you'll love it, Adrienne, it's very *you*.'

No sooner has she left the next morning than who should arrive but my old friend Mr Leeton. Dog barks as the car comes up the driveway, which is unusual as he's only a watch-dog in the most passive sense of the word. I come to the door ready to talk. But when he rolls out of his golden car and lumbers up the front steps like a belligerent rhino, I hesitate. My friendly little wave is redirected to the more useful task of tidying my hair. I stay in the doorway, ready to slip and bolt.

He's flushed with the exertion of exiting his car in such haste and is almost panting as he stands before me. I won't be surprised if he suddenly snorts and starts to paw the ground.

'Now, Missus Bennett, you and I both know —' he thunders.

'Mr Leeton! *Don't* you *dare* presume to tell me what I know and don't bother telling me what *you* know – because I'm not bloody interested! Now fuck off and find some other hill to stick your colonnades on. This one is taken!'

Leeton blinks several times. He looks bewildered for a moment, then turns, without a word, hurls himself back into his car and leaves, quietly.

Oh shit. Now I've really stuffed it.

I make a cup of tea and sit down to open Jack's bank statements. I'm going to have to start withdrawing those funds to keep going until my first pay comes through. I probably could have paid a month of Lauren's rent from this account. Not that it would have changed things between us.

Something's odd. There are still payments going out of the account every month to Finbal Pty Ltd. Sounds like a shelf company. I go online to ASIC and search company names. Not much there. Principal Place of Business: Sydney NSW. One possible lead is the former name: Jacaranda Nursing Home. I do a search on the name in the white pages and am rewarded with a phone number.

I pick up the phone and dial. It's answered by the nursing sister on duty. She can't help me. I'll need to call back after the New Year break and talk to Mrs Adams, who handles the accounts. I thank her and hang up.

Two minutes later I pick up the phone, press redial and she answers again.

'You don't have a Rosanna Martino there, by any chance?'

The heat is like a smothering blanket. I sit in the car watching the old people out on the lawn under the trees, just sitting staring. I wonder if one of them is Rosanna.

There is no one in the entrance hall. No directions, just the lingering odour of old food and old people, cheap talc and Sorbolene. I manage to catch a nurse as she strides past.

'Mrs Martino?'

'Third door on the left,' she says without slowing her pace.

My shoes sound stealthy on the lino as I creep down the hall. I peek around the door.

'I'd like to know who the hell put me in here,' calls the woman leaning forward in her bed to get a better view of me. 'There's nothing wrong with me.'

I approach her bed and see the thick plait, now grey as silk, curled across her shoulder and shrewd dark eyes that take in every detail.

'Rosanna?'

She looks at me for a long time, right into my eyes. 'Have you come to take me home?' she asks, stretching out her hands towards me.

'Do you know who I am?'

'Of course,' she says with a smile. '*Adriana*.'

It's the first time I've heard my name spoken this way. It's beautiful.

'I knew you would come,' she says, taking both my hands in hers. 'I knew you would come one day. Sit here beside me.'

She takes my face in her hands and holds it in front of her while she studies me and kisses both my cheeks. Her expression is radiant; there is such love in her eyes. Suddenly, she says plaintively, 'When is Jack coming? He hasn't been for weeks.'

'Jack?' I sit up in shock. Has no one told her Jack is dead?

'Oh, you know Jack. You said he had beautiful brown eyes. *Che bel figliolo*.'

I take her hand. 'Rosanna, I'm so sorry. Jack has died. He died a year ago.'

Her eyes fill with tears. 'Oh, yes, I forgot. Someone told me. I get muddled.' Her face has clouded over, no signs of the happiness of a few minutes ago. She looks at me closely. 'You're not Adriana, are you.'

'I'm Adrienne, Jack and Isabelle's daughter.'

She suddenly becomes restless, blinking and looking around the room worriedly as though it's crowded with memories and she just needs to find the right one. 'Jack and Isabelle's daughter,' she repeats.

I stroke her hand and say gently, 'I'm living at the farm. At Duffy's Creek.'

She brightens. 'We used to swim in the creek. We washed our hair and lay on the rocks in the sun. Bella and Rosa, the olive sisters, they used to call us. I didn't care – better than the salami sisters!' she laughs. 'Bella hated it.' The light fades and she gives a heavy sigh. 'Bella hated everything we had and wanted what she couldn't have. She took everything.'

'Well, the house is still there, and the blue rug, and the olive trees, and the creek, of course. It's all still there, probably hasn't changed a bit.'

'I knew who I was then,' she says with a slight smile. 'I was 100 per cent me. I have these little strokes now. The doctor said they're like little . . . hmm . . . little . . .' She contorts her face in a childlike pose of intense concentration. 'Grenades! They blow my mind,' she says, with the chuckle of a well-worn joke. 'So, if I forget things you'll have to forgive me. I'm starting to forget more than I remember, I think. I'll remember you, though.'

I am rather lost for words. It's not that I find this some-what circular conversation difficult – it's not unlike the ones I have with myself – but there is something about Rosanna's presence. I thought I would have a hundred questions for her, but somehow they don't seem as important any more. A part of me knows that many of my questions are simply too personal, too confronting, to be asked outright. I will have to be patient. I will have to wait and see what comes my way. At the moment it seems enough just to be here, to be with her.

I've never been a great one for too much hugging and kissing but I put my arms around her now and she hugs me tight. She hugs me as though she'll never let me go. I feel I am somehow already intimate with her, as though she's part of me. As though we've hugged a thousand times. It's as if I'm meeting a part of myself. Her skin is my skin. It's something I've never felt before. I'm amazed and devastated. I feel my face start to crumple the way it did when I was a child before I learnt to weep silently and, later, secretly. If I let myself loose I could lay my head on her lap and howl down the lost years. She holds me in her arms as though she's comforted me my whole life. She comforts me in a way my mother never did.

I don't know how to tell her I haven't come for her.

When I get home I start to quietly unravel. There seems to be nothing to stop me now. When I call Joy I'm crying so much she doesn't recognise my voice at first. She arrives within minutes.

She finds me curled on the couch, tears streaming from me, a torrent of grief. She sits beside me, wraps her arms around me and holds me without a word. I can't speak. I don't know where to start. A long time passes before my voice croaks out the only explanation that comes, 'Rosanna.'

I hear her sharp intake of breath. 'You found her?'

'Yes.'

'She told you?'

'Told me what?'

She looks into my face. 'She didn't tell you anything?'

'She said she'd had some small strokes,' I grab a wad of tissues from the box Joy brought with her and give my face a pat, my nose a good blow. 'She's in good spirits but she is somewhat befuddled and forgetful.'

Joy gets up and opens a window to let the cool night air in. Insects hurl themselves against the flyscreen, desperate to get into this stifling room. 'That's the trouble with secrets, sooner or later they get forgotten. I can imagine Rosanna wanting to forget what's gone on.' She stands at the window, looking out into the darkness. 'Somehow I always knew I'd have to be the one to tell you, some day.' She pauses, as though looking for a way out. Seeing none, she settles herself back on the sofa.

'Adrienne, I knew Rosanna well – in fact, we were good friends. We both worked at the hospital and I used to come up here and see her quite often. I would bring my eldest, Sammy, with me when he was a baby; she was very good with him. Then something changed. Isabelle came back to live at the farm with her for a time. Isabelle was a very different person – private, rather aloof.

'Rosanna suddenly left her job and when I came to see her, Isabelle told me she wasn't well. She was quite off-putting. The same thing happened the next time. I went a third time and I knew they were home but they didn't answer the door. I saw Isabelle several times in town and noticed that she was pregnant.

'Then one evening I found Jack banging on my door. He said that Rosanna needed me urgently.' She stops and gives a deep sigh. 'I think we both need a cup of tea.' She gets up and goes into the kitchen to put the kettle on. I follow her and sit down at the table under the 100-watt halo. It's too bright tonight. She makes the tea slowly and deliberately, warms the teapot, spoons in the tea. 'Would you like a nice piece of toast, dear?' I would.

Joy sips her tea. I eat my toast. 'I've been at a lot of births but nothing like yours. You decided to come a bit early and no one knew what the heck to do. Good Lord, I can still see Isabelle's face, white as my mother's best sheets. Jack was none too happy about my being there, I can tell you. Probably thought that would be the end of their little secret. And perhaps it should've been. I've always wondered if the fact of me knowing the truth is what made them stay away. I've never told a soul before today, but this has gone on far too long. The thing is, Isabelle wasn't pregnant at all.'

'Isabelle wasn't pregnant! What on earth do you mean?'

Joy slides her hand across the table and places it over mine. It's warm and soft from clasping the mug of tea. 'What I'm trying to tell you, in a roundabout way, is that Rosanna is your mother. They planned it all. Jack was your father, but Rosanna is your mother.'

My hands fly to my face; it's warm and dark and safe in here. No one can see me. No one can hear me. There is silence. And as I sit in that silence I feel relief. It is as though I have been waiting all my life to hear the truth and here it is, laid out on the kitchen table, golden as toast.

Twelve

ON HIS RETURN from the north coast, Jack was delighted to be greeted affectionately by Isabelle, to be shown the cleared vegetable garden and the abundance of sweet marjoram and wild sage that had thrived on the neglect of the past year. To have her tear open purple figs for him to taste – a gift of early summer rains – reminded him of his early days with Isabelle. His spirits lifted to see his wife so light-hearted. He had wondered if she would ever recover from the loss of the baby she had wanted so much, yet never spoken of.

Rosanna and Isabelle had made Jack a homecoming meal of rabbit stew – Rosanna's specialty. Three weeks in a primitive hut, living in a way that had once been his entire way of life, now seemed brutal. He had come to dread meals of canned food that had once seemed palatable. His companions took little interest in what they ate – often not even bothering to heat their food – just as long as there was plenty of beer to wash it down. He missed the sense of celebration around meal times and the flavours, tastes and textures he'd discovered at the Martinos' table. He craved a single sip of the sweet dark *caffè* Isabelle made for him each morning.

It occurred to him that food had become a seductress he could not resist.

Jack's homecoming felt as though it was the start of something new. Isabelle seemed more attentive. She waited, just a little shyly, for him in the double bed while he bathed and shaved his bristles. She softened in his arms in a way he had almost forgotten, all of which made her proposal even more of a shock than it might have otherwise been.

'Rosanna and I have been talking,' she began hesitantly. 'She knows what we want and about the loss, of course. And there was the problem before that, so . . .' she trailed off. 'Rosanna is younger, and she's strong. So, this is what we talked about. The problem . . . and Rosanna has offered to help.'

Offered to help with what? Jack was mystified. Isabelle was often inclined to talk in fragments but he could usually connect them together. Several of her words were smudged in a way that made him suspect she had 'fortified' herself for this discussion.

'What is it you want us to do?' he asked.

She was silent for a moment and then, her voice little more than a whisper, said, 'I want you to be with Rosa.'

'Be with Rosa? Marry her?' he said with alarm. He pulled away from her. Isabelle sat up, her face strangely luminescent in the moonlight.

'Not marry. Have a child with her. For us.'

Jack sat up, stunned at first, disbelieving, but then a fury threaded its way through his body like hot wire until he was consumed with rage. He leapt from the bed and paced the floor. His anger had him by the throat. He opened the French doors, walked out onto the verandah and stood staring into the night for a long time. He wasn't thinking about what to say or how to respond. His mind was a tangle of anger and disjointed thoughts that scrambled over one another, vying for attention. He remembered his moment of acute clarity at the wedding as he stood beside Isabelle contemplating the plastic bride and groom and his sense that he was inter-changeable with a thousand different bridegrooms. Jack was beginning to realise that Isabelle was the one with the grand plans and those around her must play their parts.

When he returned to the room Isabelle had gone. She was back in her childhood bed.

By the morning his anger was a hard lump sitting in his gut. He felt used and manipulated, outraged that Isabelle could think she could lend him to her sister like a stud bull. He had the car packed for their journey back north before breakfast, hurried Isabelle along and left without making eye contact with Rosanna.

They drove in silence for several hours, then Jack pulled off the main highway onto a side road to have a break and stretch his legs. It was hot and the road was dusty. He pulled up under an expansive plane tree that offered shade for the car.

Jack got out, walked around the car and opened the door for Isabelle. Without waiting for her to get out, he went over to the tree, the girth of which could only have been spanned by two people meeting at the fingers. Two people in agreement, reaching out to one another. He rubbed his hands over the surface, feeling its roughness on his palms. There was a moment of solace in the warmth and solid feel of the massive tree.

He took a pack of cigarettes out of his shirt pocket and pulled one out. He felt Isabelle standing behind him. 'Why do you want to do this, Isabelle?'

'I don't feel that there is any choice.'

He turned to face her. 'How can there be no choice? We don't *have* to have a child! We were happy before – we can be happy again.' He felt around his trouser pockets for matches.

She bit her lip. 'It's not enough.'

'I'm not enough?'

Isabelle looked at her feet. She carefully rearranged the thick dust on the verge of road with the toe of her shoe. Jack struck the match and inhaled deeply. They both watched the dust being pushed this way and that as though it were something important, not to be missed.

'There is no point in being married if you don't have children,' she said finally.

'*No point*!' Jack exploded. Isabelle flinched. 'I love you, Isabelle. It doesn't make any difference to me whether you can have children or not.'

She stamped her foot, creating a small cloud of dust. 'You don't understand! It matters to *me*. What will people think if we don't have children? We'll be outcasts for the rest of our lives. We'll have no children, no grandchildren . . . we will *never* stop being different.'

Jack looked at her for a long time. He had never heard her speak so forcefully. He was hurt for a hundred different reasons. And he wanted to hurt her.

'So you want me to have sex with your sister. What do you think people might think about that? Do you think they might consider *that* a bit "different" – perhaps just a little immoral? Because I certainly do. What about the child? What are we going to tell it? It's not going to look like you, you know.'

She stood quite still, her head bowed. She made no sound. Her tears were raindrops in the dust. A magpie swooped down and perched on a bough of the tree. It filled its chest and warbled as though it thought them in need of a song. Jack felt like throwing a rock at it.

'Come on, get in the car,' he said, grinding his cigarette into the dust. Isabelle walked back miserably and got in the passenger's side. Jack turned the car around and headed back to the main road.

They sat at the intersection with the motor running for ten minutes. He looked neither north towards home nor south towards the farm but straight ahead. He thought about his life before Isabelle. He thought about Rosanna shouting at him and the strength of her blow to his head. He knew he had let Marge down. He had let Dot down. He had let Franco down. Franco and his dreams. Several cars passed by but still he sat there. Finally, he pulled out onto the highway and headed back the way they came.

By the time they reached the farm he was too tired to maintain his anger. He was gratified to see that Rosanna looked quite nervous to see them return. She was without her usual bravado. He had a nap, made some tea and sat on the front verandah. Isabelle was nowhere to be seen.

Rosanna came outside and sat on the steps.

'Bella has gone to keep Dot company tonight,' she said, not looking at him.

'I see. So how do you feel about all this?' Jack regretted the question immediately, seeing he had left himself open for further insult.

Rosanna turned to look at him. 'I want to do it for Bella. This is the most important thing in the world to her.' She tilted her chin towards him. 'Your work is a lot less than mine, Mister.'

They held each other's gaze for a long moment.

Jack looked away first. 'Fair enough. Just tell me when and where.' He put his hands behind his head and leant back in his chair with what he hoped looked like cool indifference.

'First, we will have a nice meal,' said Rosanna. 'Let's be civil to each other.'

'It's not necessary, really. We can just get down to business.'

Rosanna turned to face him. She leaned forward a little and he could see the soft flesh of her breasts lift under her cotton dress. She had taken to wearing perfume since her trip and he caught a whiff of it now. It made him feel nauseous. She gave a playful pout. 'Please?'

She went into the kitchen. Jack waited. Finally, she came out onto the verandah carrying a basket. She handed it to him, went back into the house and returned with a rug.

'We'll go to the river,' she announced and went down the front steps with every expectation that he would follow. He did. He had never been invited to the river before; it was Rosanna and Isabelle's domain. During the summer they went almost every evening to bathe and wash their hair in order to save water. Rosanna swam there even during winter.

She stopped in the garden to strip a lettuce and pick a few ripe tomatoes before they set off across the paddock. The moon was rising as they reached the river. Rosanna spread the rug on the grass and took the basket from him. She took out a bottle of Franco's *vino rosso*, unscrewed the top and with an expert hand flicked off the drop of oil that sealed the wine. Jack sat down on the rug. She dropped down beside him, took a swig from the bottle and handed it to him.

'*Salute*! To the future generation.' She gave a giggle.

The night was warm and resonated with the throb of insect life. The intimacy of the darkness and a couple of slugs of wine relaxed him a little. He was reminded of another night. A wild suburban party – Mount Isa? She was an attractive dark-haired girl, her name long forgotten – if he had ever taken the time to know it – and they had a drunken tryst among the shrubbery of the back lawn. In the dark Rosanna could be anyone. She could be that girl.

'I envy you your travels,' she said suddenly, unpacking the picnic. She'd brought a candle, which she propped up in a jar and lit. 'That's where I want to go, to the Outback. I'd like to join a nomadic tribe and wander the desert endlessly.'

'You've already been halfway around the world.' He took another swig of wine and watched the tiny flame paint dancing shadows on the trees.

'Well, you can imagine how much fun I had with my mother on the ship going over. She would have stayed safely in the cabin until we docked in Genova if she'd had her way.' She broke off some bread and cheese and handed it to him absentmindedly. 'Mamma is not one of life's great adventurers. She was never happy here – twenty years and she cried every single day.' Rosanna unpacked some cold meat and salami. She got up and washed the lettuce and tomatoes in the river.

'Isabelle never told me exactly why you came back.'

'There were lots of things I loved there: different people, food – different everything. But in another way it was as claustrophobic as Duffy's Creek – worse even. I discovered that there are small-minded people everywhere, but plenty of people around here do actually mind their own business. Or at least they don't think it is their God-given right to know your business. There was a tremendous fuss about me coming back here. They got the priests round to try and talk some sense into me. Mamma cried for a week. It was only Isabelle being pregnant that finally swayed her, so then I was off as fast as I could go.'

'So she told you and not me!' snapped Jack, outraged. 'I'm her bloody husband!'

Rosanna sat down beside him and took the bottle. She took a quick gulp and handed it back. 'You don't know Isabelle very well, do you?'

'Clearly not,' he said coldly.

'Respectability and conformity are of paramount importance to her. She probably would have been happier living her life in Genova, following some primal plan laid down for her over the centuries. It's just the way she is. I wouldn't read too much into it.'

'And what about this? What should I read into this?'

Rosanna lay back on the rug. 'I don't know, Jack. Let's just be a man and a woman, on a rug under the moonlight. Let's not delve too deeply into it.' She started to laugh. 'Isn't this the silliest thing?' she said, almost helpless with laughter. She saw he was not amused and tried to be serious. 'Oh, Jack, I know you don't want to sleep with me. It's not a very nice feeling, you know. A girl likes to feel she is at least desirable. I'm not so bad, am I?'

Jack lay down beside her. She turned her face to his and he could see the moon reflected in her eyes. Tentatively he placed his lips on hers. They were soft and giving, her breath sweet with wine. He felt himself pulled towards her like a tide to the moon and he buried his face in the warmth of her neck and throat. Rosanna gave a shriek of laughter as they rolled across the rug – her mouth on his mouth, her hands in his hair, her body wrapped around his.

For Jack it felt like a long slow dive into the deep. He was breathless with fear. Afterwards he had the strangest sensation of looking down from a great height at the two of them lying naked side by side on the rug. He could see their clothes strewn across the grass, a flare of moonlight as it slid on the river, the curve of the black shadows cast by the rocks. He thought he must have dreamt that moment. Later he realised that everything was just as he had seen it.

They slept that night rolled together in the rug and swam in the river in the silvery dawn light. They walked home as the sun rose over the hills. Jack slept for an hour or two. When he woke Isabelle was home. She cooked breakfast and they sat around the table together and talked of movies and movie stars, a favourite subject of hers. She and Rosanna seemed as close as ever but somehow it felt different. It was as though by making love to Rosanna he had closed the loop. They had become a threesome. Or perhaps it was simply Isabelle's genius for pretending nothing had changed. He was relieved she couldn't see how much had changed. He needed time to think.

Rosanna hugged them both when they left. His body recognised hers and he resisted an almost overwhelming desire to bury his face in her hair, to inhale her fragrance one last time.

Over the next few weeks Rosanna was in Jack's thoughts more often than he liked. He found himself in an ongoing conversation with her. He told her things about himself – things he had never thought about before – things that would interest her. He longed to hear her voice, to feel the texture of her skin.

'I had a letter from Rosa today,' said Isabelle from the other side of the bed. He was glad it was dark and she couldn't read his face.

'Yes?' he tried to sound noncommittal.

'She checked her dates and she wants you to meet her in either one week's time or three weeks' time. She'll take the train up to Henderson and book into the Grand Hotel there. She said you should send a telegram and confirm which date. You should sign it Isabelle.' She was silent for a while, then added, 'You need to take my wedding ring with you.'

Jack tried to hide his anticipation all week. He left on the Saturday morning, farewelling Isabelle with a kiss on the cheek as though he were going to work. Visions of Rosanna danced before his eyes and his stomach churned as he drove down the highway.

They met at the station. She wore a white shirt with a little green scarf around her throat and a full skirt the colour of ripe corn. His first thought was how beautiful she was – the polished gold of her skin, the dancing light in her eyes. She was exquisite. Without even looking around him he could sense other men looking at her. Admiring her. She gave him a playful kiss. He put his arm around her and slipped the ring from his pocket.

'With this ring I thee . . .'

'Don't say it, Jack. Here, give to me, I'll put it on.'

He took her overnight bag from her and they walked arm in arm to the hotel, where they booked in under the name of Mr and Mrs Bennett.

The hotel had once been grand but now it was just a pub with rooms. Their room too had once been grand with its gold brocade wallpaper, Victorian light fittings and crimson-and-gold patterned carpet, now faded and threadbare. It was clean and had a view of a back lane with weeds and bins.

As soon as the door was closed Jack pulled Rosanna to him and kissed her. Rosanna laughed but did not push him away. 'Hold up, Jack, you're starting to take your work too seriously. The night is young and I'm hungry. Or is it the other way round?'

It was early evening and the sky still light. The bar had closed and the dining room was rank with stale beer and tobacco. They bought two packets of fish and chips wrapped in newspaper, tearing the ends open as they walked down to the harbour. The wind had dropped and the only sounds were the slap of the water against the wharf, the occasional groan of a boat creaking against the pier and the squawk of a gull. They sat on the edge of the wharf and ate, steam rising from the torn packets, and talked idly about the stretch of water before them and what lay beyond that and how far that might be. Jack couldn't remember when a moment had ever felt so perfect.

Two women and a man, obviously dressed for a party, came wandering along the jetty. One of the women came over to them.

'Excuse me, have you seen a group of people going out to that yacht?' She pointed to a yacht in the harbour festooned with lights. Jack could hear disjointed refrains of music drift towards them on the breath of the breeze.

Rosanna and Jack said they hadn't but, to Jack's annoyance, the other two party-goers drifted over to them as well. The girl who had spoken was blonde and pretty, with a high ponytail and a froth of petticoats showing under a red-and-white polka-dot dress. The man wore a suit and the other woman a dark sheath cocktail frock. The girl with the ponytail was convinced that they had missed their ride and would now miss the party.

'Perhaps we could just borrow one of the boats and row you out?' suggested Rosanna, standing up. 'It's not that far.'

'Borrow a boat?' said Jack. 'I think we'd need to ask someone.' He looked around. It was almost dark, the water shimmered silver and tiny waves licked at the sand. The beach was deserted.

'Come on, Jack. Don't be so stuffy. It'll be fun.' Rosanna

put her hands under his armpits and made a great play of trying to pull him to his feet. The women and the man laughed. Jack scowled but privately conceded that the fastest way to get rid of them might well be to row them out to their party. Reluctantly, he got to his feet and followed the group down to the beach.

A dinghy was propped up against the sea wall, its oars tucked inside. Jack suggested they push it into the water off the beach and then lead it by its rope alongside the jetty so they could all climb aboard off the steps and not get wet.

The two girls flung down their handbags with excitement and helped push the dinghy down to the water. Jack took off his shoes and rolled up his trousers and coaxed it along the shoreline. The party followed, making helpful suggestions but keeping their feet dry.

'Does your husband know about boats?' the girl with the ponytail asked Rosanna.

'What my husband doesn't know about boats, my dear, isn't worth knowing,' said Rosanna firmly.

There was an air of celebration as they all stepped into the boat; the girls gave little squeals as it rocked slightly. Jack stepped in last and took the oars.

'We are rude,' said Ponytail. 'I'm Sal, this is my friend Nina, and Harry, my brother.'

'Rosanna and Jack,' replied Rosanna. Now in a playful mood, everyone made a show of shaking hands with everyone else even if they already knew them.

As they drew closer to the yacht the music carried across the water towards them. Sal began to sing along in a warbling voice. 'When I find my truuue looove . . . Golly, we'll crank up the music when we get there.' She pulled a small, half-empty bottle of brandy from her handbag and passed it around. Jack shook his head and kept on rowing. Rosanna had a swig. 'I better have one for Jack too,' she said and took another, longer, draught.

They drew in beside the yacht and Rosanna tied the dinghy to the boarding ladder. Sal got out first and climbed aboard. 'Oh, thanks for waiting!' she called out to someone on board. 'We had to kidnap some people and steal a boat to get here.' Several faces peered over the side at them as Nina and Harry climbed up.

'Please do come on board for one teeny-weeny little drink,' said Sal, leaning over the side.

'Maybe just a little one,' said Rosanna without hesitation, and stepped onto the ladder.

'I'll wait here,' said Jack, trying not to show how annoyed he was.

'Don't be a spoilsport, Jack,' was all she said and she was gone.

He waited in the boat, seething, as he heard Rosanna's laughter rise above the music and float over the water. An hour passed. Jack let the dinghy float out to the length of the rope and sat in the darkness watching the party on deck. He could see Rosanna in the crowd dancing with a man in a black shirt. As they spun around he saw the man's hand was low on her spine. He was holding her close enough to make Jack's ears buzz with angry static. Jack stood up in the dinghy and shouted Rosanna's name. She turned slightly as though she thought she heard something over the music. She spoke into the man's ear, withdrew from his embrace and stepped back from the cluster of dancers. Jack was just about to sit down and row closer to the yacht when he saw the man had also left the dancers. He took Rosanna's hands in his and talked earnestly to her. Rosanna threw back her head and laughed. The man put his arms around her waist. Jack's whole head started to buzz and something in his chest ached. He wanted to get on that yacht and break every bone in that man's body. He saw Rosanna put her arms around the man's neck and give him a long, slow kiss on the lips. Jack's ears roared with rage. He thought he was going to vomit and retched over the side of the dinghy.

'Jack! Where are you?' Rosanna was halfway down the ladder. Jack stood in the dinghy, helpless.

The man stood at the top of the ladder. 'Leave me a shoe, at least, my princess. I shall scour the countryside and find you!' he called, clutching his heart in mock despair.

Jack pulled on the rope until the dinghy met the yacht and Rosanna climbed in, flopping down opposite him.

'What fun! You should have come up instead of sulking in the dark.'

Jack rowed in a black fury. 'What kind of whore are you?'

'Oh, Jack. I liked him, that's all. He was sweet. I'm not your girlfriend, you know. This might be the last time we have together, then it's over. You know that.'

'Do I? Do I?' His throat was so tight with anger it was a strain to speak. He wished the boat would sink right there and then and the pain he was feeling would end. He thought of tipping it over, of jumping overboard or throwing Rosanna overboard. In the end he just rowed ashore, abandoned the dinghy and stalked up the beach.

He walked a little ahead of her all the way back to the hotel and lay on the bed in the dark, fuming and feeling like a fool at the same time. Rosanna went off down the hall to the bathroom, singing. She returned damp and smelling of roses. Taking off her robe, she lay down beside him. 'In the cool, cool, cool of the evening, tell him I'll be there . . .' she sang softly. Jack took her by the shoulders and kissed her hard.

'Hey,' she whispered in his ear. 'That's more like it.'

During his drive home the car seemed as reluctant as he was. It stuttered and started and after he stopped for a cup of tea at a roadside teashop it refused to start again. He felt like kicking the living daylights out of it, but got out the crank and expended his anger on turning the handle. He wasn't relieved to hear the engine turn over. He didn't want to be stuck in that godforsaken place but he was looking for anything to delay his trip home. He prayed that Rosanna wasn't pregnant. He prayed that it wasn't the last time he would be lost in the wilds of that foreign, beautiful terrain called Rosanna.

Heading home was heading in the wrong direction. Everything was clear to him now. The farm was home. Rosanna was home. Everything had changed. He didn't know how he would face Isabelle. He could hardly even remember what he had felt for her. She seemed distant, somehow; like someone he hadn't seen for years, not a part of his world.

All the way home his mind slipped from memories of that last night to fantasies of other nights and days with Rosanna until he couldn't tell them apart. He talked to her. He reasoned with her. She agreed with everything he said.

Isabelle greeted him as casually as if he had just been out for a walk. He declared himself tired and went to bed, not waking until morning.

Life slipped back into the old routine and Jack participated without engaging. His mind was like a crazy playground with swings of exhilaration and long slides that grounded him with a jolt. One moment he was exultant in love, content to be apart from Rosanna, the next he was torn with doubt, imagining her with someone else, becoming convinced the man in the black shirt was with her that very moment and feeling quite insane with jealousy. He talked himself down, thought he saw her in the street, heard her laughter, smelt her perfume on his shirt, tasted her skin, wept in his sleep.

The hardest part was yet to come. Arriving home from work a few weeks later, he found Isabelle standing at the back door with a letter in her hand. He tried to read her expression so he could prepare himself.

'It's from Rosanna,' said Isabelle, as she watched him take off his boots.

'Yes,' he said gruffly and brushed past her into the house. He could tell she was offended even without looking at her.

'She's pregnant. It's early days but . . . yes . . .' She drifted off.

'Good – well, that's that out of the way.' He sat down in his armchair and flicked open the newspaper. 'What's for dinner?'

Isabelle was surprisingly firm about the arrangements. Jack had thought that Rosanna would come to them but Isabelle thought that absurd when they only had the one bedroom.

She would have to go and care for Rosanna as soon as she started to show. They had it all planned. Rosanna would stay at home and Isabelle would go out to do the shopping. She would wear a cushion.

'A *cushion*? You two are barking mad!' exploded Jack. He banged his cutlery down and pushed his chair from the table, leaving his meal unfinished. 'And where are you planning to give birth to this cushion?'

Isabelle pursed her lips. 'Not in Duffy's Creek, obviously. We'll have to take her up to the hospital at Tindall where they don't know us. She'll pretend to be me.'

'Honestly! You two need your bloody heads read. Do I have any say in this cloak-and-dagger plan? The voice of reason? Go on, now tell me you're both Russian spies.'

'Don't be silly, Jack. This is serious. What would people think if they knew Rosanna was pregnant?'

'And what have you told your mother?'

'Well, I can't lie to her, obviously.'

'I'm glad all these things are so obvious to you.'

'She knows I lost the baby.'

'And?'

'Rosanna will write and tell her that we have another baby on the way. That I'm not feeling well —'

'So, let me get this straight. Rosanna gets to have a baby for you *and* lie to your mother about it.'

'It's not a lie —'

'Isabelle – the whole bloody thing is a lie! We're all in it up to our necks!'

'There's no need to shout, Jack. Rosanna doesn't care; she's says it's none of Mamma's business.'

Speechless, Jack leant back in his chair and slowly shook his head to demonstrate the full extent of his disbelief. Isabelle sat silently, her head bowed slightly and hands clasped together as if in a tight-lipped prayer.

'Why does Rosanna do these things for you? Did she really "offer"?' Jack asked in a low voice.

Her eyes narrowed as she met his stare. '*You* wouldn't understand,' she replied stonily.

Jack felt like shaking her till her teeth rattled. Although it was Saturday he left the house, got into his car and drove to work. He sat at his desk – a makeshift affair in the site office that was little more than a shed – and smoked one cigarette after another. He thought about Rosanna being pregnant. He couldn't picture it. He couldn't quite imagine this part of him growing within her. Hourly, he resisted the urge to go to her.

'World on yer shoulders, mate?' Wally, the site foreman, flopped into his swivel chair with a crash and banged his clay-clagged boots on the floor. 'Something up?'

Jack turned to look at him. Almost bald, with chubby cheeks, flushed and pink, he looked as innocent as a cherub. Jack thought of telling him he was going to be a father. But it was too complicated. He'd find out sooner or later. 'Nothing, mate. Just a bit tired. Fancy a beer?'

Isabelle began to make preparations for when she would go down to the farm and he had the feeling that she couldn't wait to get away. They were courteous to each other as they had always been but Isabelle was always asleep by the time he came to bed. It seemed that was the best thing for both of them.

Rosanna, almost five months pregnant, wrote to say that the matron at the hospital where she worked had commented that she was putting on weight. Isabelle needed to come down before tongues started to wag. Jack was hungry to see Rosanna and offered to drive Isabelle down the next weekend.

Rosanna greeted them with hugs and kissed both Jack's cheeks but she wouldn't meet his eyes. She and Isabelle gloated over her round stomach and cooed through the box of baby clothes Isabelle had brought with her. Jack sat around feeling uncomfortable. He was waiting for his moment.

When Rosanna went out to collect some vegetables for dinner he offered to help. Even with her extra weight she had a manly stride and he fell into step beside her. She gave him the bucket to hold and pulled some carrots and dropped them in the bucket. He'd waited weeks for this moment and couldn't think how to start.

'Rosanna. I need you.' His voice betrayed his longing.

She looked up briefly from her search among the zucchini vines. 'Jack, don't. You don't need me. The deed is done and over.'

'Not for me. I —'

'Don't, Jack. Don't say any more.' Rosanna took a pair of scissors out of her apron pocket and snipped a handful of chives, some stems of rosemary and a bunch of basil. 'Jack, I love Bella. I want her to be happy. I am going to give the two of you a gift, the greatest gift possible. I want you both to be happy. Please, I beg of you, don't ruin it all.' She dug into her pocket, pulled out a piece of string that she used to wind around the herbs and dropped them in the bucket. She stood in front of him, looking up into his face. She put her hand on his cheek. 'I'm sorry I hit you that day.' There was a softness in her eyes he hadn't seen before. She took the bucket from him and turned and walked back to the house.

Thirteen

I wasn't with my mother, Isabelle, when she died, though I hardly left her side in the last days. She had me sit silently beside her bed in that darkened room, the curtains drawn against each new dawn. Life was just one long night except for the daylight probing the curtains and the occasional laughter of the living. I spent my nineteenth birthday in that room.

To my eternal shame, I was impatient for her to go. It wasn't as though there was an alternative. When she did go it was unexpected, and I was shocked. I had left the room for a few minutes on some domestic errand and she slipped away while I was gone.

I sat beside her all that night and when morning came I opened the curtains. Bathed in light, I saw how changed she was. The fretwork of tiny lines on her face now soft, there was a sweet relief in her smile, as though she had just consumed a deeply satisfying morsel of life. Even then, I couldn't leave. She was all I had. Now she was safe, I was terrified for myself. Terrified that my life would end up in that same place. I was afraid to leave that room.

I've spent a good part of my life running from that night. I have to keep moving, for if I stop the fear and loneliness settle on me like an insidious dust that seeps into my pores.

Despite all we'd been through together, I wouldn't ever say we were close. It's not as though each of us could anticipate what the other was thinking, let alone feeling.

When I was about six, my parents sold our little house in Elenora and my mother and I moved to a flat in Elizabeth Bay. One of her clients, Mrs Armstrong, had opened a bridal salon and invited her to come and work there as a dressmaker. Our flat was within walking distance of the shop.

The word separation was never mentioned. The fact that my father wasn't coming with us hardly registered; he had always been away more than he was home. That was the nature of his work, I had often heard my mother tell her clients.

Lately I have given some thought to the question of why she ever agreed to move to Sydney. She was not a city person, and she loathed noise and crowds. I assume that even then money was tight so the prospect of steady work must have been attractive. But I think the real reason was the possibility of anonymity it gave her. I wonder if my father asked for a divorce, and she couldn't bear our town to know. She wouldn't risk the ladies of the guild finding out.

My father still turned up from time to time. It was usually weeks after he said he would and then only for as long as it took to go up the street and have an ice-cream. We would sit awkwardly on a bench in the park and talk about school. He would study my face as though I was a stranger to him – which, of course, I was. He was always restless and on edge. He would sometimes have a cup of tea with my mother, but they were like strangers too. Once I caught him going through her mail on the table beside the telephone. I could see from his guilty start that it was wrong.

I was about twelve when my mother first became ill and her small world seemed to shrink just as mine was expanding. She had no friends apart from Mrs Armstrong, who occasionally delivered work to her at the flat, so she rarely ventured out. I was not allowed to have friends home and never allowed to stay away overnight. I realised later that it wasn't because she missed me, or even that she was lonely. It was that without me the clocks would stop, the power would be disconnected and the fridge would remain stubbornly empty; ditto the bottle of Gordon's Dry. Without me there she would lie in bed all day, the sewing machine eerily silent, swathes of abandoned satin spilling off the dining table onto the floor. She needed me to keep her connected with the world.

There are so many things I would ask her now, in addition to the obvious one – why? Why the elaborate hoax? Why didn't she tell me? But there is also a deep sense of relief in knowing the truth. It's as though I have a diagnosis for my mysterious illness. It answers a thousand questions I haven't yet articulated for myself and presents me with a thousand more. It explains the emotional chasm that existed between us – we simply weren't bonded by that primal glue. I did love her, but why didn't she love me? Perhaps she did in her own way. Perhaps she gave it her best. I should grant her that at least. And Jack? What did he see in me? A little girl who idolised her absent dad? Or a nagging reminder of his own lost hopes, and lost love?

There's been a growing sense of freedom unfurling inside me since I heard Joy's revelation, just days ago. If I'm not who I thought I was, who am I? Am I already defined as someone else? Or, freed from the constraints of 'not being like Isabelle', can I now be anyone I want to be? I feel something is opening up in me. It's not a solid feeling. It's as though I'm entering the space between who I was and who I could be. It comes and goes, tiny tremors of something that feels like courage are liberating other emotions in me – a sense of anticipation, of possibility, nibbling at the edges of my fearfulness. I'm nervous about going back to see Rosanna, now I know the truth. I almost can't bear feeling so emotional all the time.

Usually this house is cool until late in the afternoon, but not today. Outside the air crackles with heat; it gradually seems to be leaking into the house. I close the doors and windows and pull down a couple of blinds on the north side. I need to pack up my stuff. It's only three days until I leave to take up my new role and I haven't done anything about trying to rent this place out yet. It's hard to get motivated when it's so stifling. With the air a hot thick soup, to move is to wade.

Suddenly Dog starts barking and I go outside to see who's there. It's just a car accelerating down the road. But then I smell the smoke. In a moment I see wisps drifting from near the road, and there's a distant crackling like thousands of tiny explosions. I run across the garden and down the path through the trees to the orchard. Thick smoke pours off the long grass and flames lick hungrily at the dry tips. It flows towards me with a divine and dangerous grace.

I don't know what to do. I don't have time to call for help, and don't know where the hose is and doubt it is long enough. Dog barks and barks. I'm paralysed by panic. Suddenly, it comes to me. I run back to the shed and grab an armful of old sacks, see my purple sarong on the clothesline and stop to rip a wide strip of fabric off the bottom. Wrapping it around my face to cover my mouth and nose, I run to the back door and pull on my boots.

As I emerge from the trees into the orchard I can hear a rushing sound. The fire is now a curtain of flame – maybe a metre high and 10 metres wide – coming up the orchard. It has conjured up a rush of air to feed its hungry flames.

There is a trough at the top of the paddock – I dunk the sacks into it, pull them out and run towards the fire. I whip the flames from the edge with my wet sacks the way I've seen them do it on the television news. I've never worked so hard in my life. I've never been so focused. I use every muscle in my body to beat, beat, beat the flames. I run back and forth along the rim of the fire, pushing it back only to have it edge past me somewhere else. The smoke is choking and makes it impossible to see how far the fire has spread. I don't know whether I'm winning or losing. There's no time to think about it, I just keep going. I've started to work out the best way to smother the flames – too much flapping simply fuels them. I need to watch my back and not be surrounded.

The wind picks up – the promised southerly – and the hot gusts make it even more difficult to breathe. Through the haze I can see dark clouds scudding into view, like street gangs attracted to trouble. The smoke turns towards the hills. Rain, please rain.

For a time my whole world is reduced to this tiny patch of earth. My face burns radiant with heat, my body is drenched in sweat and black with soot. Just keep going. The thought occurs that someone deliberately started this fire. Bastards. Fucking bastards. Anger on top of adrenaline fuels me.

It seems hours before I hear a siren coming up the road. The fire truck drives straight through the closed gate into the orchard. People run everywhere, Keystone Cops in yellow jackets. Water, blessed water. Finally, there's just drifting smoke and black charred grass.

One of the firefighters comes over to me. 'Lucky you got to it when you did, lady. Once it hit those trees it'd just gobble up your little house there. Sorry about your gate. Gwen got a bit overexcited.' He takes off his helmet and wipes his face with his hands, smearing sweat and grime. 'Gwen! Yer stupid cow. What if that'd been the new truck?' he shouts.

Gwen's a chunky, well-built girl. She takes off her helmet to reveal a dazzling head of cropped, bleached hair. She grins at him and shows him her middle finger. 'Damsel in distress, mate – no time to worry about a fucking gate.'

I feel my legs start to give way. 'I think I need to sit down.' I lean against the truck and slide gracefully onto the ground.

'Yer right?' he says, managing to sound not at all solicitous. He looks relieved when Gwen gives him a hoy and he sprints off in her direction. A few minutes later he's back with her and the other two firies in tow.

'Got on the wrong side of anyone lately, love?' He sounds marginally more concerned. 'Bit of petrol along yer fence line there, someone's put a match to it. You didn't see anyone hanging around?'

216

I shake my head. My arm hurts.

'I'll put it in the report, so don't be surprised if you hear from the cops.'

'Well, yer don't need to be a flamin' genius to work out who it might be, do yer?' says Gwen. 'Come on, we're all done here.' She nods in my direction. 'You better go and have a cup a tea and a lie down, I reckon.'

I stagger off and lean against the fencepost as they lift the gate up off the ground and prop it against the fence. As I limp back to the house the truck heads off, the firefighters waving and tooting as though we've had a fun day out together.

I lie on the bed, covered in soot. My body has an electric current running through it. I can feel the artery in my neck thudding. My heart sounds like a rubber ball bouncing in an empty auditorium. When I wake Dog is lying on the end of the bed. He's pleased to see me alive and covers my face with wet kisses.

It's raining now; steady falling rain. Outside the sour, lingering odour of smoke is stronger than ever. I go down to the orchard to inspect the damage. The apple and the almond are untouched. A few of the orange or mandarin trees are blackened, though; their foliage was dense and green. Even now the rain is washing away the ash and soot.

I climb the fence through to the olive grove, untouched by the fire. I lift myself up into the sheltering branches of a tree and sit inside the green and silver canopy. My fingers explore the twisting limbs; I can see the points at which it was pruned long ago, forcing the tree to grow against its natural inclination. I climb down and move from one to the

217

next, holding this limb and that one, a slow dance in the rain. Dog wanders along behind, thinking his own private thoughts. All at once something wells up in me; a lightness, a feeling of intense exhilaration – pure, pure joy. I am so proud of myself. I saved the olives. I saved the house. I saved my grandfather's apple tree. As thunder rolls down the hills I can hear someone singing. It's me.

I take the curtain off the bathroom door so I can watch the rain from the bath. I've never been so happy to see rain. It clatters on the roof and gurgles down the drainpipes. I can hear the water tank filling, it must have been low. I never thought to check.

Tomorrow's Friday, and on Sunday I leave for Sydney. On Monday I start work. Next Friday night I'll be at the Summit bar with the old crowd, regaling them with the fire story and loving every minute of it.

Joe hasn't been around for two days. Perhaps he's not coming to say goodbye, though he has to come and collect Dog. I don't want to put myself through all these difficult partings. It's not as if I ever said I would stay.

I dry myself and get dressed. My shoulders ache now from my fire-fighting efforts. My arm has several angry welts on it. I flop from room to room, lie on my bed, gaze out the window.

Suddenly, I hear Joe's truck coming up the drive. I leap from the bed, fluff my hair, fling off my T-shirt and pull on a pale pink shirt I know he likes. Running down the hallway, the cool boards slap under my bare feet. His familiar lean shape and battered old hat is silhouetted through the screen door. He pulls it open and I practically leap into his arms. I've missed his slow smile, the musky smell of his skin, the strength I feel in his arms now wrapped around me. I've missed every bit of him. Damn!

Over the next day I get calls from a dozen locals. Margaret Simmonds calls to offer me a room in her beautiful house if I need to get away for a few days. Jenny from the takeaway phones to say if I don't feel like cooking I should drop by and she'll whip me up some fish and chips, whatever I like, on the house. Leonie promises to sort out any frazzled hair problems with a free conditioning treatment and would I mind if she got a photographer from the local paper along – it could be a good angle for some free PR. Stain queen Deirdre rings and offers to come over and keep me company. Walter sends his best regards. Annabelle calls to say that she has received information from her archangel about the perpetrator of the fire; he looks like a cherub but has the hooves of a devil. I think I know who we're talking about here. Joy comes and brings food, carrot cake with tangy cream-cheese icing, steak and kidney pie and homemade bread rolls. They are all dismayed to hear I'm leaving. They find it incomprehensible that anyone would choose to live in Sydney.

'We were just getting to know you,' sighs Margaret.

'What a shame! We need more bods like you,' says Jenny.

Joy doesn't remonstrate. She just has a bit of a tidy-up in the kitchen, puts the kettle on and makes a cup of tea. While we drink it she looks around the room as though she's going to miss it, although I can almost imagine that she will come and go as usual whether I'm here or not. After a while she says, 'You know, with a lick of paint you and me could transform this room, gal.'

My throat feels tight. We smile sadly at each other and I feel the tears pushing their way out. 'You've been so kind to me, Joy. I will keep in touch, I promise.'

'Of course you will – gosh, you're only a couple of hours away.' She smiles unconvincingly. We both know how far it really is.

A car pulls up outside. There's the sound of a CB radio and the slam of a door. A fresh-faced twenty-something policeman enters, looking ill at ease. Joy makes him tea. He takes notes in a tiny notebook.

'The whole town knows who did it, Toddy,' says Joy. 'So let's not beat around the bush.'

Constable Thompson makes a note. 'I'm calling myself Todman these days, Mrs Oldfield. I think it gives me more credibility; better for my image. Commands respect.'

'Todman Thompson,' says Joy without irony.

'Aren't you going to ask her who everyone thinks did it?' I say.

'I need to make my own enquiries, not be influenced by small-town gossip, Miss Bennett. Policing today is based in science, forensics, special tools and equipment. You'd know all about that with your background in corporate communications.'

'Special tools and equipment?' I ask.

He has the grace to colour a little. 'Reconnaissance. I can't reveal my source for obvious reasons. Rest assured I have my finger on the pulse of this town.'

'Never mind all that,' I say, suddenly impatient. 'This

is serious. This is arson, vandalism, destruction of private property and attempted murder! I want some action. I want an AVO out against the lunatic!'

There is a long intake of air through the constable's teeth as he considers this possibility. 'The courts would need a strong body of evidence to support any charges etcetera against the lunatic in question. He's a bit of a slippery customer.' He pauses. 'I mean, did you actually see Mr Leeton start the fire?'

'No.'

'Miss Bennett, I think you need to decide whether you want revenge – as in punishment – or if you want Leeton out of your hair, so to speak. If it's the former, you'll probably be seeing a good deal more of Mr Leeton than you'd care to. And even if you were successful in the courts, there are plenty more Leetons where he came from.'

'Well, I obviously don't want to bring the wrath of the Leetons down on me, but —'

'Why don't you go and see Mrs Leeton, then?' says Joy with the arch of a brow.

'His wife?'

'His mother.'

Todman Thompson nods his support for this plan. 'Certainly, realistically, that would be a positive move in the right direction to get some closure on this and allow us to all move on. So, I'll just make a note here that that's the line of enquiry we are pursuing right now.' He scribbles away for a moment. 'Perhaps if you and Mrs Leeton can resolve this we should keep it at a more informal level.' He rips the page out of his notebook and screws it up.

'Todman, I think you should eat that to be safe,' says Joy, compressing a smile.

Unsmiling, he balls it up and drops it into his pocket. When he's gone I ask Joy, 'Is he really a policeman? That was absolutely pathetic.'

'He's also president of the Young Liberals. I think he's planning to get into politics when his whiskers come through,' she says as she clears away the cups. 'Wouldn't want to fall out with the Leetons, I shouldn't think.'

'So I have to go and see his mother? You're serious? Is she the Leeton matriarch?'

'Let's just say that she's a woman who knows how to carry a grudge and has a very long memory. Pretty tough. She had a bit of a row with one of her boys one day – they were up Marfield way – and she made him stop the truck and she got out and walked home. I don't know how far that is, but they reckon it took her about five hours. If any-one can handle her boys, she can.'

Mrs Leeton lives in a little fibro cottage near the shops in Duffy's Creek. It has a sign out the front: Craft for Sale. Entry is via a gate and through the carport, which contains a gallery of clay pots made to look like faces; pottery cats and pigs; little baked clay signs with 'Mum's cooking, keep your distance' and the like. There is a bell and a sign: Ring for Attention. In my nervousness I do, several times.

Finally, the screen door at the back of the house opens and a woman sticks her head out. 'It's six o'clock – I'm done for the day. Yer cuttin' into me drinking time now.'

'Mrs Leeton?'

'Yeah?' She comes out onto the step and we regard each other for a moment. Easily over seventy, her hair is permed and bleached to a mustard frizz. (I do hope Leonie is not responsible.) She's wearing glossy purple short pyjamas covered in bright pink teddies atop withered legs, skin as slack as tree bark. Her feet are lizard-like – toes splayed and gnarled, nails like claws, etched with what appears to be seventy years of accumulated grime.

'I'm Adrienne Bennett.'

She looks me over. 'What kin I do for yer, girl?'

All my years of creative propositions, corporate cajoling and artful negotiation have been leading to this moment, but this time the stakes are real.

'You're an artist?'

Her furrows regroup to form a smile. 'I am. Would yer like to see me studio?' She tilts her head towards a shed at the back of the yard.

'I would love to.'

'Just hang on.' She ducks inside and is back in a moment with a bottle of Bailey's and two glasses, half full of ice.

'Lubrication,' she says with a crooked grin, showcasing an array of teeth worn to stumps, several missing in action.

She dusts off a chair for me in the shed, a filthy mess of clay and old rags, half-made pots, broken pots, yellowing newspapers and, taped to the walls, hundreds of pictures torn from magazines of urns, bowls, pots and ancient arte-facts. She fills the greasy-looking plastic glasses to the brim with Bailey's and hands me one.

'I've had five kids, got eighteen grandkids – they give me

a lotta pleasure, but I tell yer, they bring me a lotta fucking grief too.' She pats her potting wheel fondly. 'This one, she brings me nothing but joy. It's me passion.'

I nod and sip my drink. I have no idea where to go from here.

'You got a passion?' She crunches on a piece of ice.

I have to think for a long time about this. My instinct, or maybe it's just my habit, is to be glib. Make her laugh and deflect the focus from myself. In the face of her honesty, that seems like a cheap trick. One of many at my disposal.

'I've discovered, only in the last few days, that I am passionate about my grandparents' farm. *My* farm. I'm passionate about the olives, the apple tree, even that funny old house. I've discovered that I was born in that house. It would break my heart to see it all go up in flames.'

Mrs Leeton looks at me hard. 'It's good to have a passion. Keeps yer going through a lotta heartache. I knew your aunty, you know. When we was kids. Had a bit of a fist-fight with her once.' She laughs. 'Up at Deakin's waterhole there. Said the wrong thing – probably called her a wog or something – and suddenly whammo! She laid into me. She was quite something. You're the spittin' image of her.' There is respect in her eyes, almost admiration. 'So you're a local girl, eh?'

She shows me her latest creation – a vase that is almost elegant. She tells me about the clay she uses, brought to her by her sons, the by-product of various diggings. As I make to leave she puts a restraining hand (almost as lizard-like as her feet) on my arm, goes to a shelf at the back of the shed and brings me a figure of a woman moulded in clay. It's about a foot tall and has little detail; it's more the flow and suggestion of a woman. It's beautiful.

'Take this and put it near yer front door. It'll bring yer luck, you'll see. Darryl's my naughty boy. I've broken a few wooden spoons on his bum.' She gives me a shrewd grin. 'I might just have to break another one on him if he don't behave himself. He loves his mum, but.' She smiles her ragged smile.

'Thank you,' I say.

'There's always a drink on here 'round six,' she says, patting my arm. 'Remember me to Rosanna when you see her next.'

On impulse, I ask her for directions to Deakin's waterhole.

I park the ute near the bridge as instructed and walk along the bank of the creek on the high side. The low side is a stony beach populated by rocks of every size, round and pale like balls of dough. The water, a hundred shades of emerald, is clear in the shallows and deep green in the middle of the basin formed at the bend in the river.

A rope is there, looped around the branch of a huge gum. It must be an updated version, made of a thick nylon, like climber's rope. I'm alone and there are a dozen reasons not to do this. But I strip off to my bra and knickers, pull myself up the rope a little, push myself off from the tree and swing out across the water. It takes three attempts before I have the courage to let go and drop into the chill waters of the unknown.

225

Fourteen

FOR THE LAST few months of Rosanna's pregnancy Isabelle wrote to Jack every week. Her letter was waiting for him every Friday when he arrived home from work. He had become one of her set chores. She kept him informed about the weather, mild for this time of year. The crocuses were up early and they had planted the basil for summer. Rosanna was well. No mention of visitors, no mention of cushions. Jack felt as though he was in exile. Why had he ever agreed to this foolish plan? The answer was anger. He had agreed in anger. And he was still angry.

When Rosanna's time drew near he took his annual leave and, without telling a single person he was about to become a father, set off for the farm.

Unsure as to whether he should knock or not, he opened the front door of the cottage to find Rosanna alone. She lay propped up with cushions on the couch, her hands resting on an enormous belly. She wore a crimson dress, her hair fell about her shoulders and she looked like a beautiful ripe piece of fruit or the native queen of some exotic tribe.

Before he knew what possessed him, he knelt at her side,

took her hand and kissed the palm.

'Oh, Jack!' She laughed and ruffled his hair. 'Bella! Jack has arrived.' He leapt to his feet. Isabelle came quickly into the room, untying her apron as she walked.

'Hello, dear,' she said, offering her cheek for his kiss.

'You look well,' said Jack to Rosanna. He turned to Isabelle. 'You've done a good job.'

'Thank you for coming,' said Isabelle, as though he were a helpful neighbour. 'It could be any day . . .' She was watching to see where he stood on this now.

'I know. I understand.'

'Good. Let's eat, then – dinner's all ready. We were just waiting for you.' Jack and Isabelle helped Rosanna off the couch and they all sat down at the table. The meal was as awkward as any Jack had ever known. He was reminded of the early days of eating with the Martinos when he felt like a curiosity. Now he was a curiosity in his own mind; the man who sat down to dinner with his wife and his lover.

'So,' said Jack, in an attempt at conversation. 'Girl or boy?'

'I think it's a girl,' replied Isabelle.

'What about a wager, Jack?' Rosanna asked as she lazily forked up her food.

'All right, two quid it's a boy.'

'Make it worth my while! How about ten?' she said with a sly smile.

'All right, ten.' He held Rosanna's gaze as though some secret message had passed between them but she looked down, intent on her food. 'So, no doubt you two have discussed names?'

Rosanna smothered a yawn and leant back in her chair. 'Hardly – there's nothing to discuss. It's either Adriana or Francesco.'

'Adrienne or Frank,' corrected Isabelle. 'We don't want to saddle the child with the past.'

Rosanna shrugged. 'It's the saddle that helps you stay on the horse, Bella.'

It was early October and the weather was cold with clear bright skies. Rosanna seemed content to wait out her time despite her isolation. She slept, tended the garden, checked her traps for rabbits and occasionally walked in the olive grove alone. Isabelle guarded her carefully, caught the bus into the village every few days (wearing her cushion, Jack presumed) and bought essentials. They ate mostly from the garden and had still managed to keep the roadside stall stocked up with vegetables over winter.

They kept the gate locked to discourage visitors. A friend and neighbour, Joy Oldfield, had come back repeatedly to see Rosanna, not put off by Isabelle's excuses.

'She probably thinks you've murdered me,' said Rosanna. 'Good ol' Joy, she'll get to the bottom of this mystery and bring my killer to justice.'

Isabelle had been nervous and insisted they both hide in the bedroom when next she knocked at their door.

On Jack's second night at the farm, Isabelle slipped into bed beside him and he wondered if she was under instructions from Rosanna. He turned over and went to sleep. He was woken around midnight by a shout from Rosanna and leapt out of bed. He ran into her room, flailing about for the light string, swearing all the while. Finally, it was in his grasp and he gave it a tug. Rosanna sat up in bed clutching her belly. Her eyes were closed, against the light or in pain he couldn't tell. Her mouth was wide open but no sound came out. After a moment she flopped back on her pillow.

'My waters must have broken while I slept. The pains are coming so fast.' She sounded frightened.

Isabelle stood in the middle of the room, looking dazed. She clutched Jack's arm. 'What do we do? The hospital —'

Rosanna started to gasp. 'Forget the hospital! Jack, drive down and get Joy. She's a nurse, she can help.'

'No!' Isabelle's hands flew to her mouth. 'Can't we do it without her?'

'Bella, please – Joy is a good friend. She'll be fine. Please get her, Jack. Hurry!' She clasped her stomach and let out a low moan that sent Jack flying out of the room.

If Joy was surprised at the turn of events she said nothing. She took charge, sending Isabelle back and forth on errands and urging Rosanna on. Jack, pacing the hall in his role as expectant father, had to smile as he heard all Franco's old expletives revisited.

Finally Rosanna's bellowing, singing and wailing stopped and there was silence. Jack stood waiting.

'You owe me ten quid, Jack Bennett!'

Jack opened the door. The bedroom was in chaos and there was hardly room to move. Rosanna's mattress had been pulled onto the floor and bloodied sheets and towels were piled in one corner. A half-empty bottle of brandy sat on the bedside table. Propped up on pillows in Isabelle's bed, Rosanna looked exhausted but elated at the same time, wearing nothing but a sheet and a huge smile. There in her arms was his daughter, dark hair smeared to her head, mouth open in a silent scream.

Joy quickly put the metal bucket she was holding aside, covering it discreetly with a towel. She crossed the room to the bed and pulled up the eiderdown, tucking it around mother and baby.

Isabelle sat silently at the end of the bed. Her face was ashen and she seemed not to notice that she still had a blood-stained sheet tied as an apron around her waist. Joy handed her the bottle of brandy from the bedside table and, with an almost indiscernible nod of acknowledgement, Isabelle unscrewed the top and took a swig. She looked up at Jack with a wan smile.

'Bella, take Adriana,' said Rosanna. 'Let Jack hold her.'

'Adrienne,' corrected Isabelle sharply.

Joy gave her a long look, and finally turned to Jack. 'Congratulations,' she said.

The newborn slept almost constantly over the next few days, as did Rosanna. Isabelle administered to Adrienne, bathed her in an old tin bath on the kitchen table, changed her clothes a dozen times a day and brought her to Rosanna's breast for feeding. However, she never smothered the tiny face with kisses in the way that Rosanna did. Isabelle seemed a little afraid of the baby; always anxious that she was warm enough but not too hot, fed but not overfed, tired but not over-tired. Rosanna took little interest in the bathing and clothes-changing. Instead she sucked the baby's toes, murmured to her in Italian and promised to take her swimming in the river as soon as she was awake long enough.

Jack hung around the house like the family dog usurped by the new baby. There was little or no opportunity to be alone with Rosanna. Breast-feedings seemed to take up much of her time and he was not permitted to witness these. Isabelle told him that they would wean little Adrienne as quickly as possible and then they could go home as a family. The very thought of going home as a family filled him with dismay and he doubted his ability to pull it off.

From where Jack stood the immediate future looked like an impenetrable thicket. He had gone up to the town hall and registered Adrienne Isabelle Bennett but he was resistant to actually telling people. He couldn't seem to shake off the sense of unreality about the situation, as if it were a practical joke and they would all be found out at any moment. 'Joke's over, everyone – it was just a cushion!' Prompted by Isabelle, he finally sent a telegram to his parents, relieved not to have to break the news personally. Adrienne was so like Rosanna with her dark hair and eyes that it seemed impossible that his mother wouldn't put it together.

A week passed, Rosanna began to wean Adrienne and the work increased with bottles to sterilise and milk to warm. Isabelle, always fond of routine, slipped easily into feeding by the clock and weaning by the book. She changed the baby prior to every feed, waited with a warmed bottle in her hand for the chime of the clock to signal the hour before inserting the teat in the baby's mouth, seemingly impervious to her shrill cries of hunger.

Together she and Rosanna hand-washed the nappies, tiny singlets and matinee jackets, all made by Isabelle over the winter months. They hung them on the long line that stretched the length of the garden and propped it up to catch the breeze.

The November days drifted, long and warm, into early summer. Jack worked in the garden every day. He went to the river, where he lay under the shade of the paperbarks on a flat rock as white as bone and daydreamed a dozen different scenarios for his life. He waited for Rosanna. The thought of leaving her alone in the house, alone in her bed, drove him quite wild. It made no sense to him, his place was here. He would talk to Isabelle. He would tell her things had changed. The day of their departure grew ever closer and still he didn't find the words to tell her.

The night before their leaving Jack lay awake listening to the sounds of the night and Isabelle's even breathing. He heard Adrienne stir in her bassinette, now in the living room, as Isabelle was determined that she would no longer be fed in the night. The stirrings turned to whimpers and little cries and he heard Rosanna tiptoe down the hall. He slipped out of bed and pulled on his trousers and shirt.

Rosanna sat out on the verandah in a wicker chair. She had lit a candle in a jar on the table beside her. She started when she saw him; her blue cotton robe was open at the front but she made no effort to conceal her exposed breast where the baby suckled, wrapped in a rug.

'Whoops, caught in the act.' She smiled.

'How's Isabelle going to cope without you?' Jack sat down near her on the verandah, leaning his back against the wall of the house. He quietly watched Rosanna, her face infused with love and light as she gazed upon the baby in her arms, and a hazy feeling of contentment settled on him.

'She'll be fine, Jack.' Rosanna said gently. 'Dr Spock will be her guiding light.'

Jack found his cigarettes in the pocket of his trousers and lit one.

'I'll have one of those, thanks.'

'Didn't know you smoked,' said Jack. He put another cigarette between his lips, lit it from his own and passed it to her.

'I don't mind one, I might even take it up – I can do anything I like now. I've done my duty by the family. You and Bella have your daughter, and she is my daughter too – what could be better? She'll own this farm one day. You should probably know that my only condition for doing this was that Bella never sell the farm. I know she'll honour that. In fact, I've already made over my share to Adrienne so it can never be sold without her permission. And when you and Isabelle have gone, it will be hers.' She inhaled and blew a jet of smoke into the night. 'I'm free now – no one can tell me what I can or can't do any more.'

'Is that why you say you won't marry?'

'Maybe. My parents' marriage probably put me off. They started off young and in love and ended up practically hating each other.'

'You're exaggerating,' said Jack.

'I don't really know how they felt about one another, but they used to have some fearsome rows in the night. Bella and I invented a game where we would rock ourselves into another land where it was peaceful and quiet and everyone loved each other. I vaguely recall there were sweets involved too.'

Rosanna wrapped the rug firmly around the sleeping baby and pulled her robe together.

'What if I could promise you a peaceful, quiet place, where everyone loved one another – with as many sweets as you could ever want?' His voice was a hoarse whisper. He watched her, his heart thudding.

'Jack, don't. Please don't wreck everything.' She held Adrienne to her chest and closed her eyes tightly. 'Don't say any more.'

'I have to be with you, Rosanna. I love you. This is *our* child – we belong together.'

She was silent, her eyes closed. In a moment he was on his knees before her. His face was so close to hers that he could feel the warmth of her skin. He could see the silver trail of a single tear on her cheek.

Jack slept fitfully the rest of that night, his conversation with Rosanna replaying itself over and over in his dreams. He dreamt that he woke and Rosanna had gone, taking baby Adrienne with her. He was relieved to be woken by the hungry mewing of the baby and the sounds of Isabelle in the kitchen preparing the 6 a.m. bottle. He slipped out of bed, pulled on his trousers and padded quietly down the hall.

Rosanna's bedroom door was shut. He turned the handle slowly and gently pushed the door open a crack. Feathered dawn light framed the curtains and the room was dim, but he could see she was there. He slipped silently inside and closed the door. He wanted to watch her sleeping. He wanted to watch her dream. He wanted to know who Rosanna was when she was truly alone.

Still in her blue cotton robe, she lay sprawled face-down on the bed, arms hugging her pillow, her hair a tassel of black silk against the white fabric. The covers had slipped half off the bed and one side of her body lay exposed from ankle to shoulder, her robe twisted around her. In the grey light she was a charcoal landscape of woman, rolling plains of curves and shadows. His knees felt weak and he knelt for a moment beside the bed. He brushed her hair aside and kissed her neck. Rosanna lifted her head and turned sleepily to face him. She looked as though she had not slept at all, her face puffy, dark shadows under her eyes. Her eyes filled with tears. She pulled him to her and kissed him. Wrapped in her arms he felt immersed in love. Her vehement kisses contradicted everything she had ever said to him. Spilling tears told him everything he needed to know.

Jack slipped silently from Rosanna's room, his bare feet making no sound on the timber floor. Isabelle sat on the couch feeding Adrienne and he could feel her eyes on him as he crossed to the kitchen. Not for the first time, he realised that he was somehow afraid of her. Afraid in the way a child fears an adult who never loses their temper but grimly devises complex, devastating punishments. Rosanna, on the other hand, was volatile. It was sudden and wild but it was just anger, raw and real, and he almost envied her ability to give it a voice. He didn't enjoy it being directed at him but neither did he fear it. Isabelle was different – she never acted without thinking long and hard, and she had an uncanny way of quietly, covertly, getting her own way.

'Take Adrienne, please,' she said suddenly. 'She's almost finished.' Isabelle handed him the baby and left the room. He stood, startled, in the middle of the living room holding his daughter. What did Isabelle know? What would she do? What *could* she do? He waited. He heard her open Rosanna's door and softly close it behind her. He heard the key turn in the lock. Then it was silent.

Jack held the swaddled package of baby while Isabelle settled herself fussily in the front passenger seat. Rosanna stood back and refused to meet his eye. She looked ruined, her robe pulled tightly around her, her hair a tangle of knots. Jack was confused. He had imagined some sort of confrontation between him and Isabelle. He longed for her to force his hand. To make him say the unsayable. Yet there was no confrontation. Nothing had changed, apart from the sparking current of anger he could feel arcing between Isabelle and Rosanna. He felt weakened and bewildered by the force of it and by his ignorance of what had passed between them.

Ignoring Rosanna, Isabelle lifted her arms towards Jack to receive the baby but, on the spur of the moment, Jack turned and handed her to Rosanna.

'Say goodbye to your Aunty Rosanna, Adrienne.'

Rosanna's face sagged. She avoided Jack's eye and, with trembling hands, took her daughter. She gazed intently into her face and sang softly, '*Ninnaò ninnaò, questo bimbo a chi lo do . . .*' Her voice cracked. 'Goodbye, my darling, darling, darling . . .' Soft kisses were sprinkled like tiny blessings over the child's face. She gently handed the baby back to Jack, her eyes gilded with tears. 'Please go now. Please.'

She turned and walked up the steps to the house. As Jack drove slowly down the driveway he watched her through the rear-vision mirror. She stood in the shadow of the doorway, her arms wrapped around herself. He could see her shoulders heaving as she slowly sank to the floor. He could feel the thread that bound them together grow tighter and more painful by the minute, like a slow constriction of the heart. Two tears forced their way out and dried on his unshaven cheeks.

Over the next few weeks Jack planned it all. He planned it backwards and forwards and inside out until he became confounded by his own contradictory emotions. He would wake one morning, determined to ask Isabelle for a divorce; the next, he would plan to leave without telling her. But with each passing day it somehow became more difficult to extract himself from the life they had together.

He spent most evenings brooding on the back porch, a pack of cigarettes and a bottle of beer for company, flicking one glowing butt after another into the darkness. Absorbed with her daughter and her new identity as a mother, Isabelle seemed indifferent to his restlessness. It seemed to him she was too happy to notice, or care, how unhappy he was.

While Adrienne napped, Isabelle wove her magic with gossamer fabrics and tangles of threads in rich creams, butter-yellow and pale pink that coalesced into christening gowns. Her skills quickly elevated her to the sweetheart of the Church guild mothers. They came to Isabelle to have their babies' gowns made. They stayed for tea and biscuits and began to learn the finer points of embroidery, the joys of cross-stitch. Soon mothers with bundles of babies, bunny rugs and bags full of nappies and bottles tripped in and out of the house all day long.

In the company of her new coterie Isabelle was social and jovial; she had a quiet sense of confidence about her. If Jack arrived home to find a group of women in his living room they would invariably fall silent and Isabelle would say, 'Ah, here's my husband. It must be dinnertime!' And they would all laugh and begin to pack up their babies and bags. It irritated him that she always referred to him as 'my husband' as she always referred to Adrienne as 'my daughter'.

Adrienne was his daughter, yet he felt no connection with her. She seemed to be perpetually wrapped in a tight wad of blankets, transported from bed to bottle to bath and back again. Occasionally she was placed in his arms to free Isabelle for some other chore but he invariably spent these precious moments searching her tiny face for a glimpse of Rosanna.

Although desperately drawn to the farm, his plans seemed to stagnate; his courage deserted him daily. He was afraid of the repercussions for Rosanna and for Adrienne if he left Isabelle. He was afraid of the censure he would bring down on his own head from the moment he set any one of his plans in motion. He realised that scandal could become for him the same snake that had chased his father from one small town to the next.

His father had presented to the world as the perfect husband and Isabelle presented as the perfect wife and mother. Unlike his father, she tried to live up to this behind closed doors. Even when Jack was short with her, which he often was, she was unfailingly polite and solicitous. But there was one thing he knew she would never move on. She would not allow cracks to appear in the facade. She would never agree to a separation, let alone a divorce. And he knew that Rosanna would not consent to be with him without Isabelle's approval. Rosanna would never ask for it and Isabelle would never give it. These problems bumped around noisily in his head like fairground dodgems, colliding recklessly out of control until they periodically ground to a halt only to start again, around and around.

He moved through each day in a daze and felt a pang of guilt when Wally tapped him on the shoulder one morning and told him he was wanted upstairs in the manager's office. He was even more concerned when he saw Henry Mackie, one of the more senior pen-pushers from head office, sitting talking to Sid Evans, the site manager.

Henry stood, greeted Jack affably and shook his hand, gesturing for him to take a seat. The manager's office sat high above the site so Sid could watch the workings below from relative comfort. Being summoned up to the bridge was rarely a treat. Jack sat down warily, trying to gauge the mood.

'I won't beat around the bush, Jack. We've got a proposition for you,' said Henry. He took his pipe out of his jacket pocket and inspected the contents for a moment. Jack waited impatiently while he struck a match and huffed and puffed until satisfied it was lit. Sid rolled his eyes and glanced at his watch for Jack's benefit.

'You know we've been carrying out a joint exploration with Minearch out at Mount Zizan, near Broken Hill – your old stamping ground,' Henry said between puffs. Jack nodded and began to relax a little in his chair. 'We've found some lead intersections and sunk a shaft to 450 feet. We've put in a pump station at 300 feet and begun to extract the ore.' Henry paused and relit his pipe. Finally he said, 'We need a good mine manager, Jack – someone with your sort of experience.'

The drone of Henry's voice as he discussed the details was overtaken by a heraldic trumpeting inside Jack's head; the clear, clean note of freedom. His own mine. Something he couldn't turn down. Suddenly he had permission to cut loose and be free of the suffocating life he was living. He saw himself running the mine, being his own boss. Isabelle wouldn't want to come but Rosanna would; she too craved the freedom of the bush and the desert, the anonymity of a new start. He almost laughed with relief.

'Yer better sleep on it, Jack,' said Sid. 'It might be a good career move but it's not much chop for a bloke with a young wife and baby.'

'I have to be honest with you, Jack, it's a difficult site,' added Henry. 'It's in a limestone valley, so it's as wet as it gets. We'll fly you out for a look-see, if you like.'

'I need a few days to sort out some . . . family matters,' said Jack. 'Then I can give you an answer – oh, what the hell, yes! The answer is yes.' He leapt up, shook Henry's hand and then was out the door, sprinting down the rickety wooden stairs, two at a time, feeling a rush of energy and clearness of mind he thought he'd lost forever.

Isabelle accepted the news gracefully, relieved she was not expected to go. The company would pay his key money and rent for a house in Broken Hill and there would be a substantial pay increase to send home.

'Mine manager – it sounds impressive, doesn't it?' she said, rocking the baby in her lap. 'Your daddy's going to be a mine manager, little one. We'll be able to pay off our house and move a little closer to town, I should think.'

Jack ignored her comment. This new way of indirectly communicating her wishes through Adrienne simply exasperated him.

'I'm going to spend a few days down in Sydney at head office,' he lied. 'I'll drive down tomorrow and be back on Sunday. I might call in and check on Rosanna on the way. If you like.'

She looked up at him for a moment and then gazed down at the baby in her lap. A smile played around the lips of the good wife. 'Please yourself,' she said.

The gate to the farm was locked and Jack had to leave his car on the road. He had a sense of foreboding as he walked up the driveway, barely hearing the chime of the bellbirds. He began to run and stopped suddenly as he came around the bend and emerged from the trees. The house was closed up and the windows boarded over. He walked around the verandah. Every window was covered in old planks badly nailed into the window frames; Rosanna's handiwork. He could see through the cracks in the boards that the house was still full of furniture. He walked slowly down the back steps to the patio now enveloped in the verdant green of the grape. The vine-leaf table and chairs had gone and the bricks of the patio had recently been swept clean. In the centre was the outline of a heart laid out in olives.

Fifteen

MY NEW ROOM is like a cell, three floors up, with bars on the windows. It has an ensuite and is utterly pristine. No spider could survive in here. I have views over Lavender Bay and a ten-minute train ride to work. Diane has left a note apologising for not being there, but she'll bring dinner. The apartment doesn't actually look as though anyone lives here. It was a display unit for the block and Diane bought it as a job lot with elegant furniture and even a stack of *Der Architekt* magazines (I'm almost certain she doesn't speak German and wouldn't have a clue about architecture) on the coffee table. With its sleek furnishings in this season's flavours of vanilla and cocoa it looks as though it has been airlifted straight out of a catalogue. I sit tentatively on the chocolate faux-suede sofa feeling as though I'm in a specialist's waiting room.

If I wasn't so sure that this is how my life is meant to be I could easily get back in the ute and scurry home to Duffy's Creek. I'm saved by the swish of the lift and Diane coming in through the door.

'I've brought you a few of the joys of city life; some hand-made wood-fired sourdough, and look! Organic *pâté de foie*.' She plonks down a bottle of Veuve Clicquot and heads into the kitchen. 'Now, I know how you love your toast, Adrienne.' She pulls up a roller cupboard and slips a gleaming appliance out onto the black granite bench, where its brushed steel armour glows under the low-voltage lighting.

'This little baby cost me $700!' she says in a stage whisper. Even I am a little shocked. 'You need to preheat it before you put the toast in. It's not easy to operate – you have to know what you're doing,' she says importantly as she flips out a breadboard and knife and switches on the toaster. The aroma of crisping bread gives this sterile little kitchen the kiss of life.

We stack our golden slabs on outsize white dinner plates, set out crystal flutes for the champagne and settle down on the sofa.

'Welcome home!' says Di as our glasses collide with a satisfying ding.

I want to tell someone about Rosanna. There are so many things I need to get clear in my own mind before I see her again. Every time I think of her I feel a little tug at my heart. I just don't know where to start. I have brought both Jack's letters with me. Mine is still unopened but the one to Rosanna has new meaning for me. It's now a letter from my father to my mother. It's become precious. I'd like to tell Di but I'm worried she'll say something trite. Even if Lauren were here I'd be afraid to expose my parents to her harsh judgement – the judgement of youth and of someone who hasn't seriously stuffed anything up – yet. It's too tender for me and in the end I say nothing.

I'm awake early on my first day of work. I dress carefully and have to borrow Diane's reading glasses to make up my face; the closer I get to the mirror the softer I look. I blow-dry my hair and splash a little Diorissimo behind my ears. I'd forgotten how long all this takes to do.

Out on the street I can feel my sap rising as I join the people with purpose striding to the train, heads down as they determine their strategies for a challenging day ahead. This is more like it. I can't help but feel smug as I look down at my charcoal shot-silk suit, although it is a little tighter than I remember. The heels of my Brogelio Armidi sling-backs tap out a rhythm I remember well. This is me. This is *definitely* me.

My confidence sags a little as I enter the foyer of DGS and the receptionist ignores me while she takes several calls. Two people walk through the reception, neither so much as glancing at me. Finally the receptionist looks up and acknowledges me with an enquiring eyebrow. I ask to see Warren.

'Do you have an appointment?' she asks coolly. A flush that emanates from somewhere in my belly whooshes up my chest and neck and seeps hotly over my face. I feel like tearing my clothes off to escape it. I can hardly think what to reply.

'My name is Adrienne Bennett, I'm the new Senior Account Manager,' I say stiffly.

'Oh,' she says, unimpressed. 'He's not in yet.'

Warwick is not in either. I wait in the reception for a whole hour before Warren wanders through the doors. He is holding a wafer-thin mobile to his ear and is seriously sch-moozing someone on the other end. On seeing me he slides genially out of his conversation, flips his phone shut and pops it in his pocket. He comes towards me, hand extended. 'Wonderful!' he says. 'You could not have arrived at a better time – synchronicity, serendipity, call it what you will. Come, come.'

He strides off down a long corridor flanked by glass offices, identical booths that each house a desk, a computer and a person. We step into a private lift where Warren gazes at himself unashamedly in the mirrors and rearranges his hair, flicking it this way and that, as he explains that one of my new key accounts, a subsidiary of the multinational Superbrand International, is arriving shortly to brief us on a major product launch. 'Short deadline, national roll-out, seat-of-the-pants stuff, but we need some clever, clever ideas – something fresh.'

Like a tai chi instructor he uses his whole body to emphasise and illustrate with arm movements too expansive for the confines of a lift. 'Perhaps a spot-fire tactic or a scatter-gun approach – throw all we've got at it.' I stand well back, mesmerised by his flying hands.

We arrive at the penthouse boardroom. It's got white walls decorated with massive corporate artworks; great slashes of colour in rust and bronze that harmonise perfectly with the furnishings. One wall is floor-to-ceiling glass. It's as though we're at sea suspended in a blazing blue sky, the city below a distant shore, the board table as big as a boat in a dark red timber.

'Why don't you sit here, I'll sit here, and then Warwick can sit there.' Warren prances around the table giving each of the high-backed leather chairs a playful slap as it's allocated. 'We'll have the brand manager sit opposite Warwick and between you and me. Important to get the dynamics right, isn't it?' He gives a thin smile.

'It might be fun if we take one chair away, play some music, run around the table —' I falter at his frown. 'Warren, what exactly is the product?'

Now he's fussing around with the phone, buzzing one extension after another, barely giving anyone time to pick up. He glances at me with surprise. 'No idea, they have any number of products. Natalie! Thank God I've found someone, I thought everyone was dead. I need jugs of water, glasses, coffee, Danish pastries, whatever, pronto.' He listens for a moment. 'I don't care, fix it,' he hisses down the phone.

He slams down the receiver and pulls open a drawer of the cabinet. 'Lucky you reminded me,' he says. 'We do need you to sign a confidentiality agreement before the meeting.' He slides it across the table. I sign it and slide it back without even reading it.

The phone buzzes. Warren picks it up, listens for a second and hangs up. 'Gulls on the tip,' he chirps. Moments later we hear the sound of the lift rise.

Warwick leads the Superbrand marketing team into the boardroom, none of them over twenty-five. Ellie: tight suit, tight hair, tight face. Jonathan: smooth hair and a very smooth suit. Mathew: one of those people who likes to fast-track his business relationships. He and I make eye contact, a firm, dry handshake ensues, he repeats my name as a memory peg and I can almost hear the cogs turning as he creates a word association. I wonder what it is.

Last and least, Cindy, the most junior of the juniors, enters. She hasn't got it yet. Fluffy and flowery, she is disregarded by all present. Warren doesn't give a fig where she sits. A flustered young woman, presumably Natalie, scurries in behind everyone with a water jug and glasses.

'I assume Adrienne has been given a background briefing?' Warwick asks Warren as each of our visitors skims a business card towards me across the polished expanse of the board table.

'Of course,' says Warren, bowing his head as though taking part in a Zen ritual.

I open my mouth and close it again.

Mathew takes the floor. 'Because of the size of the project we have made the decision to delay the roll-out and will invite three agencies to pitch. Cindy will give you the briefing documents after our presentation, but rest assured that our media spend alone will be 2.4 million.'

The news that we're in a pitch situation is clearly a shock. Warwick purses his lips with annoyance. Warren blinks rapidly and fiddles with his pen. Mr Seat-of-the-Pants has just fallen on his arse.

Oblivious to the effect of his announcement, Mathew continues his rant. 'We're looking for creativity with a capital C. We're looking for clever solutions. We're looking for complete commitment to the brand. This —' he pauses for dramatic effect, 'will be bigger than *Ben Hur*.'

If it were possible to lay the clichés on any thicker we'd be backing this soliloquy with the soundtrack from *2001: A Space Odyssey*. My concentration wanes and I find myself thinking about what I'll have for lunch. Suddenly, Ellie takes over in the same hectoring, evangelical tone. 'We've got a great story to tell and we're looking to our chosen agency to create the narrative, relaunch the product image, new branding, new packaging across the brand range, new print and television campaign. We're tired of being number two. We are ready to own the premium category!' She's almost shouting now.

Cindy, now the magician's assistant, places a box on the table. She opens it and brings out three large steel cans. She takes a snazzy-looking can-opener out of the box and deftly opens a can as though she has rehearsed this moment. The lid comes off cleanly. She takes three beer coasters decorated with 'Superbrand' logos out and places the cans on them. She slides the cans towards each of us. Warren takes his and has an appreciative sniff. 'Hmm, new formulation?'

Ellie simpers. Mathew nods, hardly able to contain himself. Warwick gazes into his can almost lovingly. I have to stand up to reach mine and pull it over. I look into the can. Oh, fuck. It's dog food.

She gives us each a spoon.

Jonathan makes eye contact with each of us in turn, waiting to see if one of us lacks 'commitment'; watching to see if anyone has an 'I'm-not-eating-frigging-dog-food' expression on their face. I have no idea what the expression on my face is – wonderment, perhaps? Is this a typical day in the life of a marketing mercenary? It's certainly put me off lunch.

'The breakthrough!' he practically shouts. 'It will change the pet-food industry forever. The third chunk – that's what's going to differentiate us from the market. Three vertical chunks *clearly visible* from the top of the can. Real meat chunks *drenched* in vitamin-enriched gravy. Go ahead – try it, you'll love it.'

Warwick quickly picks up his spoon, digs a lump out and pops it in his mouth. Warren gives me his thin smile and does the same. He makes a show of savouring the moment. 'Grrr, I can feel fur growing on my back.' The team look at each other, clearly thrilled.

I look around the table. All eyes are now on me. The spoon sits untouched in front of me. I'm trapped. I gaze out into the blue. Out into the wild blue yonder.

Warren fiddles restlessly with his empty glass, twisting it from side to side. It catches the light off the water jug and spins it across the table where it comes to rest within my reach. I pick up my spoon and tilt it until it scoops up the light. I smile. They don't.

Warren puts his glass down sharply and the disc of light is flung to the other end of the table. I'm aware that several people shift uneasily in their seats. No one wants to artic-ulate what everyone is thinking. There is a tension in the room. Warren looks at me, his eyes narrow as he moves the glass slowly around, shifting the disc onto the stark white wall. I get up and follow it. I stand against the wall, the fila-ment of light projected onto my cheek. I close my eyes. I can actually feel its warmth. It's as warm as blood.

There is so much I want to tell these young people with their hard little faces. I want to tell them about Joy's cof-fee cake, Deirdre's hysterectomy, Mrs Leeton's lizard feet, Goldsmith's garters. About kindness and dirt, mistakes and loneliness and how fragile we become. About starting fires and putting them out. About the cathedral of olives and my grandfather's apple tree. I want to tell them about my mother, Rosanna, and about my father, Jack. About my daughter Lauren and how I miss her. I need to tell them what little I know about love and forgiveness. I miss Dog. I miss Joe. I miss Joy. I think I even miss Deirdre. I want to tell them that the woman they see here is *not* me. Finally, I have realised that *this* is La-La Land.

I look around the table; all eyes are on me. I don't know where to begin, so I begin with the end. They wouldn't understand anyway. 'Thank you,' I say. And I really mean it. I pick up my briefcase and leave.

I ring Joe on his mobile. I hear the mower engine dying as he answers.

'What's up?'

'Um, the job didn't work out.'

There is a moment's silence. I assume he's checking his watch but chooses not to comment on the fact that it's only 10.30 a.m.

'I saw the light.'

'Yeah?' There is silence between us. I can hear the echo of bellbirds down the line.

'Come on home, Baby. We've got everything you need here.'

'I'm on my way.' My voice is thick with unshed tears.

I go back to the mocha apartment, pack my things and leave an entirely unsatisfactory note for Diane. I lug my stuff down to the ute and drive out of this lovely suburb with its old trees and young cafés, espresso and friands, poodles and BMWs. I drive north for an hour on autopilot while my mind processes my thoughts into an unrecognisable puree.

I pull off the freeway into a rest stop and sit staring at the inside of the windscreen for a very long time. Jack's letter somehow makes its way into my hand. I slit the envelope open and unfold the piece of paper. It reads:

My dear Adrienne,
We've spent our lives apart and it's not your fault, it's mine. There never seemed to be a right time to tell you the truth about your birth. It seemed to get harder over the years and I couldn't find the words to explain why things were the way they were. Isabelle was my wife but not your mother. Her sister Rosanna is your mother and I hope you will understand and forgive me when I say she is the greatest love of my life. By the time you read this I will be gone, I only hope she has not.
All my love, Dad.

I take the loop road and head back to Sydney. I have one clear thought, one thought that feels absolutely right and I have no choice but to follow where it leads. I feel calm. I'm aware of being hungry and thirsty but I can't stop.

I keep driving until I reach the nursing home. The old people are parked out on the lawn. I wonder if they always sit in the same places. I wonder if they leave them out there overnight.

Rosanna is in her bed. 'There you are,' she says. 'They won't let me out of bed. Nobody talks to me.' She points towards the other bed in the room, which I barely noticed last time I was here. 'She's been dead for three years,' she says accusingly. The bed is made so tightly that the occupant, who lies on her back snoring softly, appears to be almost flat.

'We can't have that. Shall we dob her in?' I say with a smile.

'Might as well. I'm sick of all these half-dead people.' She casts a belligerent eye around the room for any other offenders.

I sit down on the side of her bed and take her hand. Her hair is loose today, it's been washed and brushed and flows thick as molten silver over her soft shoulders. She wears a faded cotton gown sprigged with flowers. She is much darker than my mother; her skin is olive, her eyes black and surprisingly alert. This time I'm the one to take in every detail. I savour her voice, her smell, the smooth plump texture of her skin. I quietly make her mine.

'Now, I know you.'

'I'm Adrienne. I'm your daughter. The baby Isabelle took away, remember?' I say gently.

For a moment it seems as though she doesn't understand me. She wraps her arms around herself and lifts her face to the heavens as if in prayer. From where I sit all I can see is the tilt of her chin, trembling delicately. Several slow minutes pass us by. When she lowers her face it has changed. She has the beatific smile of an elderly cherub. It's as if a thousand dancing blessings have indeed rained down upon her. Her eyes glow with tears but I can see the happiness runs five layers deep. She strokes my cheek and sings in a low voice, '*Ninnaò ninnaò, questo bimbo a chi lo do —*' She raises her hands to the ceiling and calls, '*Grazie*, Bella, *Grazie*.'

When she speaks it's not the slightly befuddled Rosanna but one who is completely here, completely her. 'You were so beautiful.' She laughs out loud. 'Everyone's gone but you're *here*.' The tears spill down her cheeks as she wraps her arms around me and holds me tight against her warm soft body.

'I want to take you back to the farm with me. To live,' I say as I disengage from her embrace and brush away my own tears.

'I'm not sure I can go,' she says cautiously.

'Oh? What's worrying you?'

'I tried to escape and now they've hidden my shoes.'

'Is that all?'

Her mouth turns down at the corners. She leans forward and whispers, 'I'm worried I won't remember how to put them on.'

'Well, that's okay because I know how to do those things. I'll help you. I'll take care of everything. I'll remember anything you forget.'

If only I could do that for her. If only I knew what the future held for us. My only thought is that I'm ready to take this step; ready as I'll ever be.

Epilogue

There's a frosting of ice on the grass this morning, and my breath forms plumes of white against a deep blue sky. The grove is a sea of netting that swirls around the trees like a foamy tide. Birds of every creed and colour have gathered in the cathedral to give thanks and sing the praises of the olive. Soon the pickers will come with rakes and tubs and chase them away, but it's still early, and for the moment the grove is the birds' domain.

By the time I reach the foot of the hill my boots are soaked through but the sun has climbed a little higher and warms my shoulders. Ernie's right behind me; I think he's happy to have his real name back. I take off my jacket and begin the ascent. I come here often now. I come to visit Rosanna.

Joe's built me a little timber seat up here under the wattles, now resplendent in their winter gold. It's nothing fancy, just a simple construction of split logs to create a seat and support for my back, but I'm very fond of it. From here I can see across the valley, the soft green pattern of the grove and the dark curl of the river beyond.

Rosanna's plot is beside Francesco's. I hope that one day

Jack will have a plot here too. That's something I'd like to do for him if it's possible.

She died last summer, just eighteen months after I brought her home. She was as strong as a woman half her age and when it came to how to prune an olive tree or bake a *pan di spagna*, her memory was faultless. I knew that would change.

She was often forgetful, and she was certainly eccentric, and it was sometimes difficult to tell the difference between the two. She insisted on swimming every day. In the summer I would swim with her, while in winter I would sit on a rock wrapped in a rug while she plunged into the icy water. The water seemed to cleanse her mind of confusing detritus and it was often during our walk home that she had her most lucid memories.

She would experience the past disconnectedly, like scenes in a play, but could vividly describe Isabelle notating the words of songs played on Rosanna's little brown radio; my father and grandfather playing cards by the fire; the women preserving summer fruit; Isabelle making a dress of roses for her.

It was on one of these clear, bright days that Rosanna remembered with sadness, not anger, Isabelle's threat to twist the story of the planned conception so that I became the child of an adulterous love affair, and Isabelle a martyr.

'Bella came into my room and locked the door. She was so angry. She said that I had cast a spell on Jack. I had betrayed her. I was trying to destroy her – humiliate her. How could she say that? I couldn't stop crying. If I didn't go away she would tell Mamma . . . and who would believe me? Who would believe the truth? Adultery is a mortal sin and Bella my sister – Mamma would *never* forgive me,' cried Rosanna, still dismayed that it had come to that in the end.

What a tangled web these three did weave . . . One secret became many, with fears and guilty revelations still bubbling to the surface half a lifetime later.

Rosanna often mentioned Jack and would coo with delight when she discovered the odd possession of his that had escaped my brutal throw-out phase. I know she loved him and he loved her. I'm so glad they found each other in the end. Twice a week he had visited her over the last two years of his life. Same time, same days every week, regular as a heartbeat.

I spoke on a number of occasions to Mrs O'Brien, the manager of the nursing home, in my efforts to fit together the disparate pieces of information I had about Rosanna's past. Mrs O'Brien added some pieces to the puzzle but it remains, even today, far from complete.

Rosanna, it seems, moved to Sydney of her own accord in her early seventies, and perhaps with a purpose, since she had lived out most of her adult life in South Australia. Soon after she arrived she suffered her first stroke in the dining room of the boarding house where she was staying. She was taken to hospital, where they undertook an extensive search to find her next of kin and located Jack.

'At first, when he placed her here, we thought they were husband and wife – quite the lovebirds they were,' Mrs O'Brien explained over the phone. 'We couldn't understand his reluctance to take her home, apart from the fact that he was an elderly gentleman himself and, with all due respect, she was a bit of a handful. When the paperwork came through it turned out she'd been married briefly to a fellow over in Adelaide, but never to Jack. Bit of a story behind those two if you ask me.' Never a truer word. 'She used to ask quite often for her sister – Bella? But I think Jack managed to make it clear to her that she was long gone.'

Later I managed through Annabelle Challis to track down the hotel where Rosanna had worked, which turned out to be a country pub outside Adelaide. Ron, the manager of The Royal, remembered her well – she was famous for putting pasta on the pub's menu in 1965. She worked there on and off for many years, leaving once to work as a cook for a shearing gang and again when she was poached by the owner of a new restaurant in the city. But neither of these suited and both times she returned to her old room and her kitchen at The Royal. He had no idea she had ever been married, however briefly. She had mentioned a sister, but he didn't think they kept in touch – she didn't seem to know where the sister was living. She had retired from the kitchen ten or so years earlier and had planned to travel as far as her pension would take her. That's all he knew.

'If you're ever over this way, drop in,' he said. 'We still have pasta on the menu. In fact, the restaurant's still called "Rosanna's".'

One winter afternoon, walking back from the river as the mist started to curl across the paddocks, she sang for me. Her voice rose, as clear as a girl's; when she fell in love it would be forever. She sang from the heart into the darkening sky. And I believed her.

'You still know all the words,' I said in astonishment.

'There's nothing wrong with my memory,' she replied crossly. 'I just get muddled sometimes. Not as muddled as you – you tell me one thing one day and another the next.'

Fair comment. The path of least resistance is bound to twist and turn. Rosanna was more than muddled, though. During that year she had several more tiny strokes and began drifting backwards down the corridors of her own life. Sometimes she would look into the rooms she was passing and see the ghosts that inhabited them but more and more they were wisps that eluded her grasp. Fragments of memory, familiar faces without names, scenes that puzzled and disturbed her.

Time and place began to shift for my mother and I soon learnt there was no point in correcting her. I found myself playing imaginary games I never played with my daughter. It took me a long time to accept that I had to be a part of Rosanna's world for her to be a part of mine. She always played herself and I played all the other roles. Often, late in the day as the light began to drift away, she would call out anxiously, 'Bella, where are you?'

'I'm here, Rosa,' I'd respond from wherever I was. 'I'm right here.'

In some strange karmic turn of events I ended up becoming a mother to my own mother. It wasn't easy. Rosanna could be delightful and fun, endearing and affectionate, but she could also be fractious and defiant. She once threw her dinner across the room and instructed me to tell the kitchen staff they were fired. She would leave taps on and run us dry of water. There were times she nearly drove me mad with her stubborn, difficult behaviour – on one occasion I packed her bag, flung it in the ute and ordered her into the car, determined to take her back to the nursing home. She simply refused to get in. She folded her arms and sat on the verandah steps, watching me fume from a comfortable distance. So then I called Joy and, because I was feeling very sorry for myself, I phoned Joe as well. And they came, both of them, and they made us tea and talked us down.

Whenever she saw I was upset, Rosanna would always say she was sorry, even if she couldn't quite put her finger on what it was she had done to get me so hot and bothered. I'd tell her I was sorry too and she'd hug me tight, press her cheek against mine and say fiercely, 'I love you too much.' She was easy to forgive. I knew she couldn't help herself. I knew that above all else, she did love me.

What possessed me to bring her home in the first place? Whatever made me think I could be a carer when I was clearly such a lousy mother? They were questions to ask oneself in the middle of the night, and the answers eventually came. I did it because I was lost. Confused. Lacking any purpose in my life. But I also did it for her. I did it because, even though it wasn't my thing, it was the right thing. And there is no doubt in my mind now that it was the right thing. Despite our occasional struggles, despite her own frustrations, she was happy here – deliriously happy in the way a child is happy just to wake up every morning. She loved feeding the chooks and weeding out the vegetable garden and talking all day long to Ernie, who was never far away.

The farm, with its familiarity and memories, was her saving grace. The fruits of her childhood memories had been preserved here for leaner times, and she was nourished by them.

It was raining hard the day of her accident; the sort of weather I thought would keep even Rosanna inside. I sensed the eerie silence that always meant she had left the building, and I went out onto the back verandah to find her lying on the ground. She must have slipped on the step and taken a tumble.

'Get Joy!' she shouted when she saw me coming down the steps; her catchcry whenever she was in pain. Never mind that Joy hadn't been a nurse for thirty years; she always felt better when Joy administered the Panadol.

We were both wet and muddy by the time I got her inside, our hair plastered to our heads. Rosanna was crying but couldn't seem to locate the source of her pain. I called Joy, who called the ambulance.

When we arrived home late that night, the rain had stopped and the sky was clear. Rosanna had her ankle in plaster and was nursing a broken rib. Joy and I made her comfortable in her bed but she wasn't herself. Perhaps it was the shock of the fall, or the confusion of being taken away, but it was as though the spark had gone out of her. It was as though she had seen a glimpse of the future.

She was confined to bed for a week or two to allow the bones to knit, a restriction she refused to accept. She only stayed in bed as a prisoner of pain.

Up until then, despite swimming all winter, she hadn't

had so much as a cold. Now, lying in a warm bed, she caught a virus that sped quickly to her lungs. Within days she had pneumonia. Increased medication seemed to have no effect.

She hardly spoke in the last couple of days. It was as though she had willed this illness on herself and needed all her strength to see it through. I knew better than to leave the room. I sat and held her hand, patted her face with a damp cloth. I waited and waited. But this time my vigil was not a lonely one. Joe came and stayed. He brought me tea and toast. He held my hand and told me that he loved me. Joy came and brought with her the distant sounds of the washing machine and the aroma of shepherd's pie. Margaret brought lavender from her garden. Ernie lay at my feet.

There was a moment when it seemed as though the life had flooded back into Rosanna. She squeezed my hand and when she opened her eyes they were clear and bright. She looked at me for a moment and said, 'Let Jack know where I've gone. He'll be looking for me.'

When Isabelle died so many years earlier, I was frightened and angry. My eyes were dry. I went out in the world in a sort of rage. I lived my life at full pelt. I studied and worked into the nights, utterly determined to succeed at everything I did – to prove I had a place in the world. I constructed a hard shell around me and I was, in many ways, quite heartless.

When Rosanna died I was just plain sad. For weeks I cried when I thought of her. I missed her. I missed her presence in the house. Her laughter. I missed dancing around the living room with her. I missed her coming into bed with me when she was afraid in the night. I was sad she was gone but I knew that the layers of that hard shell around my heart had been gradually peeling away, simply by loving her and by being loved by her. Far from feeling exposed, I felt freed. I discovered that my mother was wild and courageous and as flawed as any other human. I discovered that I am my mother's daughter. I left her room with a different sort of determination, with a second chance and a sense of what needed to be done.

I asked Joe to walk with me in the olive grove. As we wandered beneath the clouds of silver olives, now in summer flower, I told him that I was, at last, ready to dive into the green depths of those dangerous eyes of his and take my chances. I asked him to come and live at the farm with me, to share my life. He kissed me softly and said, 'It takes a pretty special woman to get Mohammed down off his mountain. But heck, I'm up for it if you are, sweet thing. And, I'll tell you what, I'm going to build you a really top-notch self-composting toilet to mark the occasion.'

What more could a woman ask for?

During those last days sitting in Rosanna's room I thought a lot about Lauren. I have written to her many times. They have come back marked 'Return to Sender', every one. She's unaware of the irony. I have heard from Sarah that she is finishing her degree and has been promoted. She has a nice boyfriend and a flat in Ealing. I hear everything third-hand. It's two years since we've spoken. How did I let that happen? How did I let things harden? Why didn't I see the pattern of our family? Perhaps because I never really thought of

Lauren and myself as a family; I saw myself as some sort of heroine taking on the world, smart and tough, and she was just there, tagging along behind. My sidekick. In Rosanna's room I thought a lot about the things Lauren said to me and she was right. My business *was* my hungry, demanding firstborn. It needed me and it gave me a level of respect that mothering could never hope to offer. Lauren couldn't possibly compete. I was a hopeless mother. I treated her like one of my projects. Little wonder she doesn't like me.

After Rosanna died, I wrote to Lauren. The truth. I told her I was wrong; that I was sorry. I told her just how much I love her.

I send her the same letter every week now. Each time they come back to me unopened I scrawl 'Try Again' across the envelope and send it back. It's all I can do. I haven't heard a word but I won't give up. I won't ever give up. She's my girl and I love her more than I can say.

My life now is very far from the way I thought it would be. It's not glamorous and no one admires me for the work I do around here (much of which is sheer drudgery.) Money is in short supply. And sometimes it feels just all too hard. But while it's not all sweetness and light, there are days like this that are so perfect: the magpies chortle, my morning coffee tastes good and the shimmering grove beckons. There are evenings in front of the fire with Joe and a glass of our own rough red. There are people I love in my life every day. I know this is home and for the first time in my life I feel safe, no longer held hostage by my own unhappiness.

I wish Rosanna could have been here today of all days. I've wondered many times if the work of resurrecting the grove was too much for her. God knows it nearly killed *me*. Joe worked with Rosanna and me and a couple of local lads with chainsaws all that first year, rigorously pruning the trees back into shape for this year's harvest. The years of neglect, far from being detrimental to the trees, should actually improve the crop because of the composting effect of the olives left on the ground. I'm something of an expert on the subject of olives these days. Who'd have thought, eh?

After Joe moved in, he sold Mohammed's mountain and we built a new shed where the old one had stood. Made of galvanised iron with a cement floor, it doesn't have the character of the old one but it houses the olive mill and a processing area. Two of the Leeton boys (compliments of Mrs Leeton) helped Joe construct the stone mill. Built to the specifications of the drawings made by my father and grandfather, it has two great granite wheels attached to a central rod that runs through the centre of a large metal basin that will contain the olives while the wheels grind them into a paste. Beside it sits the press that holds the stack of mats on which the paste will be poured and then pressed to exude the oil into a barrel. An ancient method of producing unfiltered olive oil – simply the juice of the fruit.

On this frosty winter's night we have an eclectic gathering of friends, pickers and even a couple of food writers from the city here to celebrate the launch of our business. It's been a long journey to this night, from my grandfather's dream to the pressing of the first oil, and it won't stop here. Our label honours Isabella and Rosanna, the two sisters reunited, arms entwined, finally delivering their father's dream to the world. I may not have the suits but I still have the skills to create a brand identity for our oil and to get it out in the marketplace. I still have that spoon from my brief foray back into the board room – I souvenired it. I'll be putting it to good use taste-testing something I believe in, something I'm passionate about.

It's a big night for us – bigger than *Ben Hur*, I suppose you could say. The shed is transformed, lit by dozens of candles propped in jars on the exposed framework of the walls, and with glowing braziers placed around the room to warm our many guests. On the tables, buckets, tins and jars overflow with silver branches from the olives and the festive gold of wattle. The tubs of olives, picked and cleaned today, are stacked along one wall of the shed.

A hush slowly falls over the gathered friends as Joe and I lift the first tub and tip it into the crusher.

'Let there be oil!' calls Joy and we all cheer wildly as Joe presses the button and the grinding wheels begin to slowly turn.

It's warm in the shed now and our guests, discarding their coats and jackets, begin to nibble at the food and help themselves to wine while we wait for the olives to be crushed and pressed. An hour later the chat has reached cicada pitch when Joe calls out: 'Ladies and gentlemen, charge your glasses for a toast – I give you "Olive Sisters' Cold Pressed Extra-Virgin Olive Oil"!'

And, sure enough, a steady stream of pale green silk

flows from the spout of the press into the stainless-steel container. A cheer goes up and there is a buzz of excitement as we hand around bruschetta (spread with a hint of garlic and a sprinkling of sea salt) on the end of an olive twig for guests to toast over the braziers. Joy and Diane move among the crowd drizzling a little of the fresh oil on each bruschetta. Diane looks quite the part, sporting a pristine pair of RM Williams chisel-toe boots.

I kneel down beside the flow of oil. I want to drink straight from the mountain stream. We've worked hard for this. So many people have waited so long for this green oil. There's a fleeting moment when I feel someone kneel beside me, but when I look there is no one. I slide my fingertip under the last long drips of oil and place my finger in my mouth. It tastes sweet, like freshly mown grass. No, not exactly *like* it; it tastes like freshly mown grass makes you *feel*.

There is cheering and catcalls in the crowd as our entertainment for the night – The Bush Brats – arrive, almost unrecognisable in beanies and winter coats. While the band sets up we move the tables and the braziers back against the walls. The room hums with conversation and the candles exude a strangely intoxicating scent.

From the first twanging chords of a country waltz, people are drawn to one another, people who have known their partner forever and people who, I'm almost certain, have only just met. There are some unlikely combinations: Joe (wearing Jack's boots, I see) steps right up to ask Mrs Leeton to dance. Annabelle and Diane both dance with surly olive pickers. Deirdre (there is no escaping that woman) and Walter are cheek-to-cheek, of course. Margaret and her husband John are tall and elegant as they swan around the cement dance floor. Soon almost everyone in the shed is part of the colourful swirl. I have glimpses of people I've never seen before. A couple of chubby, pink-cheeked women dance together. Both are dressed in satin, and one wears a red-velvet hat. A good-looking fellow with glossy black hair laughs as he whirls a beautiful honey-blonde woman around the floor. I quickly lose sight of them as they disappear into the crowd.

At the far end of the shed I notice a young woman with long dark hair enter, and a young man trails behind her. I can't think who they might be. They both wear heavy coats and I see Joe, obviously having quickly dispensed with Mrs Leeton, cross the room to speak to them. He shakes both their hands. He takes their coats and hangs them over the back of a chair. The man puts a protective arm around the woman's shoulders. All three glance in my direction but in the low light I still can't make out who they are. Intriguing.

Without further ado, Joe takes the young woman in his arms and they begin to dance, turning this way and that, always tantalisingly out of sight. A great well of emotion rises up in me. The long hair had me fooled, but I'm almost sure . . . Suddenly they're in front of me, and Joe is looking particularly pleased with himself as he swings his partner towards me. She turns with a smile, glittering tears of light in her eyes. It's my girl. My girl's come home. Without a moment's hesitation we put our arms around each other. I press my cheek to hers and our tears mingle. Blood brothers, tear sisters, our skin as one. I feel the earth under my feet, the solid flesh of my daughter's body in my arms. We're laughing and crying and spinning with the dancers, spinning and weaving the past with the future. We dance like angels, we dance our way back to each other, and now I know I have everything I need. At last.

Acknowledgements

To my muses – Jane Symons, Su Furolo, Pam Owen and Tegan Mitchell – thank you! Without your endless encouragement, this book would never have been written. Thank you also to the many others who read later drafts and offered support and criticism: Betty Palmer, Catherine Hersom, Elise Wynyard, Olivier Gonfond, Bronwyn Wall, Marian Henderson, Mavis Bates, Jan Reggett, Tracey Knowles, Nic Price, Thalia Goldspink, Darren Gittins, Colleen Kennedy, Harold Hampson and Kim Hampson.

Thanks to Gigliana Caris and Joseph Furolo for help on all things Italian; John Sydney Griffith (Griff) for generously sharing his family memoir of his career as a mining engineer; Richard Goldspink for information on business liquidation; Robyn Barrows for checking information relating to olives; Mark Holland for sharing his knowledge of olive oil; Uwe and Gaby Studtrucker for information on the *Taggiasca* olive and Julie Pride and Bryan Duffy for sharing personal experiences with me.

Thank you to Belinda Castles for her constructive critique; Dorothy Gliksman for her wonderful encouragement and support and Lyn Tranter for her honesty and insight.

A special thank you and acknowledgement to Bryce Courtenay who provided me with the tools I needed to tame my manuscript into a book. His generosity and support have been invaluable. At Penguin Australia many thanks go to publisher Clare Forster for taking the risk; Saskia Adams for her artful editing and designer Miriam Rosenbloom for the beautiful cover.

Finally, thank you to my partner Lee Wynyard and our children, Tula and Milan, for their love and support and to our dear friend, Rocco Martino, many years gone but never forgotten.

Jessica

BRYCE COURTENAY

Jessica is based on the inspiring true story of a young girl's fight for justice against tremendous odds. A tomboy, Jessica is the pride of her father, as they work together on the struggling family farm. One quiet day, the peace of the bush is devastated by a terrible murder. Only Jessica is able to save the killer from the lynch mob – but will justice prevail in the courts?

Nine months later, a baby is born ... with Jessica determined to guard the secret of the father's identity. The rivalry of Jessica and her beautiful sister for the love of the same man will echo throughout their lives – until finally the truth must be told.

Set in the harsh Australian bush against the outbreak of World War I, this novel is heartbreaking in its innocence, and shattering in its brutality.

House on the Hill

ESTELLE PINNEY

Belle Dalton has stardust in her eyes. It's the early 1920s in Far North Queensland, and the three Dalton sisters board with Mrs Sanders in the house on the Hill.

Lovely Belle, the youngest, a talented singer and dancer, tours with a vaudeville troupe as they follow the rodeos and shows of western Queensland. On the romance front, she's being pursued by handsome local Greek Nicos Alexandros, owner of the swankiest café in town. But will she choose marriage with Nicos or a life on the stage?

Molly reigns as head cook at King's Hotel, and can whip up any stylish gown down to the last bugle bead. However, happiness with her sweetheart Fred is threatened by a terrible twist of fate . . . Josie, the eldest, has bookish ambitions and a strong spirit, which will be tested to the full when her life takes an unexpected turn.

This heart-warming and colourful novel about the power of dreams brings to life Australia's exotic far north of days gone by, with its vibrant mix of cultures and personalities. *House on the Hill* follows three sisters' joys and heartbreaks – and the difficult choices they have to make that change their lives forever.

The Stockmen

RACHAEL TREASURE

Rosie Highgrove-Jones grows up hating her double-barrelled name. She dreams of riding out over the wide plains of the family property, working on the land. Instead she's stuck writing the social pages of the local paper.

Then a terrible tragedy sparks a series of shocking revelations for Rosie and her family. As she tries to put her life back together, Rosie throws herself into researching the haunting true story of a nineteenth-century Irish stockman who came to Australia and risked his all for a tiny pup and a wild dream. Is it just coincidence when Rosie meets a sexy Irish stockman of her own? And will Jim help her realise her deepest ambitions – or will he break her heart?

The Stockmen moves effortlessly between the present and the past to reveal a simple yet hard-won truth – that both love and the land are timeless . . .

Knitting

ANNE BARTLETT

It's been ten months since Jack died, and Sandra, a tightly wound academic, copes with her grief by immersing herself in the history of textiles. When she and Martha, a gifted knitter, meet over an unconscious body on the footpath, the unlikely threads of their lives tangle into each other. Sandra invites Martha to join her in a professional collaboration, but what begins as a working relationship becomes something deeply personal. Martha seems at ease with herself, in spite of her own experience of grief. But what does she carry around in those three large bags?

'Reading *Knitting* is an experience as sensual and mystical as plunging your hands into skeins of wool and colour . . . Anne Bartlett's language gives us words to taste, jewels to finger. Her characters are friends we need . . . A joyful narrative of creating and connecting.'
SENA JETER NASLUND, AUTHOR OF *AHAB'S WIFE*

Subscribe to receive *read more*, your monthly newsletter from Penguin Australia. As a *read more* subscriber you'll receive sneak peeks of new books, be kept up to date with what's hot, have the opportunity to meet your favourite authors, download reading guides for your book club, receive special offers, be in the running to win exclusive subscriber-only prizes, plus much more.

Visit penguin.com.au to subscribe.